ASH ISLAND

ALSO BY BARRY MAITLAND

THE BELLTREE TRILOGY

Crucifixion Creek

Ash Island

THE BROCK AND KOLLA SERIES

The Marx Sisters

The Malcontenta

All My Enemies

The Chalon Heads

Silvermeadow

Babel

The Verge Practice

No Trace

Spider Trap

Dark Mirror

Chelsea Mansions

The Raven's Eye

ASH ISLAND

A Belltree Mystery

BARRY MAITLAND

MINOTAUR BOOKS
NEW YORK

ASH ISLAND. Copyright © 2015 by Barry Maitland. All rights reserved. Printed in the United States of America. For information, address St. Martin's Press, 175 Fifth Avenue, New York, N.Y. 10010.

www.minotaurbooks.com

The Library of Congress Cataloging-in-Publication Data is available upon request.

ISBN 978-1-250-11320-7 (hardcover)
ISBN 978-1-250-11321-4 (e-book)

Our books may be purchased in bulk for promotional, educational, or business use. Please contact your local bookseller or the Macmillan Corporate and Premium Sales Department at 1-800-221-7945, extension 5442, or by e-mail at MacmillanSpecialMarkets@macmillan.com.

First published in Australia in 2015 by The Text Publishing Company

First U.S. Edition: November 2016

10 9 8 7 6 5 4 3 2 1

For Margaret

ASH ISLAND

ONE

ON A NOVEMBER NIGHT in 2013, two kilometres off the coast of New South Wales, a helicopter rises from the deck of a Chinese bulk carrier ship. It has just delivered a pilot to guide the 260-metre leviathan into the port of Newcastle, where it will take on 150,000 tonnes of coal.

The helicopter pilot banks away toward the coast, his last flight for the night, and checks the time. 2:16 a.m. Ahead of him he can see the white figure of the lighthouse on Nobbys Head marking the mouth of the Hunter River and the entrance to the port. To the left are the lights of the city—the city of people, mostly asleep now—while to the right lies the floodlit city of machines that never sleep. Gantries, towers, crawling scoops, and humming conveyor belts, all of gigantic size, gathering up the long ridges of coal that the trains have brought down from the valley and pumping it into the bellies of the ships.

Beyond the machines and their coal mountains the pilot can see a curious blank darkness in the general pattern of lights. It is Ash Island, an uninhabited place of saltwater marshland lying between the two arms of the river that converge in the port basin. As he turns toward his landing ground, the pilot notices one single bright point of light in

Ash Island's darkness. Puzzled, he turns back towards it. There is a three-quarter moon in the cloudless sky and as he gets closer he can make out the paler forms of pools and lakes reflecting its light—Wader Pond and Swan Pond and the meandering line of Fish Fry Creek. And there, in the crook of the stream, he sees again that unlikely spot of light. As he approaches it is abruptly extinguished. He blinks, staring into the darkness, and as he passes over the place thinks he can make out the pale rectangles of two vehicles, down by the edge of the creek.

T W O

KELLY POOL STARES DOWN into the darkness to the glow of white wave caps breaking against the base of the cliff below her. She shivers in the cool wind of Sydney's late spring. The boom of the surf rises up to her like the rhythmic chant of some primeval chorus, the chorus of the dead.

She really has had enough. For a while she thought she was coping pretty well, brushing off the sympathy of colleagues when she returned to work at the *Times*; telling them that no, everything was fine. She wondered what version they'd been given. When she asked the trainee journalist under her, Hannah, told her Catherine Meiklejohn had spoken to each of them. Kelly had been savagely attacked, she'd said without going into detail, while fearlessly doing her job. She was an example to them all of what an investigative journalist should be. But that wasn't how Kelly felt, and as the weeks and months passed her energy and will began to leak away.

The nights were her undoing. Joost Potgeiter had been killed—she'd seen it herself—but each night he visited her again in her dreams. Shredding her sleep, convulsing her in sweaty horror, her own voice screaming NO-NO-NO-NO as she struggled back to consciousness.

And so the days deteriorated too. She found it hard to concentrate, avoided leaving the office. She sat hunched at her desk staring at her computer screen, lost for ideas.

It didn't help that her flatmate, Wendy, was in much the same state. Wendy walked with a stick now, and they were both seeing therapists, but so far that didn't seem to have helped. They spent their evenings and much of their nights together locked in their apartment, and drank too much.

And now Kelly really has had enough. Sleep, release, oblivion. Just one step away.

She thinks of Donna Fenning, the pleasant, housewifely woman who drugged her and delivered her into Potgeiter's hands. Donna has vanished, seemingly without a trace; the police seem to doubt that she ever existed. And she thinks of Harry Belltree, who has also disappeared. She visited him regularly in hospital while he recovered from his wounds. Then one day he was gone, no one could tell her where.

Just one step.

She takes a deep breath, lifts up her chin. Raises her foot.

As she feels her weight tip she hears a male voice behind her roar, "NO!" and her body is checked by a tremendous jerk on her arm which brings her stumbling backwards onto her rump.

Harry! she thinks. *Harry!*

But she looks up into an unfamiliar face. He looks furious, his saliva sprays as he shouts at her, "What are you fucking doing? Don't be so bloody stupid!"

He is very agitated, shaking his head and waving his arms. She sees a dog lead in his hand and a small terrier dancing around behind him.

"I'm sorry," she says, and subsides onto the damp grass. "I'm sorry."

"For goodness sake!" He takes hold of her arm again and lifts and drags her away from the edge. "That's so stupid! So bloody stupid!"

"Yes," she gasps. "Yes, it is," and begins to laugh and cry.

THREE

AS HARRY TAKES THE wheel, Detective Sergeant Ross Bramley pulls on his seat belt beside him with an impatient grunt. Ross is an old hand, nearing retirement, pugnacious features crowned by grizzled wiry hair. He has been Harry's dour partner since he arrived. Instructed, Harry's pretty sure, to keep a close eye on him, show him how things are done up here. Maybe find out what exactly happened in Sydney.

Two months ago, after the third round of operations—when the doctors finally conceded that he was fit to go—Harry was visited one last time by his boss.

Detective Superintendent Bob Marshall, head of Homicide, got quickly to the point. "So, what are we going to do with you, Harry?"

Harry wondered about Bob, always had. Bluff Bob, Bob the Job, projecting an image of confidence, impatience with bullshit, and care for his troops. But there was a private dimension to Bob that Harry hadn't been able to pin down. He'd seen him reading novels. *Bleak House* once. Maybe it was Dickens' harsh view of lawyers that appealed to him.

"What are the options, boss?"

"Retire on full pension in exchange for a legally binding

agreement to keep quiet about what happened three months ago. Then take Jenny away somewhere to have her baby—Tasmania, say—and start again. Make a new life together. Put the past behind you."

Harry thought about that. "Is there an option two?"

Marshall sighed. "Son, if you were dead set on staying on the force, they wouldn't kick you out. But you couldn't stay here, not in Sydney. Wouldn't square with them at all. Have to be one of the bush commands. The best we could do is Newcastle."

This suggestion of impersonal forces at work, of "they" and "them," didn't altogether convince Harry. If anyone had been embarrassed by what happened it was Marshall himself. He wants rid of me, Harry thought, and who could blame him?

So now Harry is with Detective Sergeant Bramley in Newcastle. It could have been worse—here they're only two and a half hours by car or train from Jenny's family in the city. After Homicide, the work here has been very ordinary—teenage bandits, drugs, domestic violence. Lots of domestic violence. It's their campaign of the month, and it's where he and Bramley are going now.

They drive uphill, away from the coast, through suburbs of brick and weatherboard bungalows, the gardens growing larger, the verandas and trees more expansive in the headlights. The address comes up, an ambulance and a patrol car outside, neighbours peering over the picket fence opposite.

Inside the house two ambulance officers, a young female uniformed cop, and the victim's mother are gathered around the injured woman. Her face is puffy, eyes swollen shut. The other uniform is trying to calm the father, who is angrily demanding that they arrest his bastard son-in-law.

7

This is the fourth time that the parents know about; each time she's gone back. The police haven't been involved before. It seems she was picked up by a passing cab as she staggered along Industrial Drive, and brought here to her parents' place.

While Ross notes the details from the father, Harry gets a rundown from the ambulance officers—suspected broken ribs, nose and cheekbone, multiple abrasions, and blunt-force trauma. As they ease her onto the stretcher, Harry notices the extensive tattooing.

They get in the car and head back towards the inner city to find the couple's home, one of a row of cement houses in Mayfield. There are lights on in the windows, a white utility vehicle standing outside. When they ring the front door-bell they hear the click of heels approaching inside. The door opens a few centimetres and a set of long scarlet finger-nails appear. Through the narrow gap they make out blonde curls and a single eye, dark with mascara and eye shadow.

Ross checks the address again and says, "Good evening, madam. We're police officers. We'd like to speak to Mr. Logan McGilvray. Is he at home?"

"No, I'm afraid not." A soft, husky voice. "They're both out. I don't know where."

"What's your name?"

"Loretta, Loretta Smith. I'm a friend."

"I see. And you've no idea where he might be?"

"No, sorry." The door closes.

As they walk away, Harry says, "Did you notice the size of that woman's hands?"

Ross stops dead. "Yeah. And the voice." They stare at each other for a moment, then turn and head back to the front door. Ross presses the bell again. They wait, nothing happens. Ross gives the door a shove and it swings open.

"Hello? Mrs. Smith?" Silence. "It's the police again. Are you there?"

Harry says, "'Round the back," and sets off at a run.

The backyard is deserted, no one clambering over the Colorbond fence. Harry strides over to a pair of sliding glass doors overlooking a small deck and peers into the room inside. The light is off, and it takes him a moment to make out the motionless figure of Loretta Smith pressed against the far wall just inside the open doorway leading into the hall. She looks oddly proportioned, bulky torso and shoulders, thick legs in dark stockings perched on a pair of high heels. One muscular arm is raised above her blonde head, the hand gripping a very large kitchen knife.

Harry reaches for the handles of the sliding doors. Locked. Through the hall doorway he can see Ross moving forward towards the opening where Loretta waits. He shouts but it's clear neither of them can hear him. He reaches into his jacket for his gun, then notices a small Weber standing nearby on the deck. He grabs it and swings it hard at the glass door, which shatters just as Ross comes parallel with Loretta. Her arm is beginning its downward arc, the exploding door makes Ross jump back as the knife comes down and Harry barrels into the room, throws himself at the guttural roaring figure in the frock.

When they finally subdue the writhing man and the handcuffs are on, the two cops slump back against the wall, gasping for breath. Harry sees blood pouring from Ross's hand. "You okay, mate?"

Ross pulls out a handkerchief and wraps it around the cut. "Prick was gonna kill me, wasn't he?"

"Looked that way."

"Well . . . thanks." It obviously takes an effort to say the word. "Yeah, thanks."

Harry rolls their captive over to get a better look at the face. The blonde wig has gone, exposing a shaved skull covered in tattoos and a sullen male face. Saliva dribbles from between the scarlet lips. The man attempts to spit at him.

Harry gets to his feet and looks through a bedroom door at the shirt and trousers spread on the bed. There are also several packets of white crystals on a dressing table. Lipsticks, bits of makeup. He finds a wallet and checks the drivers licence. Same surly face. He returns and tells Logan McGilvray that he's under arrest for attempted murder.

When they arrive at the station the custody sergeant looks up briefly from his screen, then blinks and stares again at the bowed figure standing between the two detectives.

"Who have we got here then?"

"Mr. Logan McGilvray, aka Ms. Loretta Smith."

"Oh yes, I heard. There's a crime-scene team gone over there." He peers at the man, taking in the whole ensemble. "Jeez, Ross," he says at last, "you're a real chick magnet, aren't you?"

Ross breaks into a broad grin. "Old bloke's still got it, mate."

It's the first time Harry's seen him smile.

"But it was Harry made the arrest," Ross adds. "That dickhead was going to kill me with this . . ." He thumps a plastic bag with the knife wrapped inside onto the counter. "Harry saved me bacon."

"Did he now?" The custody sergeant looks at Harry, nods, then goes back to his computer. "So is that Loretta with one T or two, Mr. McGilvray?"

Later, after a doctor has stitched the gash in Ross's hand, they go to an interview room where McGilvray is sitting hunched at the table. He is wearing a T-shirt and shorts now, but the makeup remains, and the painted nails. Harry sees that he is as thickly covered in tattoos—arms, legs, neck—as his injured wife.

They sit down and Ross presses the ERISP recording switch. "Interview conducted by Detective Sergeants Ross Bramley and Harry Belltree . . ."

On the other side of the table McGilvray abruptly raises his head and stares at Harry. There is an odd expression on his face, startled. As Ross continues he goes on staring, his mouth twisted into something ugly that could be a smile. He ignores Ross, making not a sound as the questions drag on and finally come to a stop. All the time he has his eyes locked on Harry.

Afterwards Ross says to Harry, "What was that all about, the death stare? You ever seen him before?"

Harry shakes his head. "Never."

"Must be the drugs then."

By the time they've finished typing up their reports it's the end of their shift, and Ross says, "Well, haven't had so much fun in years, Harry. Fancy a drink?"

This is a breakthrough. They cross the road and walk past the terrace of lawyers' rooms to the Grand, opposite the old courthouse. Above them at the top of the hill looms the tower of Christ Church Cathedral. Ross buys a couple of beers and they go to a quiet corner and try to find some common ground. Ross takes the lead, telling old stories of catching people in embarrassing situations—the naked man locked out by his angry wife, the robber found pinned to the floor by the Coke machine he'd tried to break into. He's a good storyteller and Harry laughs along, not saying much. Something about Ross's manner reminds him of Bob Marshall. Same generation, same attitudes, and when Ross gets back from buying another beer Harry tells him one of Marshall's tales, then asks him if he's ever come across his old boss. Ross nods, suddenly careful.

"Sure, I knew him well once. We started out about the same time, served in Darlinghurst together for a fair while." He hesitates. "Both lost our wives to cancer the same year, too."

That was about eight years ago, Harry thinks. Ross and Marshall have kept in touch. "I'm sorry. Are you on your own now?"

"Sure. Suits me."

Harry wonders if that's true. "What are you doing for dinner? Want to come back with me?"

"Oh, your wife'll have something fixed up for you."

But he doesn't sound adamant, so Harry says, "Not a problem. I'll give her a call."

He does so, and when he's finished, Ross says, "Jenny, right? Your wife."

Harry looks at him in surprise. As far as he knows none of the Newcastle cops have met her or asked about her.

Ross goes on, "I saw her, when she was up here with your folks, three years ago. That's why you're here, isn't it? To check up on us?"

"What?"

"See if we messed up the investigation into the accident."

Harry shakes his head. "Ross, I had no say in the matter. They wanted me out of Sydney. Bob Marshall fixed it all up, told me I was being sent up here."

Ross frowns doubtfully. "Bob told me you still don't believe it was an accident."

Harry is angry now. What was Marshall playing at? "I know it wasn't an accident. I found the bloke that ran them off the road and followed the wreck down the hill with a baseball bat to make sure they were good and dead. Jenny was lucky that she was on the floor in the back and he didn't see her."

Ross looks shocked, his mouth open.

Harry goes on. "Does everybody think that's why I'm here?"

"No, no. Bob contacted me, told me to keep it to myself."

"But he told you I was coming to check on you all?"

"Well . . . no, not exactly. That was my take on it, I guess. He just asked me to look out for you, as a favour to him. He didn't mention anything about someone running them off the road. So where's this bloke now?"

"He's dead. A biker shooting."

"Jeez." Ross shakes his head. "But why'd he want to kill them?"

"That I don't know. Probably a court case my father was involved with." Harry checks himself. He's said too much, more than he told Marshall. "Ross, you've got to keep this to yourself, okay? It's an ongoing investigation, and what I've just told you is confidential. I really don't want you discussing it with anyone, not even Bob. Will you do that?"

Ross looks away for a moment, then says, "You just saved my arse, Harry. I guess I can do that."

"Thanks. So why do the others turn away when I come into a room?"

"They've been asking what a Sydney homicide cop's doing up here. Wondering if you're damaged goods."

"Great."

"You do have that look sometimes, mate," Ross says.

"What look?"

"You know, wearing the mask."

They reach for their drinks, silent. Then Harry says, "Jenny's never recognised your name when I've mentioned

13

you. She's lost her memory of the days before and after the crash. You talking to her might help. You know she lost her sight?"

"Yes, I heard."

They finish their beers and drive over to Carrington, where Harry and Jenny are renting. The inner-city neighbourhood grew up around the docks; its streets once teemed with sailors from the colliers and clippers that thronged the harbour. Now the streets are quiet and tree-lined, the old pubs and houses becoming gentrified, but beyond the rooftops the big grain silos and coal-loading gantries still loom, crowding the nearby mechanised wharfs.

Harry stops outside a small weatherboard cottage built up on brick piers on a narrow plot. They go up the veranda steps to the front door and there's a sound of barking from inside.

"You've got a dog?"

"Guide dog for Jenny, Felecia."

He opens the door and calls out to Jenny while a blond Labrador circles around them thrashing her tail. Jenny comes out from the kitchen and takes Ross's hand. As he talks she frowns suddenly and says, "I know your voice, don't I, Ross? Have we met before?"

"Three years ago. I showed you and your in-laws around when you were in Newcastle."

Over dinner he tells them about that visit. "It was a Monday, right? You drove up from Sydney and arrived at your hotel by the beach about noon."

Ross stares at Jenny's face as he speaks, at the sightless eyes, as if willing her to remember. "It was a bright sunny winter's day, kids in wetsuits out in the surf. You'd have seen them from your hotel window."

Jenny's brow creases in concentration. She says nothing.

"I met you in reception and we took my car to one of the restaurants along the harbour. Seafood—the judge wanted seafood. A big bulk carrier came in, the tugs brought it right past in front of us and away to the coal loaders on the far side of the basin. The ship was from Japan I remember, and the judge was interested. He asked lots of questions about the mines and the ships. He seemed to be quite knowledgeable."

Jenny shakes her head. "No, I can't remember."

"After lunch I left you and Mrs. Belltree to have a look around town. You went to the museum and the art gallery, did some shopping. I took the judge to the courthouse where he was meeting some of his colleagues, then later back to your hotel. In the evening I picked you all up again and took you to the Newcastle Club, up on the Hill next to the cathedral. The Law Society had put on a dinner in the judge's honour. He told me you'd get a cab back, but the next day he mentioned that you'd walked—it wasn't far.

"So, Tuesday morning. I came to the hotel about eight. There had been some doubt about whether you'd spend one night or two here, but the judge had finished his business and decided to leave straight away for Armidale. The scenic road across country on Thunderbolt's Way. We talked about the best route to Gloucester, and you all set off."

"But hang on," Harry says. "The crash happened on Wednesday, didn't it?"

"That's right. We assume they decided to stop overnight in Gloucester, then set off early the next morning. There were patches of fog on the road, and it was wet, it rained during the night—that always makes the bends tricky."

Harry thinks back to that time, the first news coming in and the shock that left him numb and unthinking—despite all his years dealing with sudden catastrophes in the police, and before that the army. Later he went to the scene and talked to the investigating team; he never questioned the timeline, or that extra day.

"Do we know what they did in Gloucester? Where they stayed?"

"Well, there were inquiries, but I don't think we ever found out. Didn't seem like an issue. The point was they were on the road by seven the next morning and crashed some time between seven-twenty and seven-thirty."

"We should go back there, take another look," Harry says. He feels the pressure of Jenny's fingers on his hand. That word *look*. "I mean, if you can recognise Ross's voice now, maybe other things will come back to you."

"It is changed a bit," Ross says. "They resurfaced some sections of the road, built crash barriers on the bends like the coroner recommended."

They move on to other subjects. Ross has become relaxed and open, a different person from the one Harry has been working with. He lives out at Kotara, he tells them, in the house where he brought up a family, too big for him now, alone.

When it's time to leave, Harry shows Ross to the door. He turns and whispers, "Is she pregnant, Harry?"

"Yes. Four months."

"Your first?"

Harry nods.

"Magic," Ross says, wistful. "You look after her, son."

FOUR

WHEN ROSS HAS GONE and the house is quiet, Jenny lies awake for a while, Harry in the bed on one side of her, Felecia on the floor on the other.

The dog has been a revelation. Jenny wonders now if she could have managed the change without her. Felecia is two distinct characters. At home she is a happy puppy, playful, teasing, a friend. But when Jenny picks up her harness she instantly focuses and becomes a responsible adult. She puts her head into the loop, waits for Jenny to fasten it, then goes to work. Aided by an audio sat nav, they have together explored every corner of this new world, from the Fishermen's Co-Op on Throsby Basin to the rail yards of Port Waratah. They've trodden and memorised the layout of every lane and shop and open space. They know each corner's distinctive combination of smells—saltwater, coffee, diesel, frangipani blossom, beer, pizza—and its sounds, from the rumble of the coal trains to music coming through the open window of a pub. And they have met the people, including their neighbours, a young newlywed couple on one side and an old ex-steelworker on the other.

Already Jenny has grown fond of this place, and finding her way around somewhere she has never seen has given her confidence. She feels for the first time that she has come to terms with her new self, no longer opening her eyes each morning hoping to see light. And while she knows that Harry feels they have been banished here and sent into limbo, she is grateful that it has taken him away from the turmoil in Sydney. The problem is that it has brought them closer to the scene of the disaster of three years ago, when their lives changed forever. And ever since they arrived here she has been dreading what finally occurred tonight. From the moment she heard Ross's voice the past came back to her in an overwhelming wave. The whole time he was talking she felt nausea and dread, as if she could hear the shuffle of something terrible coming closer.

FIVE

"YOU WERE A HOTSHOT homicide star, weren't you, Bell-tree?" Fogarty barks.

"Boss."

"Well, here's your chance to shine. Get hold of Ross and go out to Ash Island. Somebody's found a body."

They drive out of the city towards Hexham and turn off at the McDonald's onto a narrow concrete bridge across the south arm of the river. On the far side they pass through a belt of mangroves growing along the mudflats of the river's edge and emerge into the sudden empty silence of Ash Island. The sat nav goes blank, a white line twisting across empty space. Ross flicks open a battered old *Gregory's* and gives directions.

They pass signs for the Kooragang Wetland Rehabilitation Project and an area of new boardwalks and visitor-information panels. Then these indications of recent activity vanish and the metalled road ends. Now the road is a dirt causeway across the salt marsh, barely higher than the still dark waters on either side. They pass through a belt of trees, casuarinas, and paperbarks, with mangroves beyond in the salty margins, then back out into bleak open marshland.

Eventually they catch distant views across a wide black

lagoon to the yellow and orange superstructures of the giant loaders working on the coal stockpiles over at the port. Ahead of them is another copse of sparse trees, and two uniforms next to a police truck, unrolling tape to establish a crime-scene perimeter.

They park and walk over to them. Ross says, "What ya got?"

One of the GDs points to the grass at the edge of the lake. From among the tufts and muddy clumps a dirty white hand sticks up into the air. "Looks like a body, sarge."

"Certainly does. Who called it in?"

The officer points to a solitary figure standing beside a four-wheel-drive at the end of the track, a young man in green boots, his sleeves rolled up. As they walk over to him they see black mud on his arms and boots, a long-handled shovel leaning against the side of his 4WD.

He introduces himself, a young chopper pilot for the Port Corporation. Three nights ago, he says, he saw a lonely light glimmering on Ash Island.

"Two flatbed trucks or utility vehicles, looked like. They turned their lights off when I got close, so I thought I'd come out and see what they were up to. Took me a while to find the place. Over there. Once you spot it it's fairly obvious where the ground has been disturbed, but I guess in a few weeks it'd be grown over again. I sank the shovel into the mud, and that's what I turned up . . ."

They stare at the place for a moment, then Ross says, "Okay, we'll back out of here now and call in the experts."

They reverse their vehicles along the track to a place wide enough for others to pass them and Ross reports in, calling for a crime-scene team. Harry works on a statement from the pilot with dates and times. When the forensic team arrives they get him to walk them through his movements, then take his boots and shovel and prints of his tyres before letting him go.

After a couple of hours, forensics allow Harry and Ross to follow a narrow pathway they've demarcated with tape from the road to the burial site, and they follow this to where a cluster of people in mud-splattered blue overalls are working. A smell hangs in the air, something sweet and sickly lacing the sour organic odours of the marsh sediments.

One of the people is crouching over a mud-encrusted heap laid out on a stretcher. Ross introduces Harry to the senior regional pathologist, Professor Leon Timson.

"Hello, Harry. Won't shake your hand." He has a broad northern English accent. "This is interesting."

"Is that the body?"

"It is, most of it. We're still finding other bits."

On cue one of the other searchers lifts a muddy lump and cries, "Here's another one."

"Fingers," Timson explains, and calls out. "Well done. One more to go, lads." He turns back to the two detectives. "All the fingers of the right hand have been severed and buried with the body, along with various bits of clothing."

"Anything else you can tell us?" Ross asks.

"Not much until I clean him up."

"Him?"

"Yup. Not a tall person, as you see, maybe one-sixty centimetres, five foot five? Something like that."

"A youth?"

"Could be. They tell me you know exactly when he was buried?"

"Three nights ago, around 2:15 a.m."

Timson nods. "Good. Well, we'll take all this back and clean it up and see what we've got."

There is a line of vehicles now parked along the road-

21

way, and operational support group police wearing overalls and waterproof leggings are being briefed for a search of the surrounding terrain. While Ross goes over to join them, Harry moves away from the activity to explore on his own, striking out through the trees and grasses, trying to get a picture of the setting. The burial site is part of an archipelago of mounds and hillocks thickly matted with reeds and grasses and stunted, gnarled trees, threaded with watercourses and pools. Within a short distance from the activity of the search area he feels an abrupt sense of isolation from the wider world. He makes his way back to the car, where Ross is talking to another cop.

Harry looks around at the scene. "Good place for a secret burial—close to the city but completely remote. Makes you wonder."

"What?"

"If there are any others buried out here."

"Are you serious? This isn't western Sydney."

Harry shrugs. "It's pure chance this one was turned up. We should get equipment out here, do a search."

"Jeez . . ." Ross stares out at the marshes stretching away into the distance. "That could take forever."

THEY DRIVE BACK ALONG the route and come to a sign for the Wetlands Visitors' Centre. It's housed in a refurbished nineteenth-century brick building, with nursery gardens nearby for the wetlands regeneration project. Inside they introduce themselves to a woman on duty. Ross asks if they've noticed any unusual activity recently.

"No, why? What's happened?"

"We've found a body in the marshes a couple of kilometres down the track to the south."

"Oh, that's terrible. Do you know who it is?"

"Not yet. There's been a report of a couple of vehicles out there on Sunday night, after midnight. We're looking for anyone who may have seen something."

"I don't think anyone here can help you. We're only staffed during the day."

Ross asks her for a list of the people who work there, tells her to contact the police if she hears anything.

"So there's no one who lives out here?"

"Only the old couple at Copley's farm. They're not on the main route across the island . . ." she shows them on a map, ". . . but I suppose they might have seen or heard something."

They take the turn the woman indicated onto a deeply rutted tack. A couple of fields appear behind wire fences, dairy cattle grazing. The farm looks in danger of subsiding into the earth, the lean-to roofs of its sheds and barns pitched unsteadily against what might once have been a fine brick villa. An elderly woman answers their knock, wiping her hands on a dishcloth. She's short and plump, walks with a swaying limp on arthritic hips. She shakes her head as Ross repeats his questions.

"We get boys coming out here some nights in their cars," she says, "doing burnouts and that. We can hear them, on the road out by the visitors' centre. They leave us alone."

A dog growls and the two police turn to see an elderly man, thin and worn hard as a weathered tree stump, approaching across the yard with a scrawny collie loping by his side. He confirms what his wife has told them. "Keep ourselves to ourselves," he says. "Don't want no trouble from hoons."

Harry points to a ruined brick structure among the trees

23

beyond the paddock, and the old man explains, "Radar station in the last war."

When they leave they drive over that way and see an extensive concrete apron scattered with bricks and tufts of weed. A brick tower has collapsed in on itself, and nearby stand the only intact structures, two blackened curved humps of concrete shell huts. They get out and check them, their doorways and windows sealed with brickwork and old corrugated steel sheets, long untouched, then return to the car and drive back to report to Fogarty.

SIX

DETECTIVE CHIEF INSPECTOR FOGARTY is seated behind his desk, studying a large satellite image of Ash Island. He looks up as they come in and frowns.

"Well?"

Ross brings him up to date, mentioning what little they know of the victim, the probable sex, and size.

"A child? Teenager? Some mischief gone wrong, maybe?"

Ross shrugs.

Harry says, "They're doing a surface search of the immediate area, boss, but I reckon we need to think about a more thorough investigation of that place."

"What do you mean?"

"If there's one body buried out there, there may be more. We should do a search with ground radar, dogs."

Fogarty rocks back on his chair, staring at him incredulously. "What are you suggesting, a mafia mass grave? A burial site for Mexican drug cartels?" He shakes his head. "Do you know how big Ash Island is? How long it would take? How much it would cost?"

"I'm just suggesting the immediate area, boss, by way of due diligence."

"Due diligence!" Fogarty snorts. "You're the last person

to be lecturing me about due diligence, Belltree. You've only been here five minutes and you've already got a formal complaint lodged against you."

"Boss?"

Fogarty lifts a document from his in-tray.

"Mr. Logan McGilvray's solicitor has lodged a complaint alleging you used excessive force against him, caused extensive unnecessary and malicious damage to his property, and exploited his transgender issues to publicly humiliate him."

Ross laughs.

"It's not funny, Ross. He makes no complaint against you, says your behaviour was exemplary and deeply regrets that you were injured in the fracas, which he claims was due to Sergeant Belltree's mishandling of the situation."

"He tried to kill me, boss!"

"He says not. He says that was Sergeant Belltree's construction on the matter. Did you actually see him threaten you?"

"He was round the corner," Ross protests, "waiting for me with a bloody great knife. He stabbed my hand. If Harry hadn't stopped him he'd have cut my throat."

"That's not the way he describes it. There's a professional-standards team on its way to interview you both. Go back to your desks and don't talk to anyone until you're called."

SEVEN

AFTER THE CRISIS ON the headland, Kelly Pool has decided to face her nightmares. She has come back to the neighbourhood known as Crucifixion Creek in western Sydney, to Mortimer Street, where Donna Fenning drugged her and handed her over to Joost Potgeiter. But when she arrives, pulling her car into the kerb on the perimeter road, she feels a visceral shock. Behind the high chain-link fencing that now surrounds the place, machines are grinding away at the fabric of buildings, uprooting trees, collapsing roofs, pushing over walls, breaking up concrete slabs.

As she stares in astonishment, a huge truck loaded with rubble growls through the gates now erected at the end of Mortimer Street. They remain open, and she gets out and walks towards them. All the cottages down the right-hand side of the street, including the one owned by her elderly friend Phoebe, have vanished, leaving no more than a long mound of crushed bricks.

On the other side the demolition is incomplete. Old fireplaces are exposed on tottering walls, windows tilt drunkenly into space. She walks down the street feeling like the lone survivor of a devastating earthquake and comes to a patch of dirt in which one cactus remains upright, coated with white dust. This is the front garden of number eleven, Donna Fenning's house. Through the gap where the front windows used to be she sees a sheet of wallpaper curling from the shattered plasterwork. She recognises the pink rose pattern with enough force to take her breath away. She steps over the debris and tears off a section. Stares at it.

"Hey, what are you doing in there?"

The voice belongs to a man in a hi-vis vest and hard hat, gloved hands on hips.

She steps back out towards him and apologises. "I used to know this street. I had no idea . . ."

"Well, you can't just wander in. This place is dangerous."

"Yes. So it's all going? The biker compound, the factory units, everything?"

"Everything. Clean slate."

"That's good," she says, tucking the piece of wallpaper into her pocket.

The man escorts her back to the gate and closes it behind her.

A clean slate. As she walks back to her car she feels a growing sense of liberation. She sees a large billboard attached to the perimeter fence, announcing a major new urban development, Phoenix Square, with a picture of gleaming apartment towers. The developer is Ozdevco. She knows that name.

EIGHT

PROFESSOR TIMSON HAS FINISHED the postmortem by the time Harry and Ross are told they're free to go. On the drive over to the pathology department Ross grumbles about McGilvray, the professional standards officers and Fogarty.

Harry says, "Do you reckon he's got it in for me?"

"Nah, Foggy's been like that with everyone for months. Lost a good mate, a cop he knew from way back. Got killed in a shooting accident in Sydney."·

"What was his name?"

"Funny name . . . Falstaff? Wagstaff. Got shot by mistake by a couple of trigger-happy patrol officers."

After he put two bullets in me, Harry thinks, feeling the muscles in his chest tighten around the scars.

Ross goes on. "All hushed up, of course. You ever hear about it?"

"Something. And Fogarty was his friend?"

"Close as, apparently. Worked together in Sydney for years. Drug Squad."

Harry wonders how much Fogarty knows about the real circumstances of Wagstaff's death. He tries to recapture the image of Fogarty seated at his desk, glowering at him. Pointedly? Knowingly? Hard to say.

They come to the entrance of the John Hunter Hospital campus and Harry follows Ross's directions around to the detached pathology building, where they're shown into Timson's office. While they wait they examine the pathologist's collection of trophies on his desk and the wall—a plaque with the dagger and motto of the SAS, a picture of the Union Jack being raised at Port Stanley.

They're interrupted by the sound of footsteps. The pathologist puts his head round the door. "Afternoon, folks. Come and see what we've got."

He leads the way to the examination room, where a pale corpse is laid out on the steel table. As they approach they see that the postmortem operation has been repaired, the long cuts to the thorax stitched up and the scalp drawn back into place over the skull.

"Chinese," Ross says.

"Mm, mature adult, probably late twenties or early thirties." Timson turns over the intact left hand. "Accustomed to manual work."

"What are those marks?" Ross points to large dark spots on the thighs.

"Cigarette burns. Poor bastard's been tortured. I assume that's what the severed fingers are all about. There are tape marks around the wrists and ankles where he's been restrained. Cause of death is a massive blow to the back of the head with something like a baseball bat or a scaffolding pole, that sort of diameter. Time of death would have been not long before he was put into the ground.

"His clothes are over here. We've taken off enough of the mud to see what we have—cheap trainers, jeans. Check shirt with a Best and Less label. And that orange woollen beanie looks hand-knitted. No identification, nothing at all in the pockets.

"We were able to make a likely identification of some stomach contents, a meat pie and an apple, and he'd drunk whisky before he died. Other than that there's not a lot I can tell you. I doubt if the toxicology tests will tell us much, but you never know."

"So the shirt suggests he was Australian," Ross offers.

"Yep. Your people have the fingerprints and the DNA will follow shortly. You may have something on him."

He pauses, scratching his chin, then adds, "I'll tell you something that bothers me. The nature of the wounds . . ." He shows them X-rays of a hand with severed fingers. "They seem very clean, very efficient. Done by someone who's done that sort of thing before. And if that's the case you'd be wondering if they've got rid of other bodies out there before as well."

Harry nods and says, "Do me a favour, prof, and put that in your report."

"Yes, I think I will."

When they return to the car Ross radios the station, but there has still been no missing person reported within the region in the past week, and no match for the dead man's prints.

"Let's go see Sammy."

It turns out Sammy is Sammy Lee, a Singaporean who came to study economics at the University of Newcastle twenty years ago and stayed to run his own, very successful, Chinese restaurant in the city. He is also, Ross says, an active figure in the local Chinese community.

He's unable to help. "Ross, I'd have heard for sure if anybody's son or husband was missing. He must be from out of town, probably Sydney. You know, they come up here for a day out, fish off the rocks or dig up pippies from Stockton Beach. Maybe he fell out with some local fishermen."

"Or came up here to sell drugs," Ross suggests.

"Or that, yes."

They thank him and go back to the car, Harry with a copy of the takeaway menu.

"You're not saying much, Harry," Ross says. "No ideas?"

"If he came up from Sydney, where's his car? We should check the rail station cameras. But there's something else that bothers me. I don't know any twenty-something male in Sydney who'd be seen dead in those jeans."

Ross thinks about that, then says, "Okay, let's try Father McCallum."

He makes a phone call, then drives them towards the port and parks outside a two-storey brick building with an illuminated sign, *Flying Angel Stella Maris*. Inside they walk through an entrance vestibule into a large hall where Father McCallum, chaplain of the ministry to seafarers, is showing a cluster of Asian men a rank of computers set up against one wall. He leaves them with a volunteer and comes over to shake hands with Ross, who introduces him to Harry. He takes them into a small office and offers them tea, and Ross explains their problem.

"Chinese, you say? Well, we have plenty of those." He looks at the photograph of the dead man's face on Ross's phone and shakes his head. "It's possible he's one of ours, but I can't honestly say I recognise him."

Ross asks McCallum to tell Harry about the set-up, and the clergyman explains. "We've been here for well over a hundred years, ministering to the needs of visiting sailors. This building was purpose-built in the great days. Hundreds of seamen, British and Australian mainly, here in port for weeks at a time. They held dances and film nights in that hall out there and it'd be packed out. Local girls'd come in and quite a few met their future husbands here. But it's not like that anymore. Now the ships are only in port for about fifteen hours and everything's run by computers and machines. Small crews, no more than a couple of dozen men, all Asian now. Mainly Filipino and Chinese." He pauses. "Those men, well, I shouldn't call them slaves, but they have a hard life. They're away from their families for most of the year, living a lonely kind of existence onboard ship. They're earning maybe ten dollars a day, most of which they're sending back to their families, maybe extended families, even a whole village who are dependent on them.

"They come into port, they've only got a few hours and not much money. When a ship comes in we send our bus out to its berth and take on any crew that want to come out for a short visit. The main thing they want is to use the computers here, to e-mail home, catch up with messages. Then we take them out, maybe to Blackbutt Reserve to see the kangaroos, or more likely to a shopping centre. They don't buy much but they like to look around. They might buy fresh fruit, they miss that onboard ship."

"Our man had eaten an apple and a meat pie," Ross says.

"That'd be right."

"What about the pub?"

"No. Look, the nearest pub here sells craft beers, you know? One drink would cost them practically a day's wages."

"Our man had been drinking whisky."

"Unusual, unless someone bought it for him."

Harry says, "I noticed a rack of clothes out there, Father."

"Yes, they're secondhand. We invite the men to take one item each if they want. Probably made in China," he smiles, "but these are export quality."

Ross shows him a picture of the check shirt but McCallum doesn't recognise it.

"We also offer them a beanie. We have a team of ladies

across the city who knit them for us. You've got to imagine that you're far from home in a foreign port and a stranger offers you something they've made by hand for you—something useful too, because it can get bitterly cold out there on the ocean—it's a gesture they really appreciate."

Again Ross shows him a picture, this time of the orange beanie, and now recognition lights up Father McCallum's face. "Now that does look like one of ours. Let me show these pictures to one of our volunteers. Three or four days ago, you say?"

He calls in a young man from the hall, who studies the images while the priest consults his computer.

"Last Friday we met one ship from Singapore and two from China," Father McCallum says. "On Saturday one from China, one from Japan, and two from South Korea."

The volunteer peers at the image of the dead man's face. "People look different when they're dead, don't they? Kind of preoccupied. But I think . . ." He takes out his own phone and flicks through its photo album. He stops on one and shows it to the detectives, a group shot of ten Asian men together, grinning at the camera.

"Him." He points. "A galley hand. I remember him because he was anxious to Skype his friend in China and he was having trouble. No English. What was his name . . . ? Cheung, I think. It's a common name."

Harry and Ross examine the picture. It might be him. Ross asks him to text him the image.

The young man nods. "Okay. The picture was taken last Saturday the ninth, 10:36 a.m., in the hall here at the mission. That morning we picked up crew from a Chinese ship, the *Jialing*. They spent about an hour here, and that's when I helped Cheung. Then I took them to Marketown shopping centre and left them there for a couple of hours. Some of them made their own arrangements and I can't really remember seeing Cheung again."

"But if he didn't make it back to the ship surely the captain would have reported him missing?" Harry says.

"You would think so, wouldn't you?" Father McCallum says. "The person to ask would be the ship's agent. Every vessel coming into port uses one of the shipping agents based here to look after things for them. Let me see if I can find out who it was." He picks up the phone and makes a couple of calls, jotting notes. "Right, the *Jialing* was represented by Cork Shipping. Gerry Cork is in his office now if you want to talk to him."

They take the address and thank the chaplain, who shows them to the front door. "It's very sad," he says, "to think that young man might have died out here. If no one claims him and he has to be buried here, perhaps we could help with the arrangements? When you think about it, almost everything we have in this country comes to us from the sea, and it's men like Cheung that make our lives possible here. I call them the least, the last, the lost and the lonely. Men of no importance."

Cork Shipping is in a new building on the waterfront Honeysuckle Drive. Gerry Cork offers them seats in an office with a broad view overlooking the port. He explains the company's role, representing the ship owners. "We arrange for the berthing of their ship and for the cargo they want to take on, and generally act on their behalf while the ship is in port. So if there's any problems, we see to them. Like there was a fire on one of our ships last week, and we arranged for emergency repairs at short notice so they'd be able to return home safely for a refit."

He taps at his computer. "The *Jialing*, out of Guangzhou in southern China. Took on 136,000 tonnes of coal from the NRL loader for the Chongqing Power and Light Company and departed on time at 20:36 on Saturday last, November ninth. No problems reported."

"No missing crew? Wouldn't the captain report it if someone didn't return to the ship?"

Cork shrugs. "Not necessarily. It depends how important he was. If he was one of the officers or engineers, say, regulations require that the ship would have to remain here until they found him or they flew in a replacement. But that would take time and money. If he was just an ordinary seaman and the captain could do without him, he'd want to avoid the delay. Probably wouldn't report it and wouldn't wait. It's all about money, see. Yesterday I had a call from a captain to say he had a man with bad toothache and could I arrange for him to see a dentist. We phoned around and managed to get an emergency appointment at short notice. I called the captain back and told him. He asked how much it would cost and when I told him he said, 'Ah, no, he don't have toothache no more.'"

He thinks. "You could talk to Customs and Immigration. They might be able to help you. That ship was berthed at the Kooragang coal terminal. They've got an office over there."

The two detectives drive around to the far side of the port and report to the customs office covering the Kooragang berths behind an impressive array of razor wire and cameras. The duty officer is processing a queue of men coming through the checkpoint and they wait until he's finished. They introduce themselves and explain their business; he takes them into his office. Checks the computer.

He opens another file and scrolls down the screen. "Cheung, you say? We had three Cheungs through here on the ninth . . . Hang on, we have a flag against one of them—

Cheung Xiuying from the *Jialing*. He didn't return through the gate that day or the next. Immigration was notified."

"So you have his passport?"

"No. That stays on the ship. They're issued with a shore pass."

"Nobody else missing from that ship?"

"Nope. Did he have an accident?"

"Suspicious death. Could he have been trying to jump ship?"

"It happens occasionally. Without documents or money they'd need help."

"Could he have been smuggling something ashore? Drugs?"

"Unlikely. They're checked through and anyone carrying a package is usually searched. They're not ashore for long so they don't often carry bags. I suppose he might have brought something in on his person."

He offers to show them the berth where the *Jialing* docked. Another ship is there now, its vast orange hull streaked with rust. High above them they can see the small figures of crew at the rail watching as the loader pumps a black stream of coal into the hold. There is a huge sign on the gantry. *NRL*.

Harry points to it. "What's that?"

"Nordlund Resources Limited. It's their coal. They have mines and estates up the valley. And they have their own coal loader and security here." The officer points to a man in a hard hat and hi-vis vest watching the operation from the dock. "They keep a pretty close grip on things."

"Are they worried about sabotage?"

"There've been incidents—protests, environmental activists. A couple of weeks ago they blocked the shipping lanes with small boats. This is one of the biggest coal ports in the world, so it's only to be expected. Talk to NRL's security people about the *Jialing*. They may have heard something we didn't."

The NRL office is in a modern glass and steel building among the coal stockpiles set back from the waterfront. Beyond a gate in the surrounding high chain-link fence they find a space in the car park and go into reception.

Ross shows his ID. "We'd like to speak to the head of security."

"Mr. Tolliver? You have an appointment?"

"No. It's important."

They wait while the woman phones, then tells them to write their details in the book and gives them each a pass on a lanyard.

The man who comes out to them has the heavy build and thick neck of a rugby forward softening into middle age. "Officers? Jason Tolliver. What can I do for you?"

Ross introduces them and they're taken to an office. The desk is clear of paperwork and on the wall behind is a huge aerial photograph of the port.

"The *Jialing*?" Tolliver taps at his computer. "Yes, Customs and Immigration notified us of a missing crew member on the morning of the tenth. By that time the ship had gone. We have no further information. There was nothing else out of the ordinary—timetables were adhered to, no incidents reported. Would you like to speak to one of the people on the ground that day?"

He arranges coffee while they wait for an older man in a uniform tunic to join them. This one is an ex-cop, Andy Flynn, who knows Ross and shakes his hand. "Sure, I was on that day, along with Scully and Taufa. What can I say? Nothing special."

He describes the procedures for men coming off the

ships, confirming what the others have told them, then escorts them back out of the building. In the car park he points to a red sports car. "My new car. You should do what I did, Ross mate—get out while you can and find yourself a soft number like this." He laughs and waves good-bye.

"Tosser," Ross mutters. "Always was." He sighs, rubbing the dressing on his hand. "We have a name. A man of no importance. So what the hell happened to him?"

They drive for a while, then Ross says, "Anyway, what are we going to do about that slug McGilvray?"

"Nothing, Ross. Don't worry about it. You're in the clear."

"But you're not. He deserves to be squashed."

"Let it go."

"You're very calm, Harry. In your shoes I'd be mad as a cut snake."

They return to the open-plan detectives' office in the Newcastle police station. A couple of other cops there are standing at the broad band of windows that look out over the ocean, watching a whale breaching far out to sea. While Ross starts typing their report, Harry calls up the recording of their McGilvray interview. A drug test has confirmed that Ross was right about McGilvray being stoned, but still, there is that sudden moment of clarity in his eyes when Ross mentions the name *Belltree*. Harry replays it, again and again. What does he know? What does the name mean to him?

NINE

LATER, TOWARDS THE END of his shift, Harry seeks out Anna Demos, the constable who was with McGilvray's wife at her parents' house.

"Oh yes, Sarge, I heard there's been trouble from that bastard. How can I help?"

"I wondered how his wife was doing these days. Have you been in touch?"

"No. I spoke to her sister later and she said she'd gone to a women's refuge. Apparently she doesn't want to talk to us, far less press charges. Her family's furious, but what can they do? Do you think we'll still pursue it?"

"I hope so. Did the sister give you any background?"

"Well . . . did you actually see Mrs. McGilvray?"

"She was on the stretcher when we arrived. I didn't see much."

"Only it's kind of a weird experience. She's got a lot of tattoos," Harry nods, "including in her eyeballs."

"Really?"

"Yes, her eyes are bright green. It looks really creepy. It's one of the things her family hates. They say McGilvray forced her to do it. Apparently she cried green tears for two days after it was done. She told her sister he's got some sort of deal going with the tattoo studio and they've had lots of work done. The thing is, it's really good work."

"You reckon?"

"Yes. I've heard of the artist. She's well known, really talented. And expensive."

"What do they do for a living, those two?"

"She has a degree apparently, but no job. He works in the mines, a storeman. No criminal record, but he got off with a warning when he was a juvenile. You'll never guess what he did."

"Go on."

"He stuck needles in someone's pet rabbit. It was alive, they heard it screaming."

Harry shakes his head in disgust. "Can rabbits scream?"

"Apparently yes. It's a horrible sound they say, like a baby screaming. I'm just thankful the McGilvrays don't have any kids."

"Did she say what kind of deal it was, with the tattoo artist?"

"Something about getting free time, I'm not sure exactly."

He finds the tattoo studio in a side street in Islington, a blacked-out window with elaborate psychedelic lettering: DEE-DEE'S STUDIO. A sign on the door says CLOSED but there is a light on inside. Harry raps on the glass. A young woman appears, stares out at him and shakes her head, pointing to the sign. Harry holds up his ID and she sags visibly and unbolts the door.

"What do you want?"

"Just a few minutes of your time. You're Dee-Dee Perry?"

She nods and glances quickly up and down the street and closes the door behind him. He follows her into the room where she works and he's struck by how clean and orderly everything is—new furniture, a framed licence certificate on the wall along with mounted photographs of her artwork. A neat sound system, fresh flowers in a vase.

"What's this about?"

"Sheila McGilvray."

Dee-Dee's face drops. "Oh. Her mother, right? She's made a complaint?"

"Her husband's beaten her up bad. I need some background."

"He's a pig. Is she badly hurt?"

"Broken ribs, cheekbone, nose."

"He's done this before. Sometimes she comes in here with bruises."

"Does she talk about it to you?"

"No. She seems intimidated. It's hard to get her to open up."

"And you've had a run-in with the mother?"

She shrugs. "After I did her eyes her mother came storming in here and made a scene. I tried to tell her, what could I do? Sheila said she wanted it done."

"Did she?"

"Well . . . Logan was at her elbow. He was really keen, choosing the colour and everything, but I did ask her straight out if she was sure, and she said yes."

"They're regular clients of yours, yes?"

"Yes, more or less every week."

"Her sister said Logan has a special arrangement with you."

Her eyes slide away. "Not really."

"Come on, Dee-Dee, I'm not here to make trouble for you, but I will if I have to. What's the deal? Is he selling drugs through here?"

"No!" She glares at Harry. "I wouldn't have that."

"But he wanted to? So what was it? He muscled you?"

She looks away again, then says softly, "I'm just trying to run a business. All of us are. It isn't just him, he has friends. But Logan really likes my art, and we came to an arrangement. No threats, no drugs, he keeps his friends off my back and in return I give him up to five hours of work a month."

"What's that worth?"

"A thousand bucks."

"Tell me about his friends."

"I can't do that, I don't know who they are. But they're bad. They burned down the Rainbow Ink Emporium when they wouldn't cooperate. There were people inside."

Harry gives her a card and writes his number on the back. "Call me if Logan gives you any trouble."

She studies the name. "Your skin looks very bare, Harry. Maybe you should let me do something for you."

He smiles, leaves.

When he gets home Jenny is working with her second-best friend, the computer that talks to her, reading out to her what's on its screen. Harry used to call it her best friend until Felecia came along.

He kisses her and looks over her shoulder at the document she's working on.

"I'm updating my CV. I'm still getting the work from Sydney, but I'm worried they'll forget about me now we've moved away, so I'm going to apply to some local firms."

"That's good." Jenny does online research work for a couple of law firms in Sydney, and Harry knows how important it is to her.

"Oh, and I found this brilliant app," she says. "I take a picture of something and it tells me what it is. Even reads the label out to me."

"Great." Harry's sincerely pleased. One evening last week Jenny made a beef curry with a packet of dog meat rather than the beef that was defrosting next to it on the bench.

"How was your day?"

"Not too bad. I went to a tattoo parlour—sorry, studio."

"Oh, Harry, you didn't."

"Just business. But you'll have to run your new app over me to be sure. Listen, it's my rostered day off tomorrow. I think we should take a drive up to Thunderbolt's Way."

"Oh." She turns to face him. Her eyes move as if she's searching for him.

"You'd be okay with that, wouldn't you?"

"I don't know, Harry. What good will it do?"

"Something might trigger a memory, the way Ross's voice did. It's worth a try, surely?" He puts an arm around her, trying to imagine what is going through her head. If he could go without her he would, but that would achieve nothing.

TEN

IT IS ONLY AS Kelly is driving Wendy to her final checkup at the hospital that she realises this must be the place where Donna Fenning once said her husband worked. It was about the only bit of personal information she'd mentioned; Kelly had forgotten it until now.

"I don't suppose," she says, "that in all the visits you've made to this place you've made friends with anyone who would access their staff records for you?"

Wendy looks at her as if she's mad. "Of course not."

"No, of course not."

"Why?"

So Kelly tells her.

"I've no idea whether her husband was a brain surgeon or a toilet cleaner, and there probably won't be anyone with the name Fenning on their books anyway, assuming Donna's name was false. It was just a thought."

Kelly trawls the shops at the Westfield while Wendy keeps her appointment. She's having coffee when Wendy rings to say she's finished. She drives back to the hospital and picks up her flatmate at the entrance. Wendy hands her a sheet of paper.

"What's this?"

"My cousin works here in admin. There's no Fennings, but you were kidnapped on the twentieth of July, and rescued on the twenty-second, which would have been when Donna bolted, right?"

"Yes."

"Well, an electrician in the maintenance department called Craig Schaefer quit suddenly on the twenty-second. Home address eleven Mortimer Street."

"My God, Wendy, that's brilliant." She scans the sheet. "Next of kin, wife. Karen Schaefer." She looks at Wendy and feels tears well up in her eyes.

"What is it? What's wrong?"

"Nothing. Only you're smiling. It's the first time I've seen you smiling in four months."

When she returns to the office, Kelly gets to work on the dozens of databases the newspaper has access to. Eventually she discovers the details of the marriage of Craig Schaefer to Karen Suskind, fifteen years ago at Wyong on the Central Coast, ninety kilometres north of Sydney. Karen's date of birth is given as 1964. This is followed by a birth certificate for Karen Suskind, in the Mater Hospital in Newcastle, seventy kilometres further north again. Parents David and Donna Suskind of Adamstown in Newcastle. *Donna*, Kelly thinks, *she borrowed her mother's first name*.

Now Kelly does a search for David and Donna Suskind, and finds that Donna died five years ago, also in the Newcastle Mater. They still lived in Adamstown.

She finds some snippets of information about Craig Schaefer, but little on Karen. He has a trade course certificate as an electrical mechanic, and with Karen has occupied a number of rental addresses on the Central Coast and in Sydney. Apart from this job at the hospital, however, dating back twelve months, there is no information on either of them for the past ten years. They appear to have no children.

Kelly relates all this to Wendy when she returns to their flat.

Wendy says, "Have you told the cops?"

"No."

"Why not?"

"They weren't much help before. This time I want to find out as much as I can before anyone goes blundering in."

"No," Wendy says. "You're enjoying this. You don't want them to take over."

It's true, Kelly thinks. She hasn't felt this motivated since those terrible days in July.

ELEVEN

THEY SET OFF AFTER breakfast the next morning, the three of them, Felecia sitting up in the back seat. Out along the Pacific Highway until they reach the sign for the Bucketts Way to Gloucester. Not much traffic now, and the road hemmed in by bush with glimpses of rural properties scattered among the trees. Finally the landscape opens out and Harry sees the shape of the Bucketts, the range of hills that forms a western wall to the town. He tries to describe their strange humps to Jenny, like a line of craggy dinosaurs silhouetted against the pale blue sky.

They park in the main street of the country town and go for a walk, Harry commenting on things Jenny might remember. A butcher selling local beef, a café with fresh-baked pastries, a health-food store, a travel agent and bookstore, three pubs. They come to the visitors' information centre, where a volunteer, a retired man, tells them of the history of goldmining in the area and gives them pamphlets. Local walking trails, B&Bs, and other accommodation.

Harry reads their names to Jenny; none of them sounds familiar. When they sit down at a café she shakes her head. "It's no good, Harry. I can't picture it."

"That's okay," he says, trying to sound positive. "Don't try too hard. We just need to be open to the possibility that something will click."

They set off again, out of town across the Gloucester River and onto Thunderbolt's Way, named after the bushranger who once roamed the mountains up ahead. The road reaches a tight bend with a sign for a side road to Cackleberry Valley. Harry laughs. "Sounds like something out of a kid's story, Cackleberry Valley."

"I've been there," Jenny says.

He slows and pulls in to the side. "You sure?"

"There's an egg."

"An egg?"

"A mountain shaped like an egg. Cackleberry Mountain."

Harry looks out over the fields to the surrounding hills, but can see nothing like that. "Well, let's take a look."

He turns the car back to the sign and sets off along a narrow twisting branch road across wide paddocks of grazing cattle towards a wooded ridge. Tall trees close in around them. The light of open country dims into the gloom of an ancient forest. Harry slows and winds down the windows. They smell the cool forest air and hear the zip and crack of a whip bird. Jenny has an intent look of concentration on her face, but says nothing.

Ahead of them the tree canopy begins to thin and they rattle across a cattle grid and emerge into open paddocks once again. They pass a sign, PRIVATE PROPERTY. And there, on the far side of the valley, rising out of a mat of grey-green forest, is the grey dome of a mountain shaped like an egg. Harry pulls over.

"There it is, Jenny, your Cackleberry Mountain, just as you said."

"Can you . . . can you see horses?"

He looks out across the fields and sees only cattle. "Not yet."

There has been no other traffic on the road. He is about to pull out again, barely glancing at his side mirror, when he catches sight of a car bearing down on them at speed. A yellow sports car, open topped, hurtles past them. Their Corolla rocks in its wake.

"What was that?" Jenny says.

"Sports car, doing at least a hundred." He thinks how out of place it looks, diminishing down the road into this silent landscape. "Woman in a baseball cap and dark glasses."

They follow the yellow car deeper into the valley, past stands of eucalypt. Felecia gives a low growl at a mob of kangaroos loping away across a field to their right. Then up ahead Harry notices something red nestled in a copse. As the road curves towards it he makes out the dark verandas of a two-storey homestead crowned by a red iron roof. Beyond it are the white fences of paddocks in which a dozen horses trot. He describes all this to Jenny, who nods. He notices that she's clutching her fists, breathing a little faster.

As they draw closer to the house Harry sees the yellow convertible parked outside. He pulls up behind it and gets out onto the gravel drive. Looks up at the house, a classic Australian homestead but much larger than he'd imagined from the road. As they stand there a figure comes out of the front doors onto the veranda and emerges into the sunlight. A young woman, blond hair pulled back into a ponytail. Shirt, jeans, and boots; carrying a saddle and a riding helmet.

"Hello." She walks down the steps and comes towards them. "Can I help you?" Her tone is clipped, even abrupt, as if they're in the wrong place. As she speaks Harry feels Jenny's fingers squeeze into his arm.

"Her voice," she whispers.

"Hi," he says. "We're just exploring. I've never been down this way before."

"The road ends here. This is private property. Didn't you see the sign?"

"Impressive place," Harry says. "What's it called?"

The woman straightens her back, hefting the saddle impatiently. "Kramfors Homestead. Now, if you don't mind . . ."

"Only my wife has been here before. I think you've met her—Jenny Belltree."

The woman freezes in mid-step and turns to stare at Jenny, at her eyes.

"You remember her, yes?"

"I . . . I don't think so."

"Three and a half years ago. She came here with my parents, Danny and Mary Belltree. When they left here they went up onto Thunderbolt's Way and their car crashed. They were killed, and Jenny lost her sight. You must remember."

The woman seems at a loss, mouth open, looking from one to the other. Then another woman's voice, strident, calls from the house, "Amber! Hurry up! They'll be here soon."

The woman starts. "No, I'm sorry, I can't help you. We've never met before." She turns and hurries away towards the horses' paddock.

Harry takes a picture of the retreating figure with his phone and another of Kramfors Homestead and the other woman standing at the balcony rail glaring down at them.

When they get back in the car Jenny says, "She knew me, didn't she?"

"Yes."

"Why did she deny it? Her voice was so familiar, but in

my mind it was . . . welcoming. Not like today. We were here, Harry. I remember the name, Kramfors. And I don't think it was just a chance visit."

"Okay, we can find out more. Did you recognise the other woman's voice? She must be about eighty, silver hair, slight build."

Jenny shakes her head. "No, I don't think so."

As they turn back along the road the car is filled suddenly with the loud throb of rotors as a helicopter passes low above them, heading to a landing strip in the field behind the house, where a Land Rover is waiting. Harry pulls in and watches as a figure gets out of the Land Rover and runs across to open the door of the helicopter. Harry takes photos as two men in dark suits emerge, too far away to identify their features.

They return to Thunderbolt's Way and continue up into the hills of the Great Dividing Range. When they come to the place, Harry almost misses where his parents' car went off the road. There's a heavy metal barrier there now, to guard against the steep drop. A little further along the winding route they stop at a layby and get out. But there is nothing in the sighing wind or the growl of traffic or the sight of an eagle wheeling far overhead to awaken any memories. They return to the car and drive on as far as Carson's Lookout, with its panorama across the broad valley to the hills of the Barrington Tops. Then they turn back.

At Gloucester they return to the visitors' centre and speak again to the volunteer.

"Back again? How did it go?"

Harry says, "We went into the Cackleberry Valley, saw the homestead out there."

"Kramfors? Oh yes. The Nordlunds' place."

"Nordlund? The coal-mining people?"

"That and other things. We've got something . . ." He begins searching through the racks of pamphlets and finally finds what he's looking for. "This is it." He shows them a sketch of the homestead. "The Nordlunds have been big pastoralists in this area for four generations. The patriarch was Axel Nordlund. Came over to Western Australia from Sweden as a young man to try his luck in the Kalgoorlie gold rush of the 1890s. Made his fortune there, then heard of new gold finds over here in the Barrington Tops. They never amounted to anything like out west, but Axel bought land in the Cackleberry Valley, turned to farming, and built the homestead. His son was Carl, one of the old breed of pastoralists. World War II hero."

"We met a young woman, drives a yellow sports."

"That would be Amber, Carl's granddaughter. She runs the estate now."

Harry thanks him and takes the leaflet, *Cattle Kings of Gloucester Shire*.

As she pulls on her seat belt, Jenny says, "So why did she deny having met me?"

"Yes, why would she do that?" He is thinking of the timing. The crash happened at around seven-thirty that morning, and the men who caused it had come up from Sydney. How were they able to ambush them at that time? How did they know where they were? Unless someone from wherever the Belltrees stayed overnight tipped them off the night before, and told them they'd be leaving early the following morning.

"I think we should check out the hotels and B&Bs anyway," he says. "You never know. You might recognise another voice."

So they make a start on the accommodation list that the visitors' centre provided. None of the staff they speak to in the hotels and motels were working there three years ago, but two of them have records dating back that far, which reveal nothing. None of the B&Bs has changed hands since then, and all of the people they speak to remember the fatal crash on Thunderbolt's Way. They are all adamant that they would have heard if the victims had stayed in Gloucester the previous night.

When they get home Harry downloads the photos he took and enlarges the picture of the two men in suits emerging from the chopper. The image isn't clear, but one of them seems familiar. The hair—black, slicked back—reminds him of Nathaniel Horn, the Sydney lawyer of celebrity clients—rich, sporting, and criminal. But he could be wrong.

TWELVE

back at work, goes to see Fogarty.

"Boss, I wondered if there's any progress with McGil-vray's complaint against me."

"That's out of our hands, Belltree. I'm sure they'll let you know when they're ready. Just be thankful you haven't been suspended." He bends back to his paperwork. "Yet."

"Only I've come across information that he's involved with a ring extorting money and services from tattoo sa-lons and using them to sell drugs to customers."

Fogarty looks up slowly. "What ring?"

"I don't have the names of the others involved. Yet."

"How did you come by this information?"

"I spoke to the owner of the salon where he and his wife are regular customers. They have an arrangement where she gives them five hours' free work per month, worth a thousand dollars, as protection."

"You have this on record, do you?"

"No, she won't do that."

"Has Ross Bramley been involved in this?"

"No, just me."

Fogarty sits back in his big office chair, elbows on the arms, fingers steepled, and contemplates Harry. "If you'd been here more than five minutes you'd know that Detective Inspector Colquhoun here commands Strike Force Colyton, tasked specifically with investigating the involvement of outlaw motorcycle gangs and other organised criminal groups in tattoo parlours in our region, and I have no doubt they already know of any such *ring*, if it exists. More to the point, I'm wondering why an apparently rational officer such as yourself would be carrying out a private investigation into a member of the public who has made a complaint against you. Is it just bloody-mindedness and stupidity? Or are you deliberately trying to bring this command and this office into disrepute?"

"No, boss."

"I shall make a file note of this conversation, Belltree, and record that I have given you a formal warning. Now get out."

As he leaves Fogarty's office Harry bumps into Ross, who sees the look on his face.

"Foggy? Yeah, he's been in a foul mood. Professor Timson put a strong recommendation in his report on the Chinese sailor, more extensive search of the crime scene, blah blah. They're sending up specialist forensics from Sydney."

"Ah. How about Cheung? Any progress?"

"Not much. Foggy's dragging his feet till we confirm the ID. We've got CCTV from Marketown. I'll show you."

They go to Ross's desk, where he calls up a video clip of the mall. He points to a group in the crowd. "These are the Chinese." He zooms in and Harry makes out an orange beanie on one of the heads.

"That's him."

"Reckon so."

He skips to another sequence, at the entrance to the centre. The group is examining racks of clothes, but the man in the beanie has moved apart, standing in the doorway of a shop with his right hand to his head.

"Headache?"

"Or a phone. There's nothing after that. The group seems to break up. Some go back inside, some go off across the car park. No more sightings of the beanie."

When he gets back to his computer, Harry looks up the information recorded on Logan McGilvray's charge sheet. It provides a landline phone number, which he notes.

THIRTEEN

JENNY RAISES HER HEAD from the computer and removes her headphones, listening. Felecia has risen from her side and padded out to the hallway, and Jenny can hear the thump of her tail against the wall as the front door creaks open. As Harry makes a fuss of the dog she smells take-away Chinese from Sammy Lee's. It's a relief that he's home and she can put aside the thing she's been working on.

She gets to her feet and hugs him and they go together into the kitchen, each trying to sense the other's mood—what kind of day has it been? As she hears him open the wine and set out two glasses she senses his has been as un-satisfactory as her own.

"Not for me, thanks." She'd love a glass of wine, but hasn't touched it since she learned she was pregnant.

"Sorry. Not thinking. Do you mind if I . . . ?"

"Course not. How was your day?" she asks.

"Oh, fine. Nothing much. You?"

She tells him about her computer searches for the Nordlund family.

"You don't look happy. Not much to go on?"

"The opposite—too much. The various Nordlunds have been involved in so many businesses, charities, and family complications you could write a book. In fact, I wonder why nobody has. But nothing seems to relate to us. Their companies have been involved in litigation from time to time, in the Land and Environment Court, for instance, but nothing that I could find relating to your dad's cases. Did you ever hear your parents mention their name?"

"No, never."

"But there was that one reference to NRL that we found on Kristich's hard drive, remember? We thought it must be code for some rugby league player. I looked it up again, an e-mail from Kristich to Nathaniel Horn. Just four words, *Chocky will invoice NRL*."

Harry says, "Chocky. That was their name for the property developer, wasn't it? Maram Mansur. So maybe he got some kind of service from NRL. A loan, perhaps."

"The Nordlunds have many companies, Nordlund Pastoral, Nordlund Investments, and so on. But NRL is mining. What would they have to do with Mansur?"

Those names again, Jenny thinks, coming back to haunt them.

She listens to the clink of plates and cutlery as Harry sets the table for their meal. Then he says, "Could you hack into the calls record if I gave you a landline phone number?"

"Probably. But surely you can get that from work?"

"This bloke's made a complaint against me. I've been warned off."

Jenny feels a flutter of anxiety. "A complaint?"

"It's nothing. Ross and I arrested him after he beat up his wife. It seems he has some bad friends, and I'd like to know who they are."

"But won't the other police do that?"

"Maybe. But he seems to have something personal against me, and I just want to cover all the bases."

"Okay. You don't think you're being, well . . ."

"Paranoid? Yes, probably. Come on, let's eat this before it gets cold."

After a while she says, "Have they checked his social media sites?"

"Not as far as I know."

"What can you tell me about him?"

He gives her the name, address, phone number. "He's a storeman in one of the mines and is heavily into tattooing, cross-dressing, and bashing his wife."

"Interesting combination. All right, I'll see what I can do."

FOURTEEN

LATER, WHEN JENNY GOES to bed, Harry tells her he has to go out for a while. "Will you be okay?"

"Of course." She reaches down to Felecia lying on the floor at her side. "But you be careful."

"Always."

He heads to the Mayfield bungalow. It is Friday night, and Harry hopes that McGilvray will be occupied elsewhere. He leaves his car a block away and walks into the quiet backstreet where the house stands shoulder to shoulder with its matching neighbours. There is no one about. Only a few windows showing lights, McGilvray's in total darkness. Harry steps quickly onto the path running down to the back.

The glass sliding door has been repaired. Harry takes a small tool from his pocket and works the lock for a moment. The door slides open and he is met with a heavy smell of stale marijuana and old pizza. It's clear the housekeeping's taken a slide since McGilvray's wife moved out. Clothes, pizza boxes, and dirty dishes are scattered everywhere.

Harry begins to go through drawers using a narrow-beam torch. He comes across documents belonging to the wife, including her degree certificate and photographs of her younger self, coy alongside her parents and sister. It is hard to reconcile them with the framed photograph on the wall above. The two McGilvrays in bikini and Speedos, displaying their multicoloured bodies for the camera. She looks unhappy and alarming at the same time, with black and red hair and green eyes.

In another drawer, filled with men's socks and under-wear, his hand touches something hard buried at the back, and he pulls out a mobile phone. He turns it on and checks its contents. There are no numbers listed under "contacts," and only one, repeated several times, under "recent calls." It's listed as "unknown." Harry takes a note of the number and replaces the phone.

There are two wardrobes of women's clothes and one of men's, including safety jackets with the large letters NRL on the back and a safety helmet with the same logo. In a desk drawer are letters and forms relating to his employ-ment at the Wattle Gully Mine at Singleton in the Hunter Valley.

There is a laptop computer on the desk. Harry lifts its lid and hits the return bar and its screen comes to life. He becomes very still, looking at the picture of himself and Jenny. The link is to the New South Wales police site. A report of a function where he received the Commissioner's Commendation. He is dressed in uniform, wearing his medal, and Jenny is at his side smiling, full of life. It was four years ago, and she could see.

A woman's shriek. "Hey, what are you doing?"

Harry closes the laptop and switches off his torch. The front door slams and the woman cries, "Keep your hands to yourself!" then shrieks again, this time with laughter.

Harry gets to his feet and lets himself out through the

sliding door and locks it. As he steps off the deck and into the shadows, light floods out onto the boards behind him.

When he gets home he finds Jenny sitting at the computer in her dressing-gown, the dog at her side.

"His mum," she says. "He calls her every Sunday on that landline. And there are regular calls to the wife's parents and sister, their landlord, his work number and a few other everyday numbers—a telephone company, Domino's Pizza, Dee-Dee's tattoo studio, a nail bar. I haven't found anything incriminating, Harry."

"Okay." He goes to her side and looks at the screen. "Thanks. I've got another number for you to try, his mobile."

She frowns. "How did you get hold of that?"

"It was hidden in his sock drawer. Presumably he's got another one he carries around. And there was a recent call to a blocked number." He gives her the number and strokes her hair. "Not tonight, though, it's late."

FIFTEEN

NEXT DAY HARRY JOINS the forensic team on Ash Island. It is raining steadily from a heavy grey sky and he is dressed appropriately this time, in waterproofs and gumboots. The new crew from Sydney has brought a cadaver dog as well as various pieces of equipment, and Professor Timson has come out to follow the search. He is like a small boy with a box of new toys as he examines the equipment, rubbing his hands in anticipation.

"Well, that'll be no bloody use," he says, pointing to a heavy ground-penetrating radar unit on a wheeled trolley. The team tries it out on the soft ground and it promptly sinks to its axles. They concede the point, but they also have a lighter handheld model. They also have a new device with a nozzle that can be pushed into the mud to sniff for the chemicals given off by decomposing flesh. Harry senses a competitive edge to the banter between its operator and the handler of the dog, which has been trained to detect the same gases.

They crowd together into a tent that has been set up on the site, all dripping and jostling together around a map table.

"This is like camping in the fells," Timson says. "We need tea and bacon butties."

Harry promises to organise it.

After some discussion they agree on a plan, working outward from the discovery site to east, west, and south, leaving the open water of uncertain depth to the north. Harry makes a call to Sammy Lee to bring out food and hot drinks. Sammy says he doesn't do bacon butties, whatever they might be, and suggests pork spring rolls.

It is less than an hour before the operator with the sniffer device announces that he has a strong reading, in a boggy area on the edge of the lake barely thirty metres from where Cheung's body was found. Two scene of crime officers join him and begin probing carefully into the mud. Everyone else waits, motionless, not speaking, watching intently as the rain patters on the leaves and water around them.

At last one of the probing figures raises her arm. "Positive," she shouts. "We have another body." Both the dog handler and his dog look dejected. Timson beams and rubs his hands.

Timson and the rest of the crime-scene team move in cautiously with cordons and equipment, and for a while the others wait by the white tent, watching the camera flashes through the gloom, then the glare of floodlights powered from a generator. Soon the light breeze brings hints of the sickly sweet smell of decomposition.

Eventually Timson emerges through the scrub, followed by two figures bearing a stretcher. They're all streaked with dirt, the burden on the stretcher looking like little more than a heap of mud. As Timson makes his way to the white tent, Sammy Lee arrives with food. Timson peels off his gloves and pokes suspiciously at the spring rolls. "What the bloody hell are these? I said bacon butties."

"No one had a dictionary," Harry says. "I think these may be Chinese butties."

Timson takes a doubtful bite. "Hmm, not bad, not bad at all. Well then, this one is older," he says through a mouthful of pork. It takes a moment to gather that he's talking about the corpse rather than the food.

"Probably been in the ground a couple of months. Flesh falling off the bone." He picks up another spring roll. "You'll be relying on teeth or DNA. My present guess is a one-eighty-centimetre male. Not much more I can tell you at the moment."

"Cause of death?"

"Not yet."

"Oh, mate," Ross murmurs in Harry's ear. "Fogarty'll hate you even more now."

SIXTEEN

KELLY POOL FIGHTS HER way up the motorway from Sydney, buffeted by the spray from heavy trucks heading north. She takes the Newcastle exit and follows the sat nav prompts to the Adamstown address she has tracked down for David Suskind. Parking opposite the little house, she stares out through the rain at its blank windows and overgrown garden, wondering if the trail she has been following might be a dead end.

She flicks open an umbrella and runs across the street. The front gate gives a loud screech of protest, unused to being disturbed, and a curtain flutters in the window of the house next door.

She rings the bell. There is no reaction and she tries again. Nothing.

"He's not there, doll," a voice says and she turns to see a woman standing on the front step next door, looking up at the sky. "Horrible day."

"Yes, hello. Doesn't Mr. Suskind live here anymore?"

"He's gone to a home. Poor old man's gone a bit frail."

"Oh dear."

"Can I give him a message?"

"It was really Karen I was after. I was hoping to catch

up with her again and I thought he could tell me where to find her."

"An old friend, are you?"

"Yes. We've lost touch."

"Isn't she on Facebook?"

"Not that I can see, no."

"Well, I know she still visits her pop regularly. Maybe you should ask him." She smiles and turns back to her door.

"But where is he?"

"Oh, sorry. Bottlebrush Gardens in Shortland. You'll probably find him sitting outside." She peers doubtfully at the rain. "He's still a heavy smoker."

Kelly thanks her and returns to her car. She taps in the name to her sat nav and sets off. It's not far away, and there's a solitary figure sitting beneath an awning in the forecourt, smoking. Finding a parking space is more difficult.

She runs over there, umbrella tilted forward against the rain, and sits down on the seat beside the old man. His walker is beside him, a copy of today's *Newcastle Herald* in the basket.

"Mr. Suskind? Hello, how are you?"

"I'm not too bad, my dear." He gives her a look as if he can't believe his luck. "What would a lovely lady like you want with an old wreck like me?"

"Oh, don't give me that," she teases him. "You're no old wreck."

"That's what I tell them, lovey. I tell them I'm a recycled teenager, but they just laugh."

"Shame on them. Is it all right here apart from that?"

They chat for a while until he says, "And so, how do you know my name, and I don't know yours?"

"I used to know Karen, long ago."

"Ah, at Lambton High?"

"That's it."

"I thought I recognised you. What was your name again?"

"Laura King."

"Laura . . . Laura . . . yes, I think I remember. That red hair."

"We moved away, to Queensland, and then I got married and had a family, but I was down this way and I called in at your house in Adamstown and your neighbour told me I could find you here."

"You've gone to a lot of trouble, pet. I'm sure Karen will be pleased."

"So can you give me her address?"

"Oh no, I can't do that. In the first place I can't remember it, and in the second Karen specifically told me not to give it to anyone. She works in a big estate up in the valley, see, and it's very confidential."

"Oh dear. But the home here must know, don't they? I could ask them."

"No. They have a number for Karen, but only for emergencies. I know, because I tried to get it and they wouldn't tell me. Her own dad! But I tell you what, she'll be here any minute. It's Sunday, isn't it? She comes in to Newcastle and takes me out to lunch at Hungry Jack's."

"Oh, what a shame. I have a meeting with someone and can't get out of it. In fact," she checks her watch, "I'm late as it is. Oh dear, I'll have to rush. Never mind, another time."

Kelly jumps to her feet, puts up her umbrella and waves him good-bye. He calls after her, "But give me your address, and she can contact you . . ." but she hurries on across the road, pretending not to hear.

On the far side she turns the corner and finds a spot with a view of the home through a thick bush. She stands there beneath her umbrella with her phone to her ear to deter passersby, feeling slightly foolish. Fifteen minutes later a vehicle turns into the visitors' parking area in the forecourt and a woman gets out and greets the old man. He rises awkwardly to his feet to embrace her, then begins telling her something, gesturing in Kelly's direction. The woman turns to look, and Kelly takes a photo of her through the leaves with her phone. She can hardly recognise Donna Fenning now. She has lost a lot of weight, cut her hair shorter and dyed it much darker. But it's her all right. The same posture, the same way of peering intently as if a little short-sighted. It makes Kelly shiver. She withdraws further behind the foliage.

Donna—Karen Schaefer—helps her father to the car, folds the walker into the boot, and sets off. It's a white Nissan Patrol four-wheel-drive. Kelly doesn't catch the number. When it's gone she goes to her car and drives it around the block a few times until she can get a parking place with a view of the home. Then she waits.

The Nissan returns after an hour and drops David Suskind off, then swings around and exits in the same direction Kelly's facing. She moves her car out and follows, keeping well back. They head past the university campus and onto a dual carriageway heading fast out of town. At Hexham Kelly follows the Nissan onto the slip road for the bridge across the Hunter River to the Pacific Highway heading north. She still hasn't been able to make out the car's number.

After twenty minutes Karen Schaefer signals a turn onto the Bucketts Way, heading north through wooded country. It's a quiet road and Kelly pulls back, worried that Schaefer will notice her. They pass through the small country town of Stroud and she sees the Nissan slow and drive into a filling station. Kelly continues on past for a couple of kilometres until she sees a dirt track branching off ahead. She takes it, bouncing through puddles, then turns around and waits for the Nissan to pass.

Only it doesn't. Finally Kelly sets off, back along the way she came, to the filling station. The car isn't there. She continues into Stroud, checking parked vehicles, without success. She comes to a stop, wondering what's happened. She never got the car's number.

As she sits there her phone rings. It's her editor, Catherine Meiklejohn, at the *Times* in Sydney.

"Kelly? They tell me you're up in Newcastle."

"That's right, Catherine."

"Are you up there for the body in the bog? Have you heard they've found another one?"

"Er, no, I hadn't heard that." Kelly has no idea what she's talking about.

"Looks like they've got a serial killer up there. They're holding a press conference in an hour. Can you make it?"

"Yes, yes, sure."

"It's on the site, in the bog. Hope you've got gumboots, they say it's pissing down."

"Yes, it is. Can you give me the details?"

SEVENTEEN

KELLY TURNS OFF THE busy highway onto the narrow bridge across to Ash Island and is immediately struck by the atmosphere of the place. Bleak, faintly sinister. The further she goes into the marshlands the more this feeling grows, and when she sees a white truck in her rearview mirror, trailing her at a distance, she feels a flutter of panic.

Then she rounds a copse of desolate trees and sees parked vehicles ahead, a TV camera crew and police tape. She parks and makes her way through the crowd to the barrier. Beyond it she can make out two blue tents among the trees. There's a larger white tent nearby with uniformed figures going in and out.

Under a shared umbrella she strikes up a conversation with a young woman, a journalist with the *Newcastle Herald*, who fills her in on the background and identifies some of the officials.

"That one in the uniform is Detective Chief Inspector Ken Fogarty, who's heading up Strike Force Ipswich to investigate the deaths. He'll probably be the one to talk to us. Over there, talking to the men in white overalls, is another detective, Ross Bramley, an old hand. I don't know the name of the one beside him. He's new."

Kelly knows who he is. She stares through the drizzle, hardly believing she's looking at Harry Belltree.

Fogarty moves forward to address them. Yes, a second body has been found, buried in circumstances similar to the first. He says the first body is believed to be that of a Chinese national by the name of Cheung Xiuying; officials of the Chinese embassy have been notified. He refuses to discuss causes of death or possible motives, but confirms that the police are treating the deaths as suspicious. This provokes a laugh from the back of the crowd. He closes by asking for information from the public on any recent movement of vehicles on Ash Island, particularly on the night of November ninth. Photographs of Cheung are distributed and he asks the media to run them, with a request for anyone who saw him and a group of Chinese nationals in central Newcastle, and in particular at Marketown shopping centre on that afternoon, to call Crime Stoppers.

The briefing ends and the small crowd begins to break up. Last photographs are snapped and a reporter moves to the front with a microphone to speak to the TV camera. Vehicles start making their laborious turns on the narrow track. Beyond the barrier Kelly sees Harry and Ross Bramley plod off through the mud towards the blue tents. She goes back to her car and waits.

It's another hour before a group of figures in blue overalls trudge back to the white tent, and soon afterwards a figure she thinks she recognises makes his way through the barrier. She gets out of her car and waits for him to draw near. "Harry?"

He stops and stares at her. "Kelly? Kelly Pool?"

She steps over to him, wanting to give him a hug, but holding back.

"How are you, Kelly?"

"Good, good. You?"

"Yeah, fine."

"And Jenny?"

They're observing, assessing each other as they go through the phrases. Kelly hears a raggedness in his breath, and thinks he looks thinner and paler. "I had no idea you were up here, Harry. Have they brought you up specially for this case?"

"No, I . . ." He pauses, hearing the sound of voices approaching. He moves closer to her and takes her arm. "We should have a chat, Kelly."

"Yes, we must. I need to talk to you."

The others draw near and one calls out, "Coming back to the station, Harry?"

"Yeah, Ross. Just coming." Then to Kelly, "Give me your number."

She gives him a card and he hurries away. It was almost like a furtive meeting of old lovers, Kelly thinks. Her cheeks feel flushed and her heart is beating faster. Not lust, she tells herself. The atmosphere of danger she associates with Harry. It occurs to her that he might be a little unbalanced, bearing in mind all that has happened to him. But then, he probably wonders the same thing about her.

EIGHTEEN

A STRIKE FORCE IPSWICH briefing is called, and they file into the room with cups of coffee and notebooks, settling down to hear the latest. Harry recognises most of them now, and Ross introduces him to a couple of people he hasn't met before. Fogarty is down the front, conferring with his case manager and a uniformed inspector.

Fogarty gets to his feet and sets out what they know. It's all familiar to Harry. Now the immediate tasks. A manned information booth in Marketown shopping centre with enlarged photographs of Cheung's face and the group picture of the Chinese sailors. Teams taking calls from the public. Father McCallum and his volunteer worker to be re-interviewed. CCTV cameras throughout the city centre and along the highway accessing the Ash Island bridge are to be checked.

Harry recognises the litany of predictable and labour-intensive box-ticking that has to be done to keep everyone happy. Something may turn up, someone may have seen an Asian man being bundled into a car, or having a drink in a bar. Maybe not. He and Ross are told to attend the post-mortem of the second victim, and they head off to the John Hunter once again.

When they walk in, Leon Timson's assistant is painstakingly removing the last of the mud from the body, taking care to preserve the flesh. The corpse is lying on its back, the bones of the rib cage exposed through a mess of indeterminate stuff. Most of the flesh on the skull has gone.

"Hi folks." Timson walks in. There's a murmured conversation with his assistant, then he gets to work. "Well, right away we notice that three fingers of the right hand have been severed through the middle phalanx bones, perhaps with shears or a heavy knife . . . The skull is intact this time, so we have to look for some other cause of death. With the state of decomposition, however, he could have been suffocated or stabbed or electrocuted or died of heart failure and we probably wouldn't be able to tell."

"Big help," Ross grumbles.

His initial inspection over, the assistant cuts open the skull, removes the brain and weighs it while Timson pokes around in the corpse's mouth. "Good set of teeth, no fillings." He goes on with his examination, removing what remains of the liver, lungs, heart, and kidneys. They are weighed and sliced.

Finally he comes over to the two detectives. "I can't be a hundred per cent certain, but I don't think he's Chinese. He's tall, just over six foot, and there's this." He hands them a jar containing filaments of hair. "Naturally curly, I'm pretty sure. The DNA should tell us more."

"Definitely male?"

"Oh yes. Probably mid- to late thirties."

"And tortured in the same way. When?"

"It's hard to say, Harry. My guess would be some time in September, but that salt marsh ground is unusual—the bacteria, the insects, the chemical damage, and acidity, they're all different from what we're used to. We'll need to do tests, consult the literature. Oh, and you know there was no clothing this time? No rings, watch, clothing, or anything else, just him."

As they leave, Harry says, "Well, if he was a resident, we'll just have to hope for a DNA match."

"Yes." Ross nods. "The thing is, how many more of them are out there in that godforsaken place, Harry? We've never had anything like this before."

When he gets home Harry finds Jenny and the dog in a restless mood. They've been cooped up all day indoors because of the rain. It's slackened now to a light drizzle and they decide to go out for a walk. Outside they find the young couple next door having trouble trying to start their car, and Jenny and Felecia wait on their veranda while Harry pulls his Corolla alongside theirs and gets out the jump leads. When they resume their walk Harry tells Jenny about Ash Island, and she says, "I know, I could smell it on you, the smell of sour mud. And something . . . Have you been to the hospital?"

"Yes, for the postmortem."

"I thought so, the antiseptic smell." She smiles, pleased with herself, then tells him about McGilvray's hidden mobile. "I've got a record of his calls over the past two months, and the numbers all seem to be untraceable. But there's a pattern to them. He calls the same number several times for a week, then each Monday he starts a new week making a similar number of calls but to a new number. The previous numbers are never called again."

"He's calling the same person," Harry says, "and they're changing their phone every week."

"That's what I thought."

"He's a crook, this other guy, a careful crook. And McGilvray's bent too, but not so careful."

NINETEEN

AT DAWN THE NEXT day Harry wakes to the sound of rain pounding on the metal roof. A storm cell has settled over the Hunter and the radio is forecasting continuous heavy falls for at least twenty-four hours. At the morning briefing Fogarty announces the search for further bodies on Ash Island is suspended until the weather clears.

When it's over he calls Harry and Ross to his office.

"McGilvray," he growls. "Complaints Management has decided his claims against you, Belltree, have no merit. We're to apply to have his bail revoked and proceed with charges against him. He can test his claims in court if he thinks it'll do him any good."

Ross claps Harry on the shoulder. Fogarty doesn't seem particularly pleased.

"I don't want you involved in re-interviewing him, Belltree. You can do that, Ross, since he seems to have taken a fancy to you." He gives a little smirk. "Have you spoken to Kevin Colquhoun about these possible connections to the tattoo business, Belltree?"

"No, boss."

"You might like to do that before Ross speaks to McGilvray."

They go to see Colquhoun, who is interested but sceptical. McGilvray hasn't shown up on their database and has no known connections to organised crime figures.

Later that morning Harry observes McGilvray's interview from another room. Ross has adopted a patient, even compassionate manner, which Harry doesn't find altogether convincing. He outlines the charges to be laid against McGilvray, including assault on his wife and possession of prohibited drugs. He adds, sounding almost regretful, that they are still in discussion with the DPP about a further very serious charge of intent to do grievous bodily harm to Ross himself, with a thirty-centimetre kitchen knife. These charges might result in a lengthy prison term, the loss of his job, and the end of his marriage. In the light of all this, Ross invites him to consider whether he might be in a position to improve his situation by assisting the police in other matters. For example, might McGilvray be able to make a case that he acted rashly because he was under pressure from others to sell drugs? Or to extort services from, for the sake of argument, a tattoo salon?

McGilvray listens to this with head bowed, a sulky expression on his face, and says nothing.

Ross persists. Surely there must be some information that McGilvray could give Ross to take to his superiors to persuade them to go more easily on him?

Finally McGilvray raises his head and speaks. "Yes, there is something," he says, and Ross smiles encouragingly and picks up his pen.

McGilvray clears his throat. "You can tell your mate

Belltree that he's in much deeper shit than he knows." And he leers at Ross.

He refuses to say another word, and Ross finally terminates the interview.

Later, when he meets up with Harry in the office, he says, "What is it with that bloke? It's like he's obsessed with you."

TWENTY

KELLY SITS AT THE window of her hotel room, staring gloomily out at the rain as it turns the streets into streams and the ocean into a dull grey blur. Harry still hasn't contacted her.

She sent in her piece on the Ash Island murders to the paper yesterday evening and Catherine Meiklejohn asked her if she felt it was worth staying on. Wouldn't she be better returning to Sydney and relying on the agency reports? Was there any special angle she was pursuing that would give the paper a scoop on the case? And Kelly replied yes, she had the inside track with one of the homicide detectives she'd known in Sydney and hoped this would lead to an exclusive. In reality she doubted this. What she really wants is to reestablish contact with Harry so she can tell him about Donna Fenning and her transformation into Karen Schaefer. Despite all her searches, she's been unable to find any trace of the woman in this region, apart from that one sighting.

But Harry hasn't called. Lunchtime has passed, the rain hasn't let up, and she is feeling despondent. Then the phone on the table in front of her begins to trill.

"Kelly Pool."

"Hi, Kelly."

It's him, thank God. "Harry!"

"Where are you?"

She gives him the name of the hotel and he says, "Okay. Walk down to the end of Hunter Street. There's a café there. I'll see you in ten." He hangs up and she flies across the room, gathering up her coat and umbrella and notebook.

She runs down the hill and in three minutes she's in the café giving her order for a croissant and a large latte. Then she sits as the waitress brings her order and the minutes tick by. She should be used to this, she thinks. This is a reporter's life, waiting for contacts who don't show up.

But then he's pulling up a seat. "You're looking good, Kelly."

"And you, Harry."

There is a pause as they smile and absorb each other's features, searching for signs of damage, then they simultaneously disengage and Harry says, businesslike, "There isn't much I can tell you about the case. So far we don't know much more than what's been released."

She tries to focus. "Is it a serial killer?"

"We don't know."

"Do you think there's more bodies out there?"

He shrugs. "The rain's interrupted the search, but we'll go on looking once it eases up. Look, if you want an angle, there might be a human-interest story you could follow up. The first body we found was a Chinese sailor, you know?"

"Yes."

"Well, you could talk to someone who can tell you about the kind of life those guys lead. He's a priest, based at the seamen's mission in Carrington, and it was their bus that picked up the sailor and his mates from their ship that day and took them sightseeing. His name's Father McCallum, a nice guy. Don't mention my name."

"Okay." Kelly jots down the details. "Thanks, I'll pay him a visit. Can I get you a coffee, Harry?"

He checks his watch. "Better not. Time's a bit short."

"I've found Donna Fenning—that's what I really wanted to see you about."

"Donna Fenning?" He frowns, trying to place the name.

"She was the woman in Mortimer Street who looked after the kids they brought over to Crucifixion Creek from Indonesia, and who drugged me and delivered me to Joost Potgeiter."

Harry stiffens. She wonders how much he remembers, how much they've told him of the aftermath.

"I never met her."

"No, I was the only one who did. Well, me and the neighbour, Phoebe Bulwer-Knight. Her memory's pretty shot now."

"Didn't the cops try to find her, afterwards?"

"Supposedly. She vanished. Her name didn't appear on electoral rolls or tax files or anywhere, and after a while they gave up. But I couldn't forget her, Harry. Not after Potgeiter . . ."

She's aware of a wobble in her voice and tells herself this is not the time to go soft. Harry must have noticed too. He puts his hand on hers.

"Of course you couldn't. But now you've found her?"

"Yes." She tells him about discovering the identity of the woman's husband, Craig Schaefer, and following the trail back to her father, David Suskind. "Who is here, Harry, in Newcastle. And so is Donna—I mean Karen Schaefer."

She tells him about trying to follow the Nissan. "She works somewhere up the valley."

"Have you reported this?"

"No, not yet. I want to find out what I can first and be absolutely sure. So they can't just brush me off."

"You're not absolutely sure, then? That it's her?"

"No, I don't mean that. I *am* sure. But I think the police . . . well, I think they lost interest. There were a lot of much bigger players to deal with."

"Yes," he says; she senses a flicker of doubt.

"I took a photo of her, at the nursing home, look . . ." She shows him on her phone. He frowns, and she realises how small the image is, and blurry. "She's changed her hair and lost some weight, but it's her all right."

"Send it to me on this number, Kelly . . . Tell me the names again." He takes out a notebook and writes down the details. "Are you staying in Newcastle for a while?"

"I don't know. If all else fails I'll come back on Sunday in case she visits her father again."

"You should be careful, Kelly. Just leave it with me." He gets to his feet.

"I couldn't believe it when I saw you on Ash Island, Harry. I looked everywhere for you after they released you from hospital, and I couldn't find you. I had no idea where you were. Then I follow Donna Fenning up here, and here you are. It's kind of spooky, don't you think?"

"We've had this conversation before, Kelly. Coincidences happen all the time in the real world."

"But I was right the last time, wasn't I? There was a conspiracy."

He concedes the point with a smile and waves her good-bye.

TWENTY-ONE

THE RAIN STOPS ON Tuesday morning and the search on Ash Island resumes. Towards mid-morning another strike force briefing is called and when Harry enters the room he's surprised to see a familiar figure standing talking to Fogarty and Superintendent Gibb. Deb Velasco, his offsider in his last month at Sydney Homicide. Still with the flamenco dancer looks, and drumming her fingers against her clipboard. Clearly dying for a smoke.

Gibb starts the meeting, introducing Deb as Detective Inspector Velasco. She scans the room, unsmiling. Doesn't make eye contact with Harry.

Apart from her considerable experience and expertise in homicide investigations, Gibb explains, she has been assigned to liaise with Strike Force Ipswich because the second body on Ash Island has now been identified by dental evidence as belonging to a Sydney resident, thereby expanding the possible scope of their inquiries.

He hands over to Fogarty, who gets to his feet and presses the button on a remote to project an image onto the screen behind him. Harry stares. Another familiar face. He glances at Deb and she is looking at him.

"Marco Ganis," Fogarty intones, "owner of Chieftain

Smash Repairs of Mascot, Sydney; residential address nearby. Aged forty-two, divorced, no children, no criminal record. Workers on the adjoining property were alerted on September third to the sound of a dog howling at Chieftain Smash Repairs. They were unable to find Ganis and called the RSPCA, who entered the premises and found a distressed Alsatian dog severely malnourished and without water. Seems likely that Ganis had left some time within the previous week; he hasn't been seen since. According to neighbours he was known to make regular visits to Newcastle to buy and sell vehicle parts.

"While all possibilities remain on the table, the fact that Ganis has such a very different background to Cheung makes it more likely that the victims were not connected and were chosen at random. In other words, victims of a serial killer or killers. We will shortly be able to call upon the services of a psychological profiler with expertise in this area. In the meantime, there are a number of new avenues we have to explore. We need to find who Marco Ganis was doing business with up here . . ."

As Fogarty works his way down a long list of tasks, he is interrupted by a uniformed woman who comes into the room in a hurry. "Sorry, sir. I think you'll want this."

Fogarty takes the sheet of paper she offers him and scowls at it. "A third body has been found on Ash Island."

When the briefing breaks up, Ross and Harry move to the door, intending to go out to the island, but they are stopped by the case manager, who tells Ross to go on alone. "You're wanted here, Harry, room 336." He goes up to the third floor. The door marked 336 opens into a small meeting room, empty. He walks in and stands at the window. Looks out on the beach, a few people now reemerging after the rain to walk along the waterfront. He hears someone come in and turns to see Deb, alone. She closes the door behind her and comes over to shake his hand.

"Harry, great to see you again. How are you?" She says it in that meaningful way, as if he's still in recovery.

"I'm fine, Deb. And you?"

"Oh," she shrugs and pulls out a chair, "there was a big shake-up after Crucifixion Creek. I'm sure you know."

Actually he doesn't, and he feels his isolation. He sits opposite her.

"Harry, Marco Ganis was the cousin of Stefan Ganis, ex-member of the Crows who we witnessed being killed in that siege at Crucifixion Creek four months ago. You remember that?"

Of course he bloody remembers. She's talking to him as if he's lost his wits. Marco Ganis also ended up in possession of the tow truck that forced Harry's parents' car off the road on Thunderbolt's Way on the orders of the Crows president, Roman Bebchuk. But Deb doesn't know this. Nor that Harry subsequently shot and killed Bebchuk. So Harry holds his tongue and just nods.

"The Drug Squad had a red flag on Marco's name as a possible small-time dealer, low in the food chain. This changes things. We've also had a call from the Feds. It seems they had a tip-off from China about the possibility of the *Jialing* being involved in drug smuggling into Australia, so naturally they're interested in Cheung's death. Possible that Cheung and Ganis were involved in trafficking drugs from China to Sydney through the port of Newcastle."

Harry thinks of the coal chain, the relentless flow of coal from the Valley to China, and of this other flow, equally remorseless, of the drug chain in return.

"So the serial killer angle . . . ?"

"Probably a non-starter, but we're going to run with that

until we find out more, because the AFP are anxious to protect their source in China."

"Okay."

"None of the rest of the team below the rank of chief inspector are aware of this, Harry. You have to keep it to yourself."

"Sure, but why are you telling me?"

"Because I want someone with their feet on the ground here keeping an eye on things, looking for any more Sydney connections."

Harry nods.

"And because I know you, Harry." She smiles at him. "We've missed you. It's been much quieter since you left. How's Jenny?"

"She's good. She's got a dog to take care of her now. It's working out well. How's Pete?" Deb's partner is a sergeant in the Tactical Operations Unit, the black ninjas.

Deb's face goes stony. "Oh. You don't know about that? Everyone else does." She seems disinclined to go on, then sighs. "I started getting these phone calls at work from this mad-sounding woman. She'd ring the switchboard and they'd say I was unavailable, until she finally exploded and told them that I had stolen her husband and if they didn't put her through to me she'd go to the papers. So they rang me and I spoke to her. She asked me to stop ruining her life. It seems she's been married to Pete for ten years and they've got two kids. I thought that was crazy until I remembered how he was always going on TOU training courses at weekends. Turns out there hadn't been any: that's when he'd go and live with them. During the week he told them he was on secret undercover police business and couldn't come home."

"Hell, what did you do?"

"I went back to our place and gathered up all his stuff—the clothes, the signed Bulldogs shirts, the CDs, the Star Trek memorabilia—and dumped it on the nature strip outside. By the time he got home most of it was gone."

"Jeez, I'm sorry, Deb."

"Doesn't matter." She shakes her head as if annoyed with herself for talking about it. "Anyway, you'd better get over to Ash Island. Sounds like a fun place."

"Oh yes."

In fact it seems an almost magical place when Harry gets there. The sky is heavy with dark storm clouds, but a gap directly above Ash Island allows a shaft of brilliant sunlight to fall upon the scene of toiling people, to make the damp trees and grasses all around them sparkle and the water shimmer and glisten. The slightly sinister theatrical effect is heightened by a backdrop of lightning flashes from a big electrical storm out to sea.

They have established that the third corpse is as badly decomposed as the second and smells much worse, choking the still air with a sweet putrescence that makes people turn away and clear their throats in disgust. As with the other two, several fingers have been severed, but, unlike them, the skull has been smashed beyond recognition, as if it's been crushed by a great weight.

TWENTY-TWO

JENNY IMMEDIATELY SMELLS IT when Harry returns that evening, and so does the dog, following him around, sniffing his trouser legs. He strips off and puts what he can in the washing machine and packs his jacket and trousers into a plastic bag for the dry cleaners in the morning. As she puts the plates into the oven to warm, Jenny hears him in the bathroom taking a long shower. She took advantage of the break in the rain to go on a longer walk today with Felecia, exploring the streets of Hamilton, and now feels pleasantly tired. On their way back she called in to the supermarket at Marketown where she'd been a couple of times before with Harry, memorising each aisle from his descriptions. Now she enjoyed the challenge of doing it on her own, using her phone app to distinguish each type of apple or brand of spice. There was one point of confusion where they had rearranged the dairy section and she had to ask for help, but she's been able to find the ingredients for a moussaka, and assemble them—lamb, eggplants, tomatoes, bechamel sauce—without incident.

She also spent an hour on her computer working on Harry's problem with the mobile phone numbers. Over dinner she tells him what she's discovered.

"One of the phones McGilvray called was used to take a photograph."

"Yes? You have the picture?"

"No, I couldn't get that."

"Oh. No help then."

"Well, it might be, because when the phone takes a picture its GPS data is automatically recorded, and I was able to get into that. So I don't know what the picture was, but I know where it was taken."

"Can you show me?"

She brings up the image on the screen, a map of central Newcastle with the coordinates marked. Harry zooms in and switches to street view. "That's Sammy Lee's restaurant. I bought takeaway from there on Saturday night, remember?"

"Yes. So the person with the phone was probably eating there that night."

"Do we have a date?"

"Yes. If you go back to the map . . ."

The date and time are recorded with the map coordinates. Saturday October 20, 8:46 p.m.

"Will that help?"

He says yes and thanks her, sounding pleased. With any luck Sammy will have a record of his diners that night.

After the meal they listen to the radio for a while, Harry reading the papers. He seems restless, but whatever is on his mind, he doesn't want to talk about it. They go to bed and she lies for a while, thinking. Then she feels something, a light tremor deep in her belly. It takes her a moment to realise what it is—the quickening, the first movement of the baby inside her. Twenty weeks now, and according to what her computer has told her, he—for she thinks of it as a boy—now weighs about three hundred grams and is about fifteen centimetres long. She imagines his tiny hand reaching out and touching the wall of her womb. She turns to tell Harry, but he is deeply asleep. She smiles to herself and closes her eyes.

She dreams of a high dark interior, a hallway, a grand flight of stairs of polished timber, the smell of roasting lamb. She hears the tramp of boots on a timber floor and follows the sound out onto a broad veranda with a view over paddocks, white-railed. She goes down the steps to the gravel drive and hears the whinny of horses, the clump of hoofs. Looking back, she sees a red roof. A horse has come to the rail in front of her and shows huge yellow teeth.

She wakes abruptly, feeling Felecia rubbing her nose against her hand. The clock says 1:52 and she rolls over, but Felecia keeps nudging her, lifting a paw to push against her back. She's never done this before.

"What is it?" she asks her. "Is it the lightning, Felecia? Is there a storm?"

The dog is panting, agitated, and Jenny gets up and goes out to the kitchen to see if there's water in the dog's bowl. But Felecia is at the front door, scratching to be let out. Jenny opens it, but instead of going out the dog returns to the bedroom and tries to rouse Harry.

He sits up, rubbing his face. "What's the matter? What's going on?"

"It's Felecia, she's unsettled. I think she needs to go out."

"Okay," he mumbles. "I'll take her." He gets up. Slips on a pair of shoes and puts a jacket on over his pyjamas. He clips a lead to Felecia's collar and heads for the front door. But the dog pulls back, tugging him towards the harness that she wears for Jenny.

"She wants me to come too," Jenny says. "Hang on."

"Chrissake, Felecia," Harry grumbles. "You don't know what you want."

Jenny pulls on a raincoat and boots and they go out, the three of them, into the glow of the streetlight in the narrow lane. The atmosphere is humid, close, and there's no sound of traffic in the still air. Jenny slips her hand into Harry's arm and they set off.

"I was dreaming of the homestead," she says. "The red roof, the horses. I saw the inside of the house. There were portraits of the Nordlunds on the walls."

"You remember it?"

"Probably not. I was looking them up today. It was on my mind. Probably just my imagination."

As they walk Harry describes the flicker of lightning he can see out beyond the grain silos. They circle the block and return to their street. Jenny can picture the view of their cottage ahead of them. She doesn't see the dazzling white flash and blazing cloud that erupt out of it. Instead she feels a sudden heat and then a numbing silence as the shock wave hits her. When her hearing returns there is a sound of roaring and crashing, of the rattle of debris falling on tin roofs, muffled by Harry who has covered her with his body and forced her down, crouching against a wall.

TWENTY-THREE

PEOPLE BEGIN TUMBLING OUT of the houses, dark figures emerging into the glow from the burning building. Harry checks his coat pockets. He picked up his wallet, keys, and phone when he came out, and he makes a triple-0 call. Turns back to Jenny, drawing her gently to her feet, checking she isn't hurt. Felecia is beside them, sitting on her haunches watching the flickering ruin of their home as if she expected it.

He recognises the young man next door running over to them. He and his wife are okay, he says, but Harry is worried their house may catch fire too. As he's asking if the man has a hose, they hear a siren. A fire engine is clearing the people off the street as it rushes in. Helmeted figures jump out and start unfurling hoses.

An ambulance arrives and a police car, and one of the ambulance officers comes over to Harry and Jenny. Harry gets the man to check Jenny. Tells him to make sure their elderly neighbour on the far side of their block is okay. He doesn't know either of the uniformed cops. He introduces himself and gives them a quick account, tells them to call it in as a possible crime scene. He feels helpless and ridiculous, standing there in his pyjamas. He is in an absurd dream.

More uniforms turn up with a detective Harry also doesn't recognise. He stands with Harry, gazing at the ruin, shaking his head. The fabric of the building has largely gone, blown into matchwood. Only the sheets of corrugated metal roofing are recognisable, scattered precariously over the neighbours' roofs.

"Jeez, you were lucky, Harry. How come you weren't inside?"

"The dog got us up, wanted to go for a walk."

"That's a bloody miracle. Maybe he smelled the gas."

"She," Jenny says. "And there was no smell of gas."

"Yeah, but dogs, they have this amazing sense of smell. It was probably building up under the floor and then something sparked it off, boom. Could've happened anytime, these old houses."

But ten minutes later the senior fire officer comes over. He pulls off his glove and shakes their hands. He says to Harry, "Given someone the shits, mate?"

"He didn't pay his gas bill," the detective quips.

The fire officer shakes his head. "That wasn't gas. That was ANFO. I'd stake my life on it—ammonium nitrate and fuel oil. It's got a smell. I know because I worked in the mines."

"The mines?" Harry says.

"Yes, they use it all the time as a general-purpose explosive. It's cheap and easy to make when you need it, just mix up some ammonium nitrate granules with a bit of diesel. Needs a primer to set it off, Tovex or pentolite usually. The forensic blokes'll find out."

"Hang on," the detective says, "you're telling us this was a bomb?"

"Too right."

The detective turns to Harry. "Jeez, this is your lucky day, mate. You should buy a lottery ticket."

TWENTY-FOUR

JENNY FINISHES THE TEA and wonders what to do with the cup and saucer; there must be a table or shelf in here somewhere. She gets to her feet and begins to explore, her left hand stretching out for obstacles. She bangs her shin against a low table and swears softly to herself, puts down the cup and saucer, and returns to her chair.

From time to time, people look in and ask her if she's all right. They're kind and she thanks them, but they have that tone in their voice as if they're talking to an invalid and it makes her angry, not with them but with herself. She's in the middle of a crisis and all she can do is sit around and be useless. Somewhere else in the building Harry is talking to his people and one of the things they'll be discussing is what to do about her, if that really was a bomb. She still finds the idea preposterous, out of the blue like that, so dramatic. But then it's happened before, hasn't it? With Harry's parents. Murderous violence coming out of nowhere. In her darkest moments it makes her wonder if she has been a catalyst of some kind. Even a cause.

Felecia stirs at her side and nuzzles her hand. Sometimes she even catches herself hating the dog, a symbol of her helplessness.

TWENTY-FIVE

DEB VELASCO STARES AT the floodlit scene as dawn begins to glimmer in the east. She wanted to see it for herself.

"There's quite a crater," she says.

"Yes." Harry's been trying to visualise the plan of the house. The short brick piers that supported the timber floor form a shattered grid on the scorched earth. "It's directly beneath our bedroom. The kitchen, where the only gas outlet was, was over there, and the gas meter beyond it. You can still see it." He points to a blackened box, still intact.

"So you go with the bomb theory," she says.

"It seems possible."

"Motive? Who hates you that much?"

Harry hesitates. All he can think of is McGilvray, but that seems absurd. He tells her anyway.

"He'd have to be psycho," she says. "And he'd have access to detonators?"

"Maybe, in the mines. I'll go up there and check."

"I don't think so. Someone else can do that. I'm thinking we should send you back to Sydney."

"I don't want to do that, Deb. I want to get this sorted."

"But it isn't just you at risk, is it, Harry? There's Jenny, and she needs you to look after her."

"Yes."

As they turn to go they inspect Harry's car, still standing at the kerb. Its paintwork is blistered and discoloured on one side. It is all they have here now. Everything else—clothes, books, TV, household stuff, Jenny's computer—has gone.

"You don't think your Pete could have got the idea you were shacked up here with me, do you, Deb?"

She looks shocked for a moment, then realises he's joking and laughs.

When they get back to the central police station they find Ross Bramley sitting with Jenny. She looks very tired and Ross says he's booked a room for them at a nearby hotel. He's brought some clothes for Harry and arranged for his sister, an ex-cop who lives in the East End, to get some for Jenny. There'll be an incident briefing with Fogarty and Superintendent Gibb later in the morning.

Jenny and Harry, feeling like two vagrants with a dog, check into the hotel and try to get some sleep. After an hour, when Jenny has fallen into an uneasy slumber, Harry rises, showers and shaves, pulls on Ross's clothes. The suit is baggy but the shoes fit. He goes to Jenny's bedside and she stirs, reaches out a hand for him.

"I want to go to the briefing," he says. "Will you be okay?"

She nods and tells him to go. He takes the lift down to the lobby and walks out into the street. A southerly has cleared the rain clouds away and sunlight sparkles on the waves, as if everything dark and foul has been banished with the night. He gets some breakfast at a little surfers' café overlooking the beach then walks back up to the police station.

Fogarty has spoken to the fire chief, who has personally

inspected the site of the explosion. He reads in a monotone from his notes. Although it's far too early for test results, the fire chief is confident that they will support his officer's earlier suspicions. He was present when scrapings of a chemical residue were taken from the brickwork of one of the piers. It closely resembles the remains of unburnt ammonium nitrate prills or pellets. If so, they appear to be of the lighter, aerated form of explosive-grade ammonium nitrate, rather than the denser form used as fertiliser. It seems likely that the residue survived the explosion because it had been affected by the damp conditions: ammonium nitrate is highly hygroscopic, absorbing moisture from the air.

Fogarty puts down the sheet of paper and looks at Superintendent Gibb, who shakes his head and says, "Dear God. It's a miracle there were no fatalities. What are we telling the press?"

"So far, only that emergency services were called to a mystery explosion in Carrington at twelve minutes past two last night. There were no casualties, but extensive damage to one cottage and secondary damage to neighbouring properties."

"It won't take them long to find out that a police officer was living there."

"No. I suggest we withhold the name."

Harry says, "The neighbours know our names and so do the local shopkeepers. My wife is kind of conspicuous."

"Oh?" Gibb looks blank, and Fogarty murmurs in his ear. "Oh yes. Yes, of course. She must be very shaken, Belltree. How is she?"

"Shaken, yes."

Fogarty says, "Belltree's name and the cause of the

explosion are bound to come out. I suggest it will make their lives and ours simpler if they were to leave town before then."

"Leave Newcastle?" Gibb thinks about it. "Back to Sydney? Deb?"

"Yes, I think that would probably be a good idea, at least until we have some answers."

"Good. Let's agree on that, then."

Harry holds his tongue.

"Suspects?"

Fogarty looks dyspeptic. "We have the peculiar case of Mr. Logan McGilvray, arrested by Belltree and Bramley last week and on record as making threats against Harry two days ago. However, he's currently being held at Cessnock Correctional Centre on drugs and assault charges."

"So he had friends?"

"We don't know who, yet. McGilvray is only one possible line of inquiry. It might have been a case of mistaken identity. Or perhaps Belltree upset some people in Sydney before joining us." He raises an accusing eyebrow at Harry.

"Ah . . ." Gibb looks thoughtful. "But there's no connection with the murders on Ash Island, I take it?"

"Oh no. I think we can safely rule that out."

As they are leaving, Deb says quietly to Harry, "Fogarty doesn't like you?"

He shrugs. "I won't be able to help you with your drug problem now."

"Not to worry."

"Who do I report to in Parramatta?"

"Bob Marshall's still the boss. I'll let him know what's happened. But take some time off, Harry. Concentrate on getting yourself and Jenny settled again."

When he leaves, Harry gets a cab to Carrington and

picks up his car, which, despite the ruined paintwork, still functions. When he gets back to the hotel there is a parcel of clothes for Jenny waiting for him at reception. She wakes when he gets to their room and he makes her a cup of tea and tells her what he's been doing. She reaches out for his hand and says, "Let's just go home, Harry."

TWENTY-SIX

CATHERINE MEIKLEJOHN HAS RECALLED Kelly to Sydney to cover the new ICAC hearings. The Independent Commission Against Corruption is always worth attending, and these particular hearings, concerning the granting of liquor and gaming licences to organised crime figures, were inspired by one of Kelly's predecessors on the *Times* crime desk. But Kelly finds it hard to concentrate on the complicated trail of dealings that the lawyers are attempting to untangle. Her mind keeps returning to Donna Fenning. Harry hasn't got back to her. Her own attempts to find a record of a Karen Schaefer in the country north of Newcastle have produced nothing, and it's preying on her mind.

When she was maybe eight or nine, playing hide-and-seek with three younger cousins, she climbed into an old disused chest freezer in the garage. For twenty minutes she congratulated herself on her clever hiding place; then she started to get stiff and uncomfortable, the air hot and stale. She pushed at the lid and found she couldn't open it from the inside. It occurred to her just how far out of earshot the garage was from where her parents were pottering in the house. In the muffled dark her breathing became short and panicky. By the time one of the cousins heard her frantic banging on the inside of the freezer she was convinced she was going to die.

Since then, she's had a problem with confined spaces. It's been reinforced by various incidents, including the time she allowed her lover, a married man, to lock her in the boot of his car while he dropped off his wife and kids before going back to her place. It seemed a hysterically funny idea to a young, slightly pissed Kelly. Until the steel lid slammed shut.

So when Joost Potgeiter lowered her down into that dark sink hole after he'd grown tired of using her, her terror had deep roots. It was as if he had seen into her soul. Read her most paralysing fears.

And now the thought of Potgeiter's accomplice, reborn as Karen Schaefer, living untroubled by her past crimes makes Kelly feel physically ill. The only slender thread that connects Karen to that past is Kelly herself. She dwells upon it constantly. Come Sunday she will drive back up to Newcastle to wait once again outside Bottlebrush Gardens nursing home, armed this time with one of the *Times*" telephoto cameras and a furious determination to nail the bitch.

TWENTY-SEVEN

AND IT IS GOOD to be home. On their way back through the city they stopped at a maternity shop and bought new clothes for Jenny—light, cool things for a summer pregnancy. They rekindled in her a sense of hope for the future, and also a frisson of fear for what so nearly happened. Unpacking them now in the familiar surroundings of the little house in Surry Hills, she absorbs its smells and sounds. The gentle stirring of a branch of the big plane tree against the metal roof, the echo as traffic passes the end of their lane, the creak of the sash windows, the rattle of a shutter in the wind.

She knows they are probably no safer here than they were in Newcastle, but it doesn't feel like that. This house—Harry's parents' house before the crash—has been here for a hundred and twenty years, and it seems inconceivable that it won't be here always.

The front doorbell rings, her sister Nicole come to take her out for a late lunch, then a visit to her doctor for her monthly checkup. Harry won't be coming; he has things to do. Jenny has been wondering what to tell her family. Not a bomb, but a fire? But that would lead to more questions. They would assume it was her fault. In the end she has decided to say only that Harry's boss has recalled him to Sydney.

Over lunch Nicole is full of advice about maternity wear, then asks Jenny vaguely about their life in Newcastle. She went there once, Nicole says, on their way up to the north coast. It seemed strange, she says, "So . . ." she searches for the word, ". . . so *white.*"

When Jenny returns home Harry is setting up her new computer. He has taken it to her usual guy, who has installed the various special programs that she needs, and when Harry has it running she sits down and plays with it for a while. Familiarising herself with its new features, downloading files from a backup hard drive she left here in the Surry Hills house. When she's finally satisfied, she moves to the kitchen and gets on with the evening meal, loving the familiar cupboards, the old crockery, the larder smells. As each hour passes, what happened last night—*only last night?*—has become more and more improbable. Increasingly it's as if Newcastle never happened.

But when they go to bed she can't sleep. Her body, lying rigid between the sheets, seems to have its own grip on reality, regardless of what her mind pretends. Beside her Harry is silent, but his breathing doesn't sound like sleep.

"Harry?"

"Mmm."

"What time is it?'

It's 2:00. Exactly twenty-four hours since the bomb.

"We should talk," she whispers.

"Yeah. I'll make tea, shall I?"

When he returns they sit side by side for a while, thinking.

"Do you know who did it, Harry?"

"I'm not sure. I think it has to do with things that happened here in Sydney before we left."

"So we're no safer here than in Newcastle?"

"No."

"Will the police stop them?"

There's silence for a moment, then, "Yes, I'm sure they will. Given time."

"But you know things they don't know?"

"Maybe."

"So we can either try to hide somewhere, or you can go and put a stop to it."

"My first priority is to protect you and the baby, Jenny. There's no question about that."

"But what's the best way to do that? You want to go after them, don't you, Harry? It's what you do best."

"I can't leave you, Jenny, and the more I make myself a nuisance, the more danger you're in." He sounds helpless, indecisive. Unlike himself.

"And I'm so conspicuous, aren't I?" She sips her tea. "Remember my Aunt Meredith—Meri? She came to our wedding."

"Vaguely. Bit eccentric?"

"Distinctive, good fun. We always got on well. She lives inland on the Central Coast—the Yarramalong Valley. A little place where she keeps alpacas, ducks, and chickens. She came to see me when you were in hospital. She asked me to go and stay with her whenever I want."

"Yes, but not if it's going to put her in harm's way."

"I'd have to tell her, of course, what's involved. She may not agree. In a way I hope she doesn't. The thing is, I could live there without anyone knowing."

They talk it over, the risks, the consequences. Finally Harry puts the light out again and they try to sleep.

"I could take on a false identity," Jenny mumbles. "Scarlett . . . When I was a girl I wanted to be called Scarlett. Can't remember why. *Gone with the Wind*, I suppose . . ."

TWENTY-EIGHT

THE FOLLOWING MORNING HARRY reports at police head-
quarters in Parramatta. He tries to make an appointment
with his boss, Detective Superintendent Bob Marshall,
whose secretary tells him that Bob is out of the office this
morning. He has a very busy diary for the next few days
before he flies off to a conference in Perth. She promises to
try to squeeze Harry in.

He logs on to e@gle.i and checks the latest information
from Strike Force Ipswich. They have an identification for
the third corpse now, a sixty-five-year-old male, charges for
assault and affray from the 1970s and '80s. Harry stares at
the name.

"Tony Gemmell," he whispers. "Bloody hell." He remembers the last time he saw Tony, standing by his side in the
car park of the Swagman Hotel facing a crowd of bikers.

And as he remembers Tony, and thinks of him buried
in the mud of Ash Island, he hears the voice of Kelly Pool in
his head. *I couldn't believe it when I saw you on Ash Island,
Harry . . . It's kind of spooky, don't you think?*

The phone rings. Marshall's secretary. He can see Harry
at one the next day. Lunch at Argosy on Circular Quay. Does
he know it? He says he'll find it.

He phones Ross Bramley in Newcastle, who tells him Fogarty has decided to have McGilvray released on police bail. They'll track him and hope he leads them to his co-conspirators. Harry thinks that's unlikely. McGilvray isn't stupid.

He feels like a lost ghost now in the Parramatta head-quarters, avoiding old colleagues and the questions they would ask. It's a relief to leave and head back home. When he gets there Jenny tells him that she has spoken to her Aunt Meri.

"She didn't hesitate, Harry. She told me to get over there right away. I made it as clear to her as I could about the risks, but she was adamant. She told us to come this after-noon."

"Hang on," Harry says, disturbed by her enthusiasm. "We need to go through this carefully." They discuss the implications, the precautions, the alternatives. He insists they don't decide until he's seen Bob Marshall tomorrow, but agrees that they'll head down to Yarramalong together after that, to take a look.

In the afternoon he drives over to Ricsi's innocuous shoe repair shop in Petersham for some precautionary supplies. He carries a pair of old shoes in a bag, and Ricsi gives him a ticket, then takes him into the back room, where Harry buys several throw-away mobile phones and an un-used Chinese copycat Taurus sub-compact pistol, with am-munition. Ever since he was in a position to arrest Ricsi when he first arrived in Sydney some years ago, Harry has been an occasional customer, for both shoe repairs and other goods. Careful and not too ambitious, Ricsi has so far managed to avoid any further interaction with the police, and Harry knows he'll be as discreet as he is about all his customers.

TWENTY-NINE

HARRY IS SURPRISED, VERY surprised, when he arrives at Argosy—the crisp linen, the cutting-edge decor, the expensive murmur of the maitre d'," the huge glazed view of Circular Quay and the Opera House. Bob Marshall has never shouted him more than a sandwich at a team briefing. Now this.

He is led to a table in a prime spot by the window, where Marshall is looking as if he too has been out shopping for a new suit—somewhere more pricey than Harry.

"Harry." He rises and extends a hand. "Come and sit down."

"Some pub, boss."

"You haven't been here before? Not my usual watering hole, but I thought you deserved something special after what you've been through. How's Jenny doing? No physical injuries, I hear?"

"She's coping pretty well, considering."

"Yes. Steel backbone, that girl."

A waiter appears at his shoulder with leatherbound volumes. They consider them in silence.

"Glass of wine, Harry? You're on leave, right?" He orders a couple of glasses of wine and fish for himself.

Harry asks for a steak. He unfolds his napkin and says, "I'd prefer to get back to work."

"And run the bastards to ground, of course you would. But it's not on, Harry, it's not on. I blame myself for sending you up there to Newcastle. Remember my advice? Go to Tasmania or anywhere else far away and start a new life. I should have insisted. Now we have no choice. We'll put you both on witness protection, Harry. New identities, a new life."

Harry is silent, then says, "Why did you suggest New-castle, boss?"

"Bob, Harry. We're off duty, two blokes having lunch together and an off-the-record chat . . . I take it you've gathered that Newcastle wasn't a random choice. Did you see they've identified the third victim on Ash Island?"

"Tony Gemmell." He is aware of Marshall studying him. "One-time president of the Crows."

"Exactly. You knew him?"

"I came across him."

"We think he was one of the two assailants at the Swagman Hotel killing. He was a close friend of Rowdy O'Brian before O'Brian was murdered by Gemmell's successors in the Crows."

"Makes sense. Hang on, you said the Swagman Hotel *killing*, singular. There were two."

"You didn't know? Hakim Haddad is dead right enough."

This is no surprise to Harry; he shot the Crows' sergeant-at-arms himself. "What about their vice-president, Frank Capp?"

"Yes, Capp actually survived the attack with the baseball bat. He came out of hospital around the same time you did. Now in maximum security at Long Bay. He looks a mess, but his brain seems to be functioning okay. It's a fair bet he recognised his assailants, too, though he's not telling us."

Marshall lets this sink in, still giving Harry that uncomfortable stare.

A waiter approaches and sets down plates in front of them. "Complimentary amuse-bouches, messieurs."

Marshall stares at it. "What's that in English?"

"Stuffed marrowbone, sir."

"Jesus."

The waiter retreats. Harry says, "So two of the three Ash Island victims were connected with the Crows."

"Maybe all three. At first the drug squad thought Marco Ganis might be running drugs up the coast; then they thought it could be the other way round—that he was collecting drugs smuggled into Newcastle and taking them down to Sydney for the Crows."

"Surely the Crows have broken up?"

"That's what we assumed, but it's possible that Capp's been organising a resurrection, starting by settling a few old scores."

"And you think the bombing of our house was part of that?"

"The thought crossed my mind, Harry. But only you know if it makes sense."

He knows it very well, but doesn't reply, picking up his fork.

"Actually this tastes quite good."

"I'll take your word for it."

"You didn't think about telling me some of this when you sent me up to Newcastle?"

Marshall sighs. "It was all hypothesis and conjecture, Harry. You seemed to have an intimate knowledge of the Crows . . ." a raised eyebrow at this, "and we thought you might recognise a face or a name that would help us join the dots. But we had no idea about Ash Island. It was pure chance that chopper pilot led us to it."

"A Crows' burial ground?"

"Looks that way."

"So there are probably other bodies out there, past enemies."

"Very likely."

Their main course arrives.

"Anything else bothering you, Harry?"

"Yes. Newcastle's also close to where my parents died. I wondered if that had something to do with my being sent there."

"Hmm." Marshall looks uneasy for a moment. "It was another element, yes. A more personal one. You kept scratching away at that old sore. I hoped it might give you a chance to get some closure."

Marshall is concentrating on his fish, and Harry thinks there is something evasive in this reply. The word *closure* doesn't sound right coming from him.

"You know Ross Bramley, of course," Harry says.

"Yes, yes. How is old Ross?"

"Pretty good. Jenny met him and recognised his voice, and he told her he'd met her before, with my folks, just before they died."

"Ah yes. And Jenny recognised Ross from his voice, did she? That's good. Is her memory coming back, then?"

"Fragments. The thing is, Ross told us they left Newcastle the day before the crash, so they must have stayed in the Gloucester area that night. I don't remember that coming out at the inquest."

"It was certainly known. Maybe it didn't seem important. Was it?"

"Ross said it was never established where they stayed that night, so Jenny and I drove up to Gloucester to see if we could jog her memory."

Marshall looks at him intently. "And did you?"

"Maybe. We drove past a place called Cackleberry Valley and she remembered the name. She described the shape of Cackleberry Mountain, and it looks just like she said. She'd been there before. Nothing on that road except a homestead called Kramfors, and we got out there and spoke to a woman. Jenny immediately recognised her voice, we asked her if she remembered meeting Jenny, she said no. She was lying."

"Perhaps she forgot. It was over three years ago."

"No, she recognised Jenny all right, then denied it when she realised Jenny couldn't see her."

Marshall shrugs. "Didn't get her name, did you?"

"Amber. Mean anything to you?"

Marshall smiles suddenly. "Look at that." He points with his knife at a table further down the room. Harry turns and sees a familiar profile, a flushed cheek, thick waves of silver hair.

"That's Dalkeith, isn't it? The former premier?"

"Retired but still wheeling and dealing. Recognise the bloke he's with?"

"No."

"Most people wouldn't, but he's one of the most powerful people in Parliament these days—Lucan Abandonato, cabinet secretary. I wonder what they're cooking up. I'd love to bug that table. Between them they can cause more mischief over lunch than we can manage in a lifetime." He chuckles. "There are rules, of course. It's just that we don't all get to play by the same ones." And then, as if on the same subject, "No, I can't help you there, Harry. If you're going to annoy the Nordlunds you're on your own, mate."

He wipes his mouth and checks his watch. "I'd better move on. Been good talking to you, son. Take my advice and let the boys up in Newcastle take care of whoever bombed your place. I know they'll do a thorough job. Deb'll see to that."

On his way out, Harry thinks, *But I never mentioned the Nordlunds, Bob.* He wonders just how many coded messages Marshall managed to squeeze into their conversation.

THIRTY

WHEN THEY'RE ON THE freeway and clear of Sydney, Harry tells Jenny about Bob Marshall's offer of witness protection.

"So I'd have to cut myself off from my family?" she says. "My mother would never get to see her grandchild? No thanks. We can do better than that."

He wonders if that's true.

After an hour they turn off the highway and follow the road up past the Mardi Dam and into the Yarramalong Valley. At first the route is lined with hobby farms and smallholdings, but as they penetrate further, following the winding course of the Wyong River, woodlands close in around them. The sat nav tells Harry to take a small un-marked turning onto a narrow track. It climbs up the side of the valley and into a secluded hollow where a cottage lies tucked among the trees. A small dog comes bounding out onto the veranda as the car draws up, followed by a silver-haired woman wearing an apron. There is a smell of bak-ing bread in the forest air. Beyond the house Harry catches sight of long-necked alpacas in a paddock.

Later, listening to the voices of the two women in the kitchen, Harry thinks Jenny will be happy here. Felecia has immediately settled in, lying on the fireside rug next to her new friend. Harry goes out to the car and brings in the suit-cases, the dog's harness, Jenny's computer and a case of wine for Meri. He tries to persuade himself that this is a good idea.

Harry leaves late the following afternoon. He gives Jenny one of Ricsi's mobile phones and offers the pistol to Meri, who looks startled. She says, "No, dear, I have a shotgun—for the foxes. I'll stick to that. Don't worry, I'll use it if I have to."

THIRTY-ONE

HARRY RETURNS TO THE freeway and presses on to New-castle, the twilight fading as he reaches the suburb of May-field. He parks on a side street with a long line of sight to the McGilvray house, where a light is showing in the front window. After half an hour Logan McGilvray emerges and walks out to the white utility vehicle parked at the kerb. Harry follows at a distance as it makes its way into the west end of the city centre, slowing at a pub around which people are milling. The utility vehicle circles the block and eventually finds a park. Harry does the same, keeping a view of McGilvray's car. He checks that there are no cameras in the street, then settles down to wait. Four long hours with the radio.

Some time after 1:00 a.m. a figure emerges from the shadows into the pool of light under a street lamp. The hunched bulk of Logan McGilvray is recognisable, lurch-ing off the kerb, swaying towards the utility vehicle. Harry switches off the radio and gets out of his car. McGilvray fum-bles his keys in the lock, finally opens the door. As he stoops to get in Harry heaves him across to the passenger side and gets in behind the wheel. McGilvray yells, twists around, and focuses on Harry's face, then the gun in his hand. "Oh fuck."

Suddenly he is all movement, his whole ungainly body squirming as he paws at the handle on the far door. Harry reaches across and smacks him on the knee with the gun. He howls as Harry handcuffs his wrists behind him, slides back the seat and pushes him down into the well. Harry feels in McGilvray's pockets and finds his mobile phone. He reaches across to the passenger window and throws it into a bed of shrubs beside the footpath, then starts the car.

He sets off, out of the city, fast beneath the steady rhythm of lights until they come to the turning onto the Ash Island bridge. The electric dazzle of the highway fades as they cross the dark water, and McGilvray, twitching and restless until now, becomes very still. On the far side Harry kills the car lights and slows, feeling his way between the dark masses of mangroves beyond the river margin. His eyes adjust. He picks up speed as the space opens up and they reach the dirt road, a pale ribbon stretching away in the moonlight between sheets of black water. He follows it for a kilometre until they reach a copse of twisted trees. There he stops and switches off the engine. McGilvray stirs and groans. Harry steps out of the car into the cool pungent dark. He opens the passenger door and hauls McGilvray out onto his knees on the rim of the grassy bank. Watches him flinch as he sinks into the cold swamp, mumbling an incoherent protest.

Harry squats beside him and speaks softly. "Tell me everything."

McGilvray makes a big thing of clearing his throat, then says, "You're a dead man, mate."

"Who says so?"

"Yeah, you'd like to know, wouldn't you?"

Fast and hard, Harry's hand grabs the back of the other man's head. Arcs it forward and down, pushing it deep under the black water.

Harry is struck by a sudden bleak feeling as he counts silently to himself, holding the struggling man down. This has happened before.

Finally he hauls him out and watches him. Glistening black from the mud, spewing dark liquid, choking, struggling for breath.

"Now, Logan. Everything."

"Somebody . . . in Sydney . . . wants you dead."

"Who?"

"Dunno."

Harry tightens his grip on the man's neck.

"No! I don't know who . . . They got people in Newcastle to bomb your place."

"*You* bombed my place, Logan. You tried to kill me and my wife."

"No, no, swear to God. I . . . These people, they made me get them a bag of nitrate and a detonator from the mine."

"What people?"

"Oh, Jesus, I can't . . ."

Harry forces his head into the mud again. Holds it down longer this time. When Logan comes out he is barely conscious. Harry has to pump his back to get the fluid out and bring him round. When he is finally capable of speech the words come tumbling out.

"There's these blokes, call themselves the Dark Riders, like they're bikers only they don't advertise it . . . keep under the radar, cops don't know about them. They bring drugs in from the ships. Work with the Crows in Sydney."

"Names?"

"The big boss is called Tyler . . . Tyler Dayspring."

"You talk to him?"

"No, no, never seen him. My contact is just a little guy like me, a bloke called Sammy, runs a Chinese restaurant.

I go there and he gives me drugs to sell for the Riders, and I take the cash back to him."

Harry makes him go through it again in more detail, the amounts involved, the outlets for the drugs, up at the mines and in the city. "How do the Riders get the drugs from the ships?"

"I don't know and I don't ask." Either the cold or the foetid water in his lungs is getting to him and he's shivering and panting. He coughs, hawks up something dark. "Jeez, I'm sick."

"What about the bomb?"

"Two guys, Sammy arranged for me to meet them, Riders. Hard men, real hard men, balaclavas. No names. They told me to get the stuff from the mine stores for them, show them how to make a bomb. I overheard them say a name, Belltree, and laugh. Meant nothing until that time you interviewed me in the cop shop. Then I realised."

"But you said nothing, Logan. You built the bomb and knew the target and you said nothing. That makes you as guilty as them." Harry draws the pistol from his belt. "My wife is four months pregnant."

"Oh Jesus, I didn't know that. I didn't know anything, mate, not really, I just pinched a bit of stuff from work and . . ." Harry presses the pistol to his temple and the words are replaced by sobs.

He puts his mouth to McGilvray's ear and says, "There is only one way I will let you live, Logan. Are you listening?"

"Yes, yes."

"We'll drive back to your place, and you'll call your contact on your other phone. You'll tell them that you have to see the Dark Riders, tonight."

"They won't come, man."

"Yes they will. You'll tell them that I'm with you and

I know who they are, and I want to make a deal. You understand?"

"Yes, yes, okay. I'll do it. I'll do whatever you say." He is weeping, the pale track of tears visible on his black cheeks.

"Get in the car."

They drive back onto the highway. McGilvray, arms still locked behind his back, sits slumped against the car door, coughing and spitting from time to time.

When they reach his house McGilvray sits up with a start, looks around, and croaks something.

"What?"

"The cops . . . They don't like you. Sammy told me. You should watch your back too."

Harry unfastens his handcuffs and helps him out of the car, leading him up to the front door, taking his keys and pushing him inside. McGilvray staggers along the hallway, then lurches towards the bathroom door and collapses on the floor. Harry turns him over. He looks a mess, covered in black mud, face pale and sickly.

"Come on, let's clean you up." He hauls McGilvray into a sitting position and wets a towel to wipe his face. McGilvray makes a retching noise and reaches for the toilet bowl as a gob of black fluid spills out of his lips. "Water," he gasps.

Harry looks around for a container. There's nothing in the bathroom. "Hang on."

He goes outside, finds the kitchen and takes a dirty cup out of the sink, runs it under the tap, fills it, and returns to the bathroom. McGilvray is gone.

A couple of muddy footprints lead to the back room, where the glass doors stand open. Harry runs out, down the small yard to the rear fence, nothing, then back, around the house to the street. McGilvray's utility vehicle is still there, no sign of him. Harry gets in and sets off through the streets, the side roads, searching for him.

He widens the search, seeing only a lone couple, then a group emerging from a pub. As he passes the end of Dangar Park he thinks he sees a single dark figure crossing the far end, but when he turns up there he finds nothing. After an hour of fruitless searching, he gives up and heads back to the street where his own car is parked. He retrieves McGilvray's phone from the nature strip and leaves it in the utility vehicle, which he cleans up as best he can, then sets off in his own car back to Sydney.

THIRTY-TWO

KELLY INTENDED TO ARRIVE early at the nursing home, but there is an accident on the motorway up to Newcastle and long delays so it's lunchtime before she arrives and no sign of David Suskind sitting outside. She gets a park not far away and settles down to wait, hoping Karen Schaefer has come to see her father again.

Towards two she sees the white Nissan pull into the driveway. Kelly picks up the camera and takes pictures as Karen Schaefer gets out and helps her father down from the passenger side. She's wearing jeans and a check shirt and there are streaks of mud down the flanks of the 4WD. She helps the old man to the front door of the home. Once Karen returns to her car Kelly starts her own.

They follow the same route as before, across the Hunter River to the Bucketts Way and on to Stroud. In the town Kelly gets close enough for a clear sighting of the Nissan's number plate and she puts a call though to Harry.

"I've found her again, Harry—Donna Fenning, Karen Schaefer. I'm on the road north of Newcastle, following her. She's in a white Nissan Patrol, and I've got the number."

She gives it to him and he tells her to be careful and he'll get back to her. They continue out into the open country and on towards Gloucester. The humped silhouette of the Bucketts comes into view as Kelly's phone rings.

"Kelly? Harry. Are you still following her?"

"Yes, we're nearly at Gloucester."

"Listen, I want you to turn back."

"What?"

"I don't want you to follow her anymore."

"What are you talking about, Harry? What's going on?"

"Please just do as I ask. I can look after this."

"I'm not going to lose her again!"

Harry begins to tell her again and she cuts in, "Okay, okay. I've got the message. The signal's not very good here. I can hardly hear you. I'm pulling in."

She hangs up and comes to a stop on the hard shoulder. Ahead of her she sees the white vehicle reach the top of the next rise and vanish over the crest. She thumps the steering wheel, then mutters "Bugger it!" and pulls back onto the road. She puts her foot down. Maybe Harry's arranged for the police to stop the Nissan and doesn't want her involved. But she can still follow and make sure.

Kelly spots the Nissan again in Gloucester, at the far end of the main street, turning left onto Thunderbolt's Way. There are no police cars waiting on the other side of town and the road ahead seems clear, with very little traffic.

Suddenly the Nissan slows and turns onto a side road. Kelly pulls to a stop at the sign to Cackleberry Valley, wondering what to do. If the cops are waiting up ahead on Thunderbolt's Way they're wasting their time. She has no option but to follow the Nissan.

After a while she reaches a forest just at the point where the road becomes dirt. She has to slow down, avoiding potholes, but she can see the cloud of dust kicked up by the Nissan ahead. They emerge at last into a broad green valley dominated by the lowering grey dome of the mountain far ahead. She rattles across a cattle grid, hits tarmac once again between fields of grazing cattle, and sees a distant red roof nestling in a copse of dark trees. A sign says NO THROUGH ROAD. She pulls to a halt and calls Harry's number again. No signal. She drives on.

The road ahead ends in a circular driveway around an ornamental fountain in front of the homestead, but Kelly turns off before she reaches it, into a yard beside an old timber barn. She comes to a stop. No one seems to be around and there's no sign of the Nissan. She checks the phone again without success and gets out of the car. There's a strong smell of silage and horses and, from somewhere beyond the barn, the sound of hooves. She walks cautiously to the end of the barn and peers round the corner, then jumps as a voice close behind her says, "Ah, you must be my old schoolfriend, Laura King."

Kelly spins around. "Donna Fenning." There's a man by her side.

"And you are Kelly Pool." Karen Schaefer peers at Kelly in that mildly troubled way of hers that Kelly once found reassuring. "Craig?" she says. The man takes hold of Kelly's arm in a firm grip. "Let's go inside."

They march her into the sudden darkness of the barn. Motes of dust float on the beams of sunlight that shaft through the ancient timbers. As her eyes adjust Kelly sees an old tractor and an even older sedan, covered in dust and the fine webs of bush spiders. Craig Schaefer pushes her roughly against the car and pats her down, finding her phone in the pocket of her jeans. He hands it to Karen, who flicks through to recent calls.

"Who's Harry?" she asks.

Kelly says nothing.

"You called him on the way here. Who is he?"

Kelly looks her in the eye and says, "He's a police officer. He's on his way."

"That's crap," Craig says. "Cops don't give out their mobiles. Anyway . . ." He raises an eyebrow at Karen and taps his watch.

"Yes, I know. We'll have to continue this conversation later." She looks around, frowning, then nods at the boot of the ancient Holden. She strides over and fiddles with the latch and the hood swings up. "Put her in here."

"No," Kelly cries, and jumps away from Craig, desperate to get to the barn door, but he grabs her arm and swings her around hard against the side of the car, knocking the breath out of her. Before she can recover he hoists her up and tumbles her into the boot and slams down the lid. She screams and kicks, the sounds deafening inside the steel shell, until at last she forces herself to be still, and her world shrinks to the suffocating dark silence of a coffin.

She reasons with herself. She has done this before, she can handle it. She must concentrate on controlling her breathing, she must think ahead. But when they've done whatever they have to do, what then?

She begins to explore her coffin with her fingertips. She encounters an old piece of carpet, musty with age, and several nuts and bolts. No sign of a jack handle or a tyre lever. What else does she have? She feels in the pockets of her jeans: some coins, keys, wallet, a small notebook, and a ballpoint pen.

Then the silence is broken by the muffled sound of the barn door creaking open. She stiffens. *I can't let this happen again.* And then, *The pen is mightier than the sword.* She grips it in her right hand as there is a click and a flood of light, a dark silhouette against the light and a figure looming down to take hold of her. She lashes up at it with her pen. Feels it sink into something soft and hears a shriek, *a horrific shriek* she dictates to herself, a howl cut abruptly short. She hauls herself upright and sees Craig Schaefer stretched out on the barn floor. His legs twitch and then are still. Kelly's pen is buried in his left eye.

Kelly clambers out of the car boot and stares down in horror at the motionless figure. She crouches by his side and tries to feel for a pulse in his neck. Nothing. *Dear God, I've killed him.* Her phone is sticking out of his pocket and she snatches it and runs for the door. There is no one around, no sign of Karen. The still air, the distant whinny of a horse seem unnaturally innocent. She runs to her car, scrambles in, starts the engine, and lurches into gear.

Her eyes flick continuously to the rear-view mirror, but no following vehicle is visible through the cloud of dust she raises. She presses her foot down hard and doesn't let it up even when she hits the rocks and potholes of the dirt road through the forest. The main road appears at last and she swings towards Gloucester, wondering what to do. At the roundabout at the head of the main street she sees a sign to the police station up to the left. Hesitates. Turns right, forcing herself to slow down across the pedestrian crossings until she is clear of the shopping area and on the road back to Newcastle, expecting the howl of police sirens any moment at her back. But they don't come, and on she drives, through Stroud and then into Newcastle, where she becomes lost. She has no idea where she is and finally pulls into a pub car park. Only then does she turn off the engine and, with a shaking hand, ring Harry.

"Harry? Harry, is that you? I've killed him. I've killed Craig Schaefer."

"Hang on. Slow down. What happened?"

She tells him the whole story.

"Where are you now?"

She peers out and reads the name of the hotel.

"Stay there, Kelly, and don't speak to anyone. I'll be with you in fifteen minutes."

THIRTY-THREE

THAT MORNING, SUNDAY 24 November, Harry woke at home after two hours' sleep, went out for a run through the empty streets of Surry Hills, had breakfast, and rang Jenny. She sounded positive, said she was missing him, and described going out at dawn with Meri to gather eggs from the chicken pen and check the eight alpacas. Harry told her that he'd not made much progress but asked her, if she had time, to get on the computer and check the social media sites for any postings by Logan McGilvray. When he rang off he made a coffee and went outside into the small courtyard, sat down to think.

In a way, the Crows, the bomb, Logan McGilvray all seemed like a distraction from the central question. What did they have to do with the death of his parents and the blinding of Jenny? Roman Bebchuk, president of the Crows, had carried out the murders, but he was no more than a paid assassin. Before Harry killed him, Bebchuk implicated the New South Wales Police Minister, Derryn Oldfield; Oldfield had arranged the contract on behalf of someone else but had refused to give Harry the name. He too was now dead, suicide. But somewhere there was evidence, there had to be evidence, of the compelling reason that had made all this necessary.

Harry finished his coffee and went indoors, climbed the stairs to his father's study in the attic. After his parents died he had had to search for any documents relevant in winding up their estate. In the drawer of his mother's writing desk he had found an envelope addressed to *Harry*, written in her hand. Inside was a small sheet of writing paper with a message that made his throat close: *Harry darling, we are so proud of you. With all my love, Mum.*

There was nothing like that in his father's study upstairs. Just shelves stuffed with old files and books and bundles of papers. No doubt his father had known where everything was, but Harry could see no order in it. After a cursory search, enough to satisfy him that there were unlikely to be any recent wills, instructions, or bank statements buried in it all, Harry had retreated, unwilling to disturb it. Later, when he became convinced that his parents had been murdered, he had returned to look over his father's recent rulings for some motive. But again, the complexity and fragmentary nature of the documents defeated him. It would have been different if Jenny had not lost her sight. She would have gone through it all with her legal researcher's mind and perhaps found something, some clue to what had happened. But Harry had baulked, intimidated by it all. *One day*, he thought, *I'll get the State Library in and they can take the lot for their archives.*

When he entered the study he looked for a moment at the framed photographs on the small areas of unshelfed walls. Danny and Pearl Belltree in 1965, young revolutionaries on the Freedom Ride, standing alongside Charles Perkins and Jim Spigelman; Danny with long sideburns, addressing a rally of Sydney University students in 1968; Danny and

Pearl on his admission to the New South Wales Bar, and again twenty years later on his elevation to the bench of the New South Wales Supreme Court. A splendid progression, whose atrocious end has left this room untouched.

On the long cedar desk below the window there was an in-tray, piled high with loose papers. Harry had gone through it on his early search: requests to speak, invitations to events, charity appeals, newspaper cuttings, a shopping list.

He read it again, the sad flotsam of a moment in a life interrupted: *printer cartridges, my muesli, chocolates for P, shoe polish*. The word *polish* was stained yellow by magic marker ink soaked through from the reverse side, and Harry turned the page over to find a photocopy of a page from an old book. The words that had been highlighted were *Egg Mountain*.

He read the whole paragraph:

"The Worimi Tribes of the Upper Manning," by The Reverend T. J. Bartholomew, The Journal of NSW History, Vol. 16, 1930.

In the year 1888 I travelled in the upper reaches of the Manning, Gloucester and Barrington Rivers and encountered several full bloods and many half-castes. A head man, named "Billy," then about seventy years of age, was not only an initiate but was also the ruling spirit of a local group, or "nurra," of the Worimi Clan, who spoke the "Kutthung" or Kattang language. He referred to his nurra as the "Yoon-goo-ar," and their territory, or "burri," as that of "Kuppoee-Yoongoo" which I translate as "Egg Mountain," which abuts the lands of the Geawegal Clan to the west.

Harry read it again, then put the sheet of paper down

carefully. Justice Danny Belltree was the first *Aboriginal* judge of the New South Wales Supreme Court. Is that what this was all about? An Aboriginal land claim?

And at that point the phone rang. He heard Kelly's voice. "I've found her again, Harry—Donna Fenning, Karen Schaefer. I'm on the road north of Newcastle, following her. She's in a white Nissan Patrol, and I've got the number."

Harry logged into the police intranet with his iPad. The Nissan was registered to the Kramfors Estate.

This makes no sense, he thought, and called Kelly to tell her to back off.

He checked his watch, grabbed his gear, and ran out to the car.

Two and a half hours later he was on the freeway and approaching Newcastle when he got Kelly's second call, telling him that she had killed Craig Schaefer. Thirty minutes later he turned into the car park of the hotel and found her sitting inside, half hidden behind a bank of pokie machines, hunched over a vodka tonic.

THIRTY-FOUR

SHE LOOKS VERY PALE, hair awry, dirt on her clothes.

"You okay? You're not hurt?"

She nods blankly.

"Okay." He stretches out an awkward, comforting arm to her and she suddenly falls against him, sobbing quietly.

When she sits up straight again, wiping her nose, he gets her to take him through it once more.

"So, this must have happened what, about two hours ago?" He gets out his iPad and taps into Northern Region police. So far there's no report of an incident at Kramfors.

"Should I report to the police, Harry? Will you come with me?"

He thinks about that. "Do you have a lawyer?"

She shakes her head.

"How about your paper? You could say you were following up a story, couldn't you?"

She frowns, thinking. "Ye-es, I suppose so. Oh yes, they have top lawyers."

"I think that may be the way to go, Kelly. But let's not rush into anything." He nods at her glass. "How many of those have you had?"

"My second."

"Singles or doubles?"

"Doubles. Chrissake, Harry, I've never killed anyone before."

"Do you think you can drive?"

"Yes . . . yes of course."

"We'll take the old Pacific Highway, nice and slow, away from the cameras on the freeway. You okay with that?"

The sun is setting, a red glow on the western horizon, as the two cars reach Kelly's suburb in Sydney. He goes with her to the front door, which is opened by her flatmate. She stares at Kelly, looking exhausted and bedraggled, then at Harry, and immediately grabs Kelly and hustles her inside. Harry follows, listening as Kelly blurts out her story. It would be better if she didn't, Harry thinks, but it can't be avoided.

"I suppose you've reported it?" Wendy says at last, staring accusingly at Harry.

"Not yet. We're going to get Kelly a good lawyer, but first I need to check a few things."

Wendy turns to Kelly. "What can I get you, love?"

"Vodka."

Wendy looks at Harry, who shakes his head. "She may need to make a statement."

"Strong coffee, then," Wendy concludes, while Harry gets to work on the iPad. A report has now been flagged up from Gloucester police. An accident at Kramfors Homestead, reported by the crew of the Westpac Rescue Helicopter. They've transported a Craig Schaefer to John Hunter Hospital in Newcastle with a serious eye injury.

"He's alive, Kelly," Harry says. "At least he was an hour ago."

"But . . . he wasn't moving. I felt the pen go into his brain!"

Wendy is studying diagrams on her computer. "I don't

think so. The eye cavity is like a cone of bone going back into your head, with the pointy end at the back. If the ballpoint got all the way to the back it would have hit the carotid artery there, which would have finished him off straight away for sure. You probably just gouged his eye."

Kelly jumps to her feet, gagging, and runs to the bathroom.

Wendy says, "Have they mentioned Kelly's name yet?"

"Not that I can see. At the moment they're calling it an accident."

"Why would they do that?"

"They'll need to take statements. It may take time. We still don't know what the Schaefers were doing there."

He returns to his iPad, this time searching for any mention of Logan McGilvray on the police net in the past forty-eight hours. There is nothing. Finally, toward 3:00 a.m., Harry finds an updated report from the Gloucester police on the Kramfors incident. It is now described as an industrial accident. The victim, an employee at Kramfors, fell into agricultural machinery and suffered a ruptured left eye. Involvement of a third party is not suspected.

He shows Wendy the report and she shakes her head. "How is that possible?"

"I don't know. I'll go up there tomorrow and see what I can find out. In the meantime, I think Kelly should do nothing."

"Right, I'll tell her. She'll be just so relieved."

But she returns in a moment and says, "She's fast asleep. Reaction, I suppose."

"Yes. I'll get going."

At the front door Wendy says, "Thanks, Harry, for looking after her. She's had a bad trot lately. She always told me that you were a good friend, but I wasn't sure till now."

THIRTY-FIVE

KELLY WAKES AT FIRST light, and immediately her mind fills with dread. It seems she's still in her own bed, but for how long? How long before the banging on the front door, the raised voices, the handcuffs on her wrists? She imagines the shame, her case reported in her own newspaper.

She gets up and shuffles through to the kitchen to make a cup of tea. What a luxury, to be able to make a cup of tea in your own kitchen. She wonders which prison they'll send her to. Silverwater first, probably, then who knows. She's been inside several, with the luxury of the outsider—thank God I'm not one of them! How long will they give her? Ten years? Fifteen? *My life is finished. Jesus, I should have jumped.*

She hears Wendy go to the bathroom. *How long will she keep visiting? Six months? A year? I'll have to tell her not to waste her time.*

"Hi. You had a good sleep. You needed it."

Kelly turns to her friend. "Yes. I just flaked out. I can't remember what happened." Then, the involuntary words spilling out, "How long before they come for me, Wendy? How long have I got?"

"Oh, Kelly." Wendy wraps her arms around her friend. "Harry was here till three last night, waiting for news. Then

we got the police report. He's in John Hunter with a ruptured eyeball, and they're treating it as an industrial accident."

"What?"

"I know, we can't figure it out either. But it seems you're
in the clear."

Kelly sits down heavily on a kitchen chair. She doesn't
dare to believe this is true. There'll be a twist, she thinks,
like an old movie where the condemned man is reprieved at
the last minute only to discover it's a mistake, and is hauled
off to the firing squad after all.

"You don't look happy."

"I just can't believe it."

"Phone Harry. Talk to him yourself."

But she doesn't dare, and it's another hour before he
phones her. "It's true, Kelly. I've checked again this morning. As far as the Gloucester police are concerned the case
is closed. They've flagged it as an industrial accident to be
reported to Workcover. The only thing I can think is that
the Schaefers were up to something at Kramfors that they
want to keep under wraps. I'm going up there to see what
I can find out."

"Oh, Harry. I can't tell you what a relief this is."

"I know. Go out and celebrate. But bear this in mind:
Karen and Craig Schaefer know what really happened, and
they're not going to be happy about it. Plus, they know that
you know they were at Crucifixion Creek as the Fennings. I
think, once the dust settles, you could be in trouble, Kelly."

"Yes, yes, point taken," Kelly says, but there's a wild grin
on her face. *I'm free! I'm not going to Silverwater!*

She hangs up and turns to Wendy. "Come on, let's go."

Wendy laughs at the transformation. "Where to?"

"I'm going to buy us a huge champagne breakfast."

THIRTY-SIX

SMOKE DRIFTS ACROSS THE freeway as Harry drives north. It's a hot morning, an early warning of a dire bushfire summer ahead. He stops for a coffee and a pie in Gloucester, watching the passers-by in the main street outside the café window, their untroubled pace, their quiet self-sufficiency. Decides against arousing curiosity by calling at the police station, heads straight for Cackleberry Valley. It seems another world today, hidden beyond the forest, a bowl of still, warm air below the Egg Mountain. Kuppoee-Yoongoo.

He passes the barn that Kelly described—deserted, peaceful, no police tape—and comes to the house, its red roof burning bright beneath the midday sun. In the shade of the veranda he is about to reach for the brass knocker when the door swings open and he is confronted by a boy, perhaps eight or nine years old, who stares up at him with big inquisitive eyes.

"Yes?"

"Hello. I'd like to speak to Amber."

The boy frowns at him for a moment, then turns and calls, "Mum. Someone for you."

Beyond him Harry sees a large hall panelled in dark

timber with an elaborate staircase rising on the far side, painted portraits hanging on the walls.

The boy turns back to Harry. "Are you a policeman?"

"Yes, how did you guess?"

"It's pretty obvious. About the accident, I suppose."

"What accident is that?"

"You don't know? Craig stabbed his eye out yesterday."

"Yuck. That sounds bad."

"Pretty bad. He'll be blind in one eye. I expect he'll have to wear a black patch, like a pirate."

"Right. Does Craig live here?"

"He works for us, our estate manager. Are you carrying a Glock?"

"Yes."

"Can I see it?"

"We're not allowed to draw our weapon unless we intend to use it."

"Oh, right. Cool."

Amber Nordlund appears in the hall behind him and says, "Dylan? What are you doing?"

"This policeman wants to talk to you, Mum."

As the light from the doorway catches her face he sees recognition strike her.

"You've got work to do, Dylan."

"I finished my maths and Karen isn't here to help me with my project."

"Well go and read your history book for half an hour, then we'll have lunch."

He turns and walks away with a heavy limp on a stiff right leg. It strikes Harry with a new force that he is soon to become a father, perhaps of a child like this: smart, inquisitive, vulnerable.

"What do you want?"

"To talk to you, Amber."

She seems about to refuse, then sighs and steps back for him to enter. The hall is cool, their tread muffled on a broad Indian carpet. Amber leads the way to a sitting room with a view over a shady garden.

He takes the seat she offers and says nothing, giving her a chance to speak. She seems jittery, avoiding his eyes. "Yes, I thought you'd come back. I . . . I wasn't prepared for your last visit. You took me by surprise. I'm sorry."

"Well, let's start again."

"I didn't recognise your wife—Jenny—at first. She's changed, hasn't she? Not just her . . . her eyes. She was so effervescent before, so full of life. We immediately hit it off. Of course she must have had a terrible time adjusting. I'm sorry I was so rude. I just . . . I didn't want to go back there." All this comes out in a rush.

"All the same, I'd appreciate it if you would go back there for me now."

"Yes . . . Well, your parents and Jenny just arrived one day. They were interested in history, the history of the homestead and so on." Her fingers pluck at the tassels on the brocaded cushion at her side. "And we hit it off, and I invited them to stay overnight, and the next morning they left, and . . . well, you know. I didn't hear till later that afternoon, when I drove into town, what had happened. I was so shocked."

"There was an investigation afterwards, of course."

"Yes, of course."

"Did you tell anyone they stayed with you that night?"

"No . . . well, I didn't think it was relevant. No one came to ask." She gives a helpless, nervous smile.

"So they just turned up out of the blue, you hit it off, and you invited them to stay?"

"That's right."

"Who else was staying in the house at that time?"

"Um, well, Dylan. That's all, really."

"What about elsewhere on the estate?"

"There were people in the staff cottages—the stable hands and so on, I'm not sure who exactly."

"A housekeeper?"

"Oh yes, Karen. And her husband Craig, they have their own cottage too."

"Have they been with you long?"

"Ages. Karen's looked after Dylan since he was born. I'd have been lost without her."

"Dylan told me that Craig's been injured recently."

"Yes! Poor Craig. He hurt himself with some machinery. They've taken him to hospital. Is there anything else? This is beginning to feel like an interrogation."

"Sorry, a bad habit of mine, comes from my job."

She glows an unconvincing smile. "Yes, I suppose so."

"The other thing that my job does is teach me to know when someone's not telling me the truth."

A flush rises in Amber's face and she looks away.

"My parents didn't just turn up here at random, did they?"

He sees confusion and embarrassment on her face, but not denial. "What? Was my father here on business?"

"I haven't the faintest . . ."

"Did he represent a threat, Amber? Was that it? To you and your family's interests? Is that why they died?"

"What!" Her whole frame stiffens as if he's slapped her. "You bastard! How dare you come in here and accuse me!" She jumps to her feet. "Get out. Get out right now!"

"There will be phone records, a money trail, fragments of evidence. There always are. It just needs someone to look in the right places. And that's what I'm doing."

"Get out!"

He stands and says, "Think about it." He places a card on the side table. "Phone me when you're ready to tell me the truth."

He goes to the door and steps out into the hall, Amber following, then stops as a door opens on the far side of the hall and he recognises the silver-haired woman who was on the balcony last time. She has the chin-up stance of someone posing for the camera. The skin on her face is stretched tight, the lips pumped up.

The woman stares at him, then at Amber, and says, "What was that noise, Amber? We thought we heard shouting."

Harry sees that a man is following her—dark suit, tie, black hair slicked back on a lean skull. The lawyer Nathaniel Horn.

Horn meets his eyes and says, "Well, this is a surprise, Sergeant Belltree."

"Mr. Horn."

"Belltree?" the elderly woman says. "Belltree?"

"Yes." Horn comes closer to Harry, examining him as if for evidence. "What brings you here, sergeant?"

"Personal business, Mr. Horn. What about yourself?"

"I am the Nordlunds' family lawyer, and I shall be happy to advise them of their legal rights in relation to unwelcome visitors." He looks beyond Harry. "Is he here by invitation, Amber?"

"No, I've just told him to leave."

Horn nods. "On your way, Sergeant."

As Harry reaches the front door, Horn, following him, says, "I heard you'd left Sydney. Have they posted you to the country now, Belltree?"

Harry turns to face him. "Newcastle."

Horn nods. "Hmm, you must be running out of friends. You should be careful." He shuts the door on Harry's back.

When he reaches Gloucester Harry decides after all to visit the police station. A middle-aged uniformed sergeant is leaning over the front desk, doing the crossword in the local paper.

"G'day."

The sergeant looks up. "And g'day to you. How's yours been so far?"

"Pretty much as expected. Yourself?"

"Yep." He folds the newspaper. "And what can I do for you?"

Harry shows his ID and the man raises an eyebrow. "Oh yes? Belltree? Would you be related to the judge?"

"He was my father."

"Oh, right. Condolences." He offers a big slab of a hand. "Tommy Jordan. I was one of the first at the scene that morning. Nothing any of us could do for your folks, but at least we were able to save the young woman."

"My wife."

"Ah. Covered in blood she was. How is she now?"

"She lost her sight."

Sergeant Jordan shakes his head. "Yes, I heard that. Is that why you're here now, to revisit the place?"

"My wife has only hazy memories of that time, but she has it in her mind that the three of them spent the night before the crash at Kramfors Homestead."

"Really? First I've heard of that."

"Any idea why they would have done that? Anything going on around here that would interest a Supreme Court judge?"

Jordan shakes his head slowly. "Can't think of anything."

"My father was Aboriginal, you know. Interested in Aboriginal issues. Nothing like that? A native title land claim, say?"

"No, not recently. The one for the Crown lands of the Cackleberry Forest was settled a dozen or more years ago. Local Aboriginal land council owns it now. You cross through the forest to get to Kramfors Homestead. Why don't you go over there? Young Amber'll talk to you."

"I did that, but she wasn't much help. What's she like?"

"Oh, bright girl, I guess."

"You don't sound enthusiastic."

"Well, it's just that the homestead is a sad place now compared to how it was. The girl does her best to keep it going, give her that, but it's not like it was when her father was alive. Martin Nordlund was a real force around here, big benefactor—local hospital, schools, charities. But he was killed eleven years ago in a plane crash. You've heard of Flight VH-MDX?"

"Don't think so."

"One of Australia's great aviation mysteries, a Cessna 172S Skyhawk, Martin Nordlund's pride and joy. He had his pilot's licence, flew himself to business meetings all over the state. Anyway, in August 2002 he was coming back with his solicitor from a meeting in Sydney, almost home, and he went down somewhere around Cackleberry Mountain. It was dark, but the weather was fine and clear. No remains ever found."

"How is that possible?"

"Difficult country up there—dense bush, steep ravines. No trails. They reckon the plane's wings would have sheared off when it hit the tree canopy, so the wings and fuselage would have speared down straight into all this mongrel thick undergrowth, you see. No sign from above. Doesn't appear to have been a fire. There's been any number of search parties—I was on three of them—and we might have gone within a few metres of the overgrown wreckage and never seen a thing.

"Amber would have been fourteen or fifteen back then, I guess. She went a bit crazy after it happened." His voice drops, confidential. "Got kicked out of a couple of expensive boarding schools down in Sydney. Drugs, you know. Then they sent her abroad for a while and she got pregnant. When she came back she was a grown woman with a kid. Took over the running of the estate. She keeps pretty much to herself, and home-schools the boy, so we don't see much of him either. Kind of sad."

"Another Ms. Nordlund was there—much older?"

"That would likely be Trixie Nordlund. She was a movie star back in the fifties, married Amber's grandfather Carl. Her home's in Sydney, but she comes up on visits. Parading down Church Street like she owns the place."

"And she had a lawyer with her that I recognised—Nathaniel Horn. Heard of him?"

"Horn? That the one you see on TV, scumbags' lawyer?"

"That's him. I wondered what would bring him up here."

"Well, it must be the smell of money, eh? The Nordlunds are big money. Not Miss Amber so much as her uncle, Konrad. You'll have heard of him in Sydney I dare say."

THIRTY-SEVEN

KELLY DECIDES TO TAKE the day off, phones in sick to work. She needs time to relish her reprieve, and to think. And as she thinks, something occurs to her. She picks up her phone and rings Harry.

"How are you, Kelly?"

"Better, much better, thanks to you." She can hear the background noise of his car. "Listen, why did you tell me to stop following her yesterday, Harry, after I rang you?"

There is a slight hesitation. He says, "When I checked her car registration I saw where she must be going. It's isolated, and I thought you could get into trouble following her in there."

But Kelly's journalist's ear picks something up in the way he says this. He's hiding something. "Have you been there before then, Harry?"

Another pause. "Yeah, I know it."

"What, it's known to the police?"

"No, nothing like that."

"What then?"

"Doesn't matter. Just forget it and move on, Kelly."

"Harry, I'm a journalist. I know when I'm having a door

closed in my face. You want me to dig on my own? What's the place called?"

"I've got to go."

Then inspiration strikes her. "When I was following her I saw signs for Thunderbolt's Way, and I thought, that's where Harry's folks died. Is that it?"

Another, longer pause before his reluctant reply. "It's called Kramfors Homestead. My parents stayed there the night before they died."

Kelly feels a cold finger stroking her spine. "Harry," she whispers. "Remember what I said about coincidences?"

"Yes."

"Karen Schaefer, formerly of Crucifixion Creek, turns up in the place your folks spent their last night alive? Are you kidding?"

She can imagine him shaking his head as she waits for his answer.

"No, I'm not kidding. Her car's registered owner was Kramfors Estate."

She explodes, "Why?"

"I don't know. I've just been there. The owner says that Karen has been the housekeeper there for years. Are you quite sure that she's Donna Fenning?"

"Of course I am! She recognised me straight away, knew my name. Jesus, Harry! Who is this owner?"

"Just leave it to me, Kelly."

"No! That woman's tried to get me killed—twice! I'm going to look into this with or without you."

They're both silent. Five beats, then Kelly says, "Sorry. You tried to warn me. But we should work together on this. You don't want me messing up your investigation, do you?"

"No."

"So who owns Kramfors?"

"The Nordlund family."

Kelly whistles.

"The woman who runs the place is Amber Nordlund, twenties, kind of . . . highly strung."

"So what now?"

"More digging I guess. Kelly, that thing about my parents staying there. It's personal. I don't want that made public. I want to follow it up my own way. Keep it to yourself, okay?"

"Sure, Harry."

THIRTY-EIGHT

HARRY DRIVES BACK TO Newcastle with the window down, the hot country air billowing into the car. He has found no mention of Dark Riders or Tyler Dayspring on the police databases, and decides it's counterproductive to try to keep out of sight. When he reaches the city he heads for the port and the suburb of Carrington, and stops at a pub, the Marine, at the crossroads in the centre. Over a beer he talks to the landlord about renting a room. He's taken upstairs, making a note of access points and fire escape, and checks out a room right on the corner of the building. It overlooks the crossroads and the long perspectives down to the grain silos on the docks in one direction. In the other he can see the bridge over Throsby Creek, connecting the district to the rest of the city. He is less than a hundred metres from the bombed-out ruin of their cottage. His car, sitting outside on the kerb with its scorched paintwork, is like an advertisement to whoever wanted him dead.

"This is perfect," he says.

He brings up his bag, unpacks his few belongings, and makes a call to Ross Bramley.

Ross seems surprised and pleased to hear from him. "Where are you, mate?"

"Back in Newcastle."

"On your own?"

"Yep. What are you doing tonight? Fancy a beer and a Chinese at Sammy's?"

Ross suggests they meet at a French wine bar first, a new venue he wants to try. Harry wouldn't have thought it was Ross's kind of thing, but apparently it brings back memories of a European trip with his wife.

"So how's work?" Harry finally asks.

"No more bodies on Ash Island so far, but no leads to the killers either. Foggy's cranky as ratshit, as usual. Your friend Velasco is keeping out of his way. Nothing on McGilvray—his phone's dead, no one knows where he is, reckon he's done a runner. No, it's been pretty quiet—same old same old. String of service station hold-ups, nasty suicide in Stockton, kid missing in Bar Beach."

They drive to Sammy Lee's place and park across the way. Harry pauses outside the Asian grocery store next door to the restaurant. Looks in at the shelves of packages with Chinese, Vietnamese, and Thai labels.

"This Sammy's business too?"

"Sure. It does well."

They go into the restaurant, where a woman at the front desk checks Harry's booking in a fat diary, then plucks menus from a stack. "This way, please."

Harry says, "I'll just use the gents," and as the other two walk away he quickly turns the diary towards him, flicking back through the pages to 20 October, the date of the photograph on McGilvray's contact phone. He finds the page, full of names and numbers for a busy Saturday night, and quickly takes a photo on his phone.

It is a Monday and the restaurant's quiet. Sammy himself isn't there. At a lull in the conversation, Harry says, "I keep thinking of what Leon Timson said about the Ash Island victims: all three of them had been worked over professionally, as if the killers were after information. The two oldest victims were linked to the Crows, so that's understandable, but what about the sailor, Cheung? What could some poor dumb kitchen hand off a Chinese bulk carrier know that would be of the slightest interest to those guys?"

"Pure sadism, I reckon. So does the profiler they've got in. 'Sadistic cult murders' is one of his lead possibilities."

"Okay, but supposing it wasn't. Supposing it's cold-blooded business—drug business. Supposing the *Jialing* was trading drugs as well as coal, and Cheung found out something he shouldn't have."

"You heard what the customs guy said—it could only be small quantities, smuggled out by the odd person."

"Remember when we went onto the NRL berth? There was a van there making a delivery to the ship. There must be lots of stuff they need when they come into port—toilet paper, light bulbs, bottles of water."

"Yeah, but they're not smuggling drugs *into* the ship, surely? They'd have to be taking it off. How could they do that?"

"Maybe in the empty containers, once they've taken the supplies on board. They do it regularly, month after month, year after year. Customs searches them thoroughly the first few times, then they just wave them through. What do you reckon?"

Ross shrugs doubtfully.

"Where did Cheung work, Ross? He was a kitchen hand. Worked in the galley, among the food. Tell you what, humour me. Call Gerry Cork's office and find out who supplied food to the *Jialing*."

Ross chuckles and says, "This is what shit-hot homicide

cops in Sydney come up with is it, Harry? Okay, let's give it a try." He takes out his phone and calls the shipping agent's number. One of Cork's assistants is on duty. He checks the computer. Harry watches the smile on Ross's face fade. He rings off and stares at Harry. "Sammy Lee supplied the *Jialing*. He's one of the main providores to the Asian ships. That's why you suggested coming here, isn't it? You knew, didn't you?'

"No, I didn't know. But when I saw the grocery next door it made me think."

Ross is shaking his head. "No, not Sammy. I've known him for twenty years. He's too smart to get mixed up in something like that. He's got an MBA for goodness sake."

"And a business that would be perfect for laundering drug money."

"You're serious."

"Remember the CCTV of Cheung at Marketown with his hand to his ear, on the phone? But he didn't speak English. So who was he talking to? Has to be someone who speaks Chinese."

Ross thinks. "I don't buy it, Harry. I know the guy. I'll do a few checks, and I'll prove you wrong. Want to make a bet? A hundred bucks Sammy's in the clear."

They shake on it.

THIRTY-NINE

JENNY SITS ON THE rear veranda of the cottage, holding tight onto Felecia's harness, the three of them listening to the anxious hooting noise that the alpacas are making as the shearer moves in among them.

"They recognise Drew," Meri says, "he comes every year. They don't like it."

She tells Jenny what Drew is doing, grabbing each one in turn, tripping it to the ground, binding its feet, and getting to work with the electric shears, slicing in steady arcs through the thick fleece.

"It's a good year—three, maybe even four kilos off each one. Thirty kilos, Jenny; that'll keep us busy."

Meri will spin the fibre on a wheel in the main room, which is the combined kitchen, dining, living, and work room of the cottage. She explains the process, first spreading the fleece out over the polished wooden floorboards to pick out any bits of stray vegetable matter, any fibre that isn't from the animals' premium "blanket"—the back, shoulders and flanks. She won't need to wash the fibre before spinning, it's not oily like sheeps wool, and she'll pack it into open-topped bags so that it can breathe. She'll tease out the fleece from the bag with a comb and spin it.

Jenny is to help her. She's been practising at the wheel with fibre left over from last year's shearing, enjoying the feel of the fine fleece slipping through her fingers, the total concentration needed to keep the yarn running.

Fernando, the dominant male of the small herd, gives out a furious trumpeting as his turn comes. Meri laughs, describing the scene, and Felecia gets to her feet, tail thumping.

Jenny feels the heat of the sun on her face, a slight breeze from the hills above them. It would be easy to feel happy here if it weren't for the thought of Harry out there in the harsher world beyond this bubble. He has been too careful in what he tells her. She knows something happened on Saturday night, she heard it in his voice when he called her the next morning. But he laughed it off.

Was it to do with the Nordlunds? Or perhaps the tattooed man, McGilvray. She has been following McGilvray's social media messages. Prolific until Saturday, strangely nothing since. She has a list of his Facebook friends and has been following them too. Several of them have queried his silence. Has something happened to him?

FORTY

AT SOME POINT DURING the night Harry is wakened by the noise of an engine in the street outside the pub. He sits up, swings his feet to the floor and steps to the window. There's someone on a bike down there at the crossroads, just across the street from his own parked car. The engine rumbles, idling for a moment, then breaks into a roar and speeds away. It is 1:30 a.m.

When morning comes he walks around the corner to a café for breakfast. There is no sign of damage to his car as he passes it, but later he kicks the rear wheel and drops to his knees to check the underside for a bomb before he gets in and drives away.

He has no role here. The police don't want him and all he can do is wait. He drives over to Beaumont Street and gets some cash and a bottle of Scotch, and calls in to MacLean's bookshop, where he picks out a couple of volumes—histories, not novels. He feels his real life is fictitious enough.

He returns to his room above the pub, and sits by the window, reading and watching the passers-by in the streets below.

Toward lunchtime he gets a call on his mobile. Deb Velasco.

"Harry, I hear you're back in Newcastle."

"That's right."

"On your own?"

"Yes."

"Where's Jenny?"

"Somewhere safe."

"I hope so. How would you like to come out with me?" For a horrible moment Harry thinks she means a date, but then she adds, "A prison visit, to see Frank Capp."

"Oh yeah? Long Bay?"

"Yep. I've arranged to go down tomorrow."

"Think there's any point?"

"Won't know until we try. Interested?"

"Yes, if you think I can help."

"Where are you staying?"

He tells her and she whistles. "Why don't you just put a notice in the paper? Want me to tell the local boys to keep an eye on you?"

"No."

"Okay. I'll pick you up tomorrow morning at eight."

He goes downstairs to the pub and orders lunch, and while he's there he gets a second call. A private number, blocked.

"Is that Sergeant Belltree?" It's a woman's voice, one he recognises.

"Yes, Amber. What can I do for you?"

"I was planning to come down to Newcastle this afternoon. Would it be possible to meet you?"

"Okay. Where?"

"Do you know the Nobbys Beach Surf Pavilion? I'll be there at three."

He arrives early, finds a free bench and sits down to watch the heads of swimmers bobbing under the dazzling sun. Further along the sweep of beach the surfers glide in on the swell that curves around the outcrop of Nobbys Head. Gulls swoop and dive. High overhead hang-gliders circle and a biplane putters across the blue.

He checks his watch, after three, and wonders if she's changed her mind. Then one of the swimmers pads up towards him across the sand. Fluorescent pink bathers, brown limbs, long blonde hair, a white towel across her shoulders.

"Hi." She sits down beside him.

"Water good?"

"Beautiful. You should try it." She rubs her hair with the towel. "You're a smug bastard, you know that? Going around throwing accusations at people about things you have no idea about."

"Enlighten me."

"I wonder if you even really knew your own parents. You suggested your father was a danger to my family. Well, I only knew him five minutes, but my impression was that he wouldn't be a threat to anybody. He seemed to bend over backwards to understand both sides of every issue—a compromiser, a reconciler, someone who didn't really enjoy conflict. That's probably why they made him the first Aboriginal judge of the Supreme Court—a safe pair of hands."

Harry goes to speak, but she ploughs on.

"Your mother, now—different matter entirely. Passionate, committed, decisive. *She* could be a threat if she put her mind to it."

"What was she being passionate about?"

"I'll show you—if you can be bothered learning what was really going on instead of jumping to wild conclusions."

He nods. "Fine, okay."

"Tomorrow."

"Can't do tomorrow."

She thinks. "All right, the next day, Thursday. The heliport in the Steel River industrial estate. Know it?"

"I'll find it."

"Thursday morning, ten o'clock. Don't be late."

She gets to her feet and walks off towards the pavilion. He watches her go, slightly astonished, wondering if she's right. He remembers discussions at the family dinner table, his mother throwing down a challenge and his father, his voice calm, reasonable, making the counterarguments. He remembers times when his father would disappear for days into his study, and his mother would tell Harry not to bother him. "He's wrestling with his conscience." He can hear her inflection now; it was not the tone of someone with the same problem. And he thinks of the picture in his father's study of the Freedom Ride. His mother wearing a bandana, her fist in the air; his father at her side, looking cautiously excited. Has he made a fundamental error, assuming it was the judge they wanted to kill? Or was it perhaps the two of them together? The drive and passion of one, the balance and influence of the other.

He goes for a walk along the breakwater, past Nobbys to the very end, the mouth of the harbour, and phones Jenny.

"Harry, I'm going crazy down here. The house is full of wool—sorry, fleece—and that's exactly how I feel, wrapped up in thick, soundproof fleece, out of touch with the world. Isn't there something I can do to help you? Some research I can do?"

He hesitates. "Thing is, love, I don't want you doing anything that'll let them figure out where you are. Maybe you should give the computer a rest for a while."

"That's rubbish, they won't be able to track me. I'm not

connected to any location finder. The computer's well protected."

"You sure?"

"Positive."

"Well . . . Deb Velasco has asked me to go see Frank Capp in jail tomorrow. We have all the stuff on his criminal history of course, but I was wondering about his private life. You reckon you could dig into that?"

"I can certainly try."

He gives her what he's got—previous addresses, known associates, date of birth. Then he says, "I've also got a list of the people who made bookings at Sammy Lee's restaurant the night McGilvray phoned someone there, remember? If you could find out who they are that would be good. It may be no help—it was probably Sammy himself that McGilvray was calling. But you never know."

"Fine. Do you know what's happened to McGilvray? I've been following him on Facebook, and there hasn't been a chirp since Saturday."

"I saw him on Saturday night, Jenny."

"What? You didn't tell me!"

"I didn't want to worry you, love. It didn't work out the way I planned."

He tells her what happened.

"Harry, you mustn't keep this stuff from me. He and his mates tried to kill me too. I want to help you get the bastards."

"Okay. The only things he told me were that Sammy Lee was involved in dealing in drugs brought in from the port, and the names Dark Riders and Tyler Dayspring."

"I'll look into it. What else?"

He tells her about meeting Amber Nordlund again. Repeats what she said about his mother.

"I wouldn't be surprised, Harry. Your mum was a formidable woman. I always thought your dad's landmark rulings had her fingerprints all over them."

"Really? I just never thought of it like that. You can't remember her saying something on that last trip that might have a bearing on this? A native title dispute, maybe? I found a cutting on Dad's desk about the Aboriginal history of the area."

"I can't remember anything like that. And now Amber Nordlund is going to take you off in her helicopter?"

"Maybe."

"Is she pretty?"

"Hideous."

"Liar. What was she wearing today?"

"A bikini, fluoro pink."

"What!"

"We met at the beach. It was a perfect disguise."

"You be careful, Harry. I mean it. We don't know anything about her. Where does she plan to take you, anyway?"

"I don't know. Don't worry, I'll be very careful."

FORTY-ONE

KELLY RETURNS TO WORK with a new sense of purpose. At the morning meeting Catherine Meiklejohn notices the change and speaks to her as they break up.

"Yeah, I'm feeling good, Catherine. Ready to get stuck into something challenging. You've been very patient with me."

"You've got something in mind?"

"I do. I'll tell you when I've put some thoughts together."

"Okay. But no more running off on your own and getting into trouble like last time. We've got a new intern who looks like he can take care of himself. Matthew. He can work with you and Hannah."

The three sit down together and Kelly lays a photograph on the table between them. "Matthew, there's some background to this that Hannah's familiar with, but I'll run over it for your benefit. This is a picture of four men drinking together in the bar of the Le Meridien Hotel in Jakarta, taken in April of this year. They are: Alexander Kristich, here, a shonky financier and conman; Joost Potgeiter, a local councillor for the area of Crucifixion Creek in south-west Sydney; Derryn Oldfield, state police minister; and this one's a property developer called Maram Mansur. Kristich, Potgeiter, and Oldfield are all dead now, implicated with the Crows outlaw motorcycle gang in the trafficking of children and drugs. As far as we know Mansur is still alive, whereabouts unknown, and he's never been accused of complicity in the ring, although he was certainly friendly with the other three. His company, Ozdevco Properties, is now carrying out the major redevelopment of the Crucifixion Creek site.

"Okay, that's past history. Several of the surviving Crows gang members are in jail. The story is dead."

Kelly is aware of Hannah watching her closely, and she goes on more firmly. "However, there is at least one loose end. A woman by the name of Donna Fenning was living in the Creek and looking after the trafficked children in transit. She was never traced, but it seems she's now living and working in a country property up north under the name of Karen Schaefer. That property is owned by the Nordlund family, who of course have business interests all over the place, including here in Sydney. I want to know if there are any connections between the Nordlunds and the other players I've mentioned."

Hannah is frowning. "I don't quite get it, Kelly. Just because this woman ran away and got a job on their property, why does that make them involved? Why don't we just tell the police where she is and let them sort it out?"

"I think there's more to it. It seems she worked there before she came down to Sydney." She realises how thin this sounds without the connection to Harry's parents. "The police have been informed, but Karen Schaefer isn't my primary focus. It's the possibility that the Nordlunds may have been connected to the Crucifixion Creek mess that interests me."

She sees how sceptical Hannah is, imagines the thought going through her head: *Is this some private obsession of Kelly's?*

Matthew has been making careful notes. "Shall I make a start on the business profiles of Mansur and the Nordlunds? See if there's any cross-ownership or anything?"

"That's good, Matthew, yes. Hannah? What about this redevelopment of the Creek—Phoenix Square? Want to get us some background on that? I'm going to follow up the research we did last July. We got lots of letters from the public about their dealings with Ozdevco."

FORTY-TWO

DEB VELASCO GETS HARRY to drive the police car down to Sydney. She sits in the passenger seat and smokes; works on papers from her briefcase. Harry thinks about what Jenny told him when she called him this morning with her latest research. Finally Deb stuffs the papers away and they talk. He tries to pump her about developments on the Ash Island killings, but she can't or won't tell him anything new.

"So what do we hope to get from Capp?" he says.

"I want to find out what he knows about Ash Island."

"He knows everything about Ash Island. At least two of those bodies—Marco Ganis and Tony Gemmell—are Crows victims for sure."

"Maybe. We've got no hard evidence, although Capp doesn't know that. The truth is, Harry, that the case against Capp is starting to look shaky. DPP's getting cold feet."

"What? Frank Capp tortured Rowdy O'Brian and burned him to death. Capp was the vice-president of an outlaw motorcycle gang that imported slum children from Indonesia to sell to perverts, and their premises were stuffed to the roof with weapons and drugs. What more do they want?"

"The trouble is, we haven't been able to find any evidence to link Capp to O'Brian's death, and we've been unable to get any convincing prints or DNA placing Capp in the sealed area adjoining the clubhouse where the kids' bodies and the contraband were found. He's claiming he was kept in the dark by Bebchuk and Haddad, who were freelancing and using the Crows as a front; they're both dead and can't deny it."

"Bullshit."

"And our star witness, Peter Rizzo, has become increasingly vague since he realised Frank Capp might be going to survive. He's retracted some of his earlier statements, claiming he got mixed up."

"Capp's been putting pressure on him."

"Well, yeah. The thing is, Capp's lawyer doesn't know yet about the DPP wavering, but he will. This may be our last chance to get him to give us something."

"I see. And why did you bring me?"

"I just want you to be there. You don't need to say a thing, just sit there. I want him to see that you're fit and well and that the bomb—if that was his baby—achieved nothing except making things more problematic for him."

They reach Sydney and head out along Anzac Parade to Malabar. Capp is in maximum security, in the Metropolitan Special Programs Centre of Long Bay Correctional Centre. They are shown into an interview room. When Capp's brought in, Harry barely recognises him, the left side of his face is caved in like a Francis Bacon portrait. He and Deb study that face, the shocking contrast between the normal right side and the grotesquely distorted left, the tight white skin, the fixed snarl, the collapsed skull. This was the work of Tony Gemmell with Harry by his side, confronting sixty-odd bikers in the car park of the Swagman Hotel. Unless the bashing scrambled Capp's memory he knows this, but Deb does not.

"G'day, Frank," Deb says. "Not had any more work done?"

Capp has his eyes fixed on Harry. "I'm thinking I might leave it like this," he says, his voice slurring in the ruined left half of his mouth. "Seems to make a big impression on people." He turns to face Deb. "What ya want?"

"I want to offer you a last chance to give me something I can offer the DPP to go easy on you."

"The cunt's all heart."

"Who put the bodies in the Ash Island marshes, Frank? Give me a name."

"Newcastle? Don't know nothing about Newcastle."

"You knew Marco Ganis and Tony Gemmell. Who killed them?"

Capp settles back in his chair and folds his arms. Deb takes out her cigarettes and the two of them light up, Capp sucking at his with the good side of his mouth.

Deb starts again. "Marco Ganis used to make regular trips up to Newcastle. Was that for Bebchuk and Haddad? Who was their partner in Newcastle?"

It drags on. They finish their smokes and light up again. Deb tries a different tack. "Someone tried to blow up Sergeant Belltree here, Frank. Maybe they did it to please you. Stupid, though, to target a police officer like that. All it's done is turn more heat onto you. Give us their names."

Eventually, when it's clear Deb's getting nowhere, Capp nods at Harry and says, "Doesn't say much, does he? Tell you what, give me his head on a stick to put up in me cell and maybe I'll give you a coupla tips."

Deb seems to run out of words. She switches off her

recorder and begins to put her papers back in her bag. Harry says softly, "How's Kylie?"

They both stare at him, not sure who he's talking to. He's looking at Capp.

"Your sister. Half-sister, I should say." He turns to Deb. "Frank looked after her when their mother shot through. Later they stole a car, which Frank crashed—he was so young his legs hardly reached the pedals. Smashed his sister up. She's in a wheelchair now. Frank pays for her carer, two thousand dollars a week. Kylie is very vulnerable. Like my Jenny, blinded in a car smash. You see the parallel, Deb?" He turns back to Capp, who is glaring intently at him. "Both very vulnerable."

Harry gets to his feet. "Shall we go?"

When they get outside to the car park, Deb says, "That sounded like a threat, Harry."

"Did it? The interesting thing, though, is that Kylie's carer is a niece of Maram Mansur. It was their family took Frank and Kylie in after their mother left. They lived next door, in Lakemba."

"Have I heard of Maram Mansur?"

"Course you have. Went to Jakarta with Oldfield and the others. His company is redeveloping Crucifixion Creek."

"Oh yes, of course. *That* Maram Mansur. The property developer. So how does that help us?"

"Connections, Deb. It's all about connections. What we need is a great big computer tracking everyone's connections from birth. Failing that, use Facebook and Friends Reunited."

"Is that how you found Kylie?"

"Mm."

"How about the two thousand a week to the carer?"

Harry smiles. "Just a guess."

FORTY-THREE

ON THE WAY BACK to Newcastle, Harry gets a call to say he's required to attend a meeting with Superintendent Gibb at four. Harry checks his watch; they should just make it. A moment later Gibb's office makes the same call to Deb.

"Don't they know we're together?" Harry asks.

"Seems not."

"What do you reckon, another body on Ash Island?"

But it isn't that. They are directed to a meeting room, where Ross Bramley and Fogarty are already waiting. Fogarty gives Deb a brief nod, then goes back to studying the thick file in front of him. Ross looks at Harry and shrugs. Kevin Colquhoun comes in next, talking on his phone.

Finally the superintendent bustles in and takes the seat at the head of the conference table. He turns to Fogarty. "Ken? You've called this meeting. What's it about?"

"Sir, I apologise for taking your time, but we need to straighten a few things out, and I thought it best to do it in this format."

Gibb looks as puzzled as everyone else. "Very well. Go ahead."

"I'd like to ask Sergeant Belltree a couple of questions." He stares hard at Harry. "Logan McGilvray switched off his phone at two-fifteen last Sunday morning and hasn't been heard of since. Do you know anything about that?"

"I've no idea where he is."

"That isn't exactly what I asked. Did you see McGilvray last Saturday night?"

A camera, Harry thinks. *There must have been a bloody camera. Or an unmarked car I didn't spot.*

"Yes."

Fogarty gives a chilly smile and eases back in his chair, spreads his hands on the table in front of him as if he's about to leap at Harry. "We don't seem to have any record of that meeting."

"No, it wasn't productive. I was on leave at the time."

"Tell us about it."

"I spotted McGilvray leaving the Cambridge Hotel late on Saturday night. I went over to see him as he was getting into his utility vehicle. He was obviously over the limit, so I offered to drive him home."

"And he consented to this?"

"Yes."

"Go on."

"I didn't take him directly home. I drove around for a while, trying to get him to talk."

"And how did you do that?"

"I told him this was off the record, I had no means of recording his words. I put it to him he'd been involved in the bombing of my house, and he eventually confirmed that he supplied ammonium nitrate and a detonator from the mine where he works to the people who made the bomb."

"He just confessed this? Did you threaten him, assault him?"

"No. He seemed pretty pleased with himself. He'd had a good few drinks."

"Who were these people?"

"Two men. He said he didn't know their names, but they belonged to a group, like bikers only without colours, not attracting the attention of the police. He said they were involved in running drugs from the ships coming into the port, working with the Crows in Sydney."

"What?" Colquhoun is leaning forward in consternation.

"Yes. He said they called themselves the Dark Riders, and their leader was someone called Tyler Dayspring. I checked those names later and couldn't find anything on our databases. I reckoned he was spinning me a yarn."

Colquhoun is on his phone, growling to someone on the other end, repeating the names. They wait until he's finished, then he says, "What else?"

"McGilvray claimed he distributes drugs for these Dark Riders, through a restaurant belonging to someone called Sammy. It was Sammy who put him in touch with the two bombers. That's about it." Harry is aware of Ross staring at him.

Fogarty takes over again. "What happened then?"

"He became a bit ropeable, so I drove him back to his car and let him go."

"And how long did all this take?"

"Maybe an hour? The last I saw of him was about two a.m. I haven't heard from him since."

Colquhoun says, "How were these Dark Riders supposed to be getting drugs off the ships?"

"He said he didn't know."

"And this 'Sammy?' "

"He wouldn't give me any more details, but I reckoned maybe Sammy Lee. He has an Asian restaurant."

Colquhoun shakes his head, looking pained. "We all know Sammy Lee's restaurant."

His phone beeps and he puts it to his ear and listens. "Comics?" he mutters, and listens some more, then rings off. He turns to Superintendent Gibb, who by now is looking bilious. "It seems the Dark Riders were a group of comic book supervillains, published by Marvel Comics in 1991. They were mutants and 'inhumans' apparently, and one of their number was called Tyler Dayspring."

Harry says, "As I said, I thought he was spinning me a yarn. Which is why I didn't think it worth reporting."

"In fairness, sir," Ross speaks up through clenched teeth, "Sergeant Belltree did ask me about Sammy Lee. It seems he is the providore to many of the Asian ships, including the one that Cheung Xiuying came in on. I was going to take that further, but there were more pressing matters."

Gibb checks his watch. "I'm short of time."

Fogarty says, "Perhaps if Belltree and Bramley leave us, sir, we can wrap this up."

When they get outside the room Harry says, "Sorry, Ross. I didn't want to get you involved."

Ross spins round on him and moves in close. "You could have put me in the picture, Harry. All that bullshit at Sammy Lee's place." His voice drops to a hiss. "You didn't top McGilvray did you? Tell me you didn't take him out to Ash Island and bury the bastard."

"Of course not."

"Then where the bloody hell is he?"

The silence that hangs in the air is broken by the sound of raised voices from inside the meeting room.

The door opens, and everyone comes out except Superintendent Gibb. They all avoid his eye except for Deb, who regards him with a sad shake of her head as she passes. She says, "Go in, Harry."

Gibb is standing staring out of the window. He turns and

says, "I don't know what you're doing here, Belltree. You've succeeded in muddying the waters of two strike force investigations and alienating all of your colleagues up here. Detective Inspector Colquhoun is incensed that you failed to report information that could be material to Strike Force Colyton, while Detective Chief Inspector Fogarty is similarly furious that you ignored his direct order to keep away from Logan McGilvray. I don't know how you do things in Sydney, but we don't work that way up here. Your colleagues here feel they can no longer trust you. Have you really been completely open with us about the reasons that your house was bombed? We don't know. We can't be sure, just as we can't be sure that you've told us the truth about your meeting with McGilvray.

"So take this as a formal disciplinary warning. I shall be making a report to the Northern Region Commander, who will no doubt be in touch with your senior officers in Sydney. You are supposed to be on compassionate leave in Sydney. Go back there and stay there."

FORTY-FOUR

WHEN HE TELLS JENNY about this she seems unfazed. "You're a free agent, then."

Without thinking he says, "Free, but running blind."

She replies, "I'll be your eyes, Harry."

"Yes . . . yes, okay." He settles down. He's in the bar of the Marine, a beer in front of him and one eye on the footy on the screen in the corner.

She says, "I found out that your Dark Riders and Tyler Dayspring are characters in a comic strip."

"Yes, it took them two minutes to work that one out. Pretty dumb, eh?"

"Not necessarily. In the story Tyler Dayspring liked to disguise himself as another identity, a weapons dealer who wears a rubber mask."

"So?"

"That character's called Tolliver. You know there was a Jason Tolliver on your list of diners at Sammy Lee's? He booked a table for eight people."

"I know that name. I've met him. He's head of NRL security at the port."

"I'll see what I can find out about him, shall I?"

FORTY-FIVE

IT'S A HOT NIGHT, and Harry stirs in his bed, dreaming of a helicopter coming down over the ocean. He wakes to the sound of its rotors throbbing, and realises it's the motorbike again, passing beneath his window. He checks the time. One-thirty, same as before. Someone coming off shift from the docks maybe.

THERE REALLY IS A helicopter, sleek as a fish, waiting for him when he arrives at the heliport at ten. As he gets out of his car he sees Amber Nordlund emerging from the demountable that serves as the heliport office, accompanied by a young man with a clipboard who looks as if he should still be at school. She introduces him as their pilot. They walk towards the machine. When they get close, Harry sees the words *Nordlund Pastoral* printed in small letters along its flank.

They strap themselves in, put on headsets and dark glasses, and rise into the air. Ash Island unfurls beneath them; Harry sees the police tents and small figures still working among the trees. In the other direction is the port, the black fields of coal, the crawling machines and the mouth of the Hunter, and on its other bank the cathedral on its hill above the city centre and the suburbs spreading away towards the distant sparkle of Lake Macquarie.

They follow the dark ribbon of the river, its undulating curves, its tributaries, a great writhing organism reaching back into the green-brown hinterland. Amber says little through the deafening chatter of the engine, and Harry just sits and waits for whatever revelation she has.

After twenty minutes he sees first one, then a chain of enormous black lesions hacked into the green mat of the wide valley floor. She points them out, giving them names and listing their dimensions. The chopper drops lower and Harry makes out tiny trucks—each as big as a mansion, she tells him—crawling along the contours of the vast pits. Further along the chain they see paddocks and farms teetering on the rim of black cliffs that have been gouged out of the land.

After ten minutes circling over this panorama, her voice comes over the headphones. "Got it?" He assumes he has, whatever *it* is. What is the message? The vast, earth-changing power of the Nordlunds? The curse of coalmining? He waits for the polemic, but she says no more. They wheel away towards the hills that contain the valley to the north.

The landscape beneath them changes. Farmland gives way to the duller, darker green of untouched forests rising into the Barrington Tops. He peers down at the unrelenting canopy, broken here and there by the grey eruptions of rocky cliffs like the stumps of ancient teeth. It is up here, he knows, that the lost wreckage of flight VH-MDX and Amber's father's remains lie hidden, but she says nothing.

They see the dome of Cackleberry Mountain clear

ahead, and the helicopter drops lower until Harry can make out the pale grey trunks rising beneath the crowns of the trees below their feet and feels that they might brush against them. Then the forest drops abruptly away, falling down the reverse slope of the range towards a green valley, in which the red roof of Kramfors can be made out. The helicopter banks away from the homestead, towards the forest that bounds the far side of Cackleberry Valley, and drops towards a field at its edge.

As the rotors whirr to a stop they unstrap themselves and get out onto the solid earth. Amber asks the pilot to wait. She leads Harry towards a gate in the fence along the tree line and onto a rough track that leads up into the trees.

"There are snakes," Amber calls back over her shoulder.

"Aren't there always?"

The track becomes steeper. They clamber over large roots and eroded gullies, the foliage closing overhead, until they reach the base of a rock wall, shearing upward through the forest. Amber leads him along the base of the cliff until she comes to a break where a worn trail leads up through a cleft in the stone and they resume their climb, harder now.

When they reach a broad shelf Amber pauses, panting, and points at a faded black circle on the boulder in front of them. "That's Nayantinla, the all-seeing eye that guards the approach to sacred sites."

The way ahead now forms a series of rough stone steps, which they mount until they reach a level platform sheltered by the broad sweep of a rock overhang. It forms a natural shallow cave, almost like a performance shell, facing out over the forest treetops. They turn and take in the view, a broad vista across the valley towards the dome of Cackleberry Mountain.

"Kuppoee–Yoongoo," Amber says, "Egg Mountain. Now look at this."

She points back at the rear wall of the cave, and as Harry's eyes adjust to the shadow he makes out paintings on the rock face. In the centre, dominating the wall, is a large red ochre figure of an eagle, the guardian of the valley, Amber explains. Around it are the shapes of other animals in black charcoal and red ochre—goanna, turtle, snake—and prints of hands. They are all quite faded.

"We don't know how old these are," Amber says. "Some of them hundreds of years old, and beneath them the faint traces of even older paintings. The people who made them didn't *own* the land, they didn't fence it and seal it up in legal deeds. They just lived in it, and cared for it, and then passed it on to the people who came after them. It's like the opposite of what we just saw from the helicopter— carving up the land to make a quick buck."

She pauses to catch her breath and fix Harry with a fierce glare. "Those black holes we saw will never be restored. They've shattered the water table and ruined the rivers and when all the coal is gone the holes will be filled with dead rubble that'll be sterile forever. It's not even as if we make a lot of money from it. A few, a very few of us do, but eighty per cent of the wealth is taken abroad, by foreign companies who have no connection with this land at all."

Harry watches her. Where is this leading? She is becoming more and more agitated, stopping and taking a deep breath before she goes on.

"Not far beneath the surface of Cackleberry Valley there's over fifty metres of high-quality black coal seams, maybe five or six billion cubic metres in all. You can work out what that's worth—hundreds of billions of dollars."

He says, "And you own the valley?"

"Yes, I do. But in Australia the owner of the land only owns the surface. What lies beneath belongs to the government. And the government can sell the mining rights to anyone they like—*particularly* the people they like—big multinational miners. And their Australian cronies."

That last word comes with a sneer and a significant pause, as if she expects Harry to know who she means.

"When my great-grandfather came to Australia he went to Kalgoorlie and dug holes in the ground and pulled out lumps of gold. He was lucky. He moved over here and used the gold to buy this valley and become a pastoralist. That's what we've been ever since, nurturing the land from generation to generation. But my grandfather Carl needed stone to build a road, so he dug a quarry, over on the other side of the hills, and began to sell the stone to other people as well. Then he bought into a mining business, just a small affair. When Carl died my father took charge of the pastoral business, and his younger brother, my uncle Konrad, ran the smaller mining and quarrying interests. He was a very good businessman and that side of things grew quickly, so he expanded into construction and real estate. Formed Nordlund Resources Limited for the mining, and Nordlund Investments for the rest, and he moved to Sydney, where his business contacts were. And the politicians. He became very wealthy and influential, and he donated a lot of money to his political friends and their parties, and in due course they awarded him the mining rights to Cackleberry Valley."

"Your uncle wants to dig up the valley?"

"Yes. He says it's progress. And the politicians love it—they'll get their mining royalties without the usual political fights. No longstanding farmers or residents to embarrass them like they have over in the Hunter Valley.

Here the devastation will be invisible to the outside world. There's only one landowner—me—and I'll bugger off with my compensation blood money, and that'll be that." She's rigid with fury.

A family feud, Harry thinks. He sighs and says, "Why are you telling me this, Amber?"

"There's a snag, you see. To mine the valley, NRL will have to build a highway and a railway through the forest. And the forest was the subject of a native title claim a dozen years ago and now belongs to the local Aboriginal land council, which is governed by a board elected by the traditional owners. So NRL made them a generous offer for the right to drive a corridor through their forest. The council walked the route, and then came up here. Konrad made a big presentation, tried to sell it as a choice between the past and the future. And they were split. The money would transform their lives, start up new businesses, build special schools, send their kids to university. But the valley would be destroyed forever.

"Painful choice. So in the end they decided to get the advice of a wise man, someone they respected, one of their own."

"My father," Harry says.

"He came up here with your mother, four years ago. He stood on this spot, and walked through the forest, and talked to the elders, and then went back to Sydney to study precedents and case law, talk to geologists and mining experts, and get the best possible financial advice on the likely outcomes. He was open-minded, impartial."

Harry nods.

"Listening to every point of view, asking sensible questions, hosing down the more furious arguments. The people loved him, and felt that they could trust him to find the right answer. Your mother . . . she stayed in the background, but you could tell she had an opinion. Her eyes were blazing.

"So come June of that year, your father told us that he was coming up to Armidale on Supreme Court business and wanted to meet with the land council again to go over some details. It all had to be very confidential. We decided to hold the meeting at Kramfors, and have your parents spend the night there. That evening, the twenty-fifth, your father told the council that he'd almost completed his final report. He was going to present it to them on his return from Armidale early in July." Amber pauses, with an apologetic shrug. "Well, the next morning he and your mother were dead. And no trace of a report has ever been found."

She steps closer, lowering her voice to a hoarse whisper. "The last thing your mother said to me as they drove off that morning was, 'Don't worry, Amber, I wouldn't be calling in the removalists any time soon.'" Another pause. "That's why they died, Harry. The stakes were too high."

"You're saying your uncle had them killed?"

"What other explanation is there?"

"Why didn't you or the land council report this to the police? Or bring it up at the inquest?"

"The council were scared. They didn't want to accuse NRL of something like that unless there was evidence it was something other than an accident, and the police didn't come up with any. Also, they still hoped they could get hold of your father's report and use it anyway, follow his advice. They hired private detectives, searched for it everywhere. Found nothing."

"Everywhere? What do you mean?"

"His law office, his study at home . . ."

"What? They broke into our house?"

She dips her head, embarrassed. "Yes, I believe so."

He thinks back to the chaos of those days after the crash, his parents' funeral to be dealt with—a state funeral no less—and Jenny in hospital. He'd hardly been home.

"It wasn't malicious, Harry. They were desperate."

"So how do things stand now?"

"They were in limbo for a while. Then NRL increased the pressure, upped their offer a bit. There were new elections for the land council, and now it looks as if they're going to agree to Konrad's terms.

"Harry, I'm ashamed of what my family has become, what they're planning to do. I want to stop Konrad. And you want justice for your parents and for Jenny. We both want the same thing."

"So what are you suggesting?"

She grips his arm. "I'm a member of the NRL board. Access to company documents, confidential internal information, family trust accounts. You're a police officer, with all those resources behind you. The evidence that'll destroy Konrad is out there. Corrupt deals with politicians, bribery, extortion. I mean, I've had employees of the family companies come to me over the years. They've seen things, they've been concerned. I always felt helpless, unsure what to do about it. But if we work together, we can do it. I'm sure of that."

He steps away from the sweaty heat of her anger, looks out across the treetops to the bald mountain, thinking.

Finally he says, "Okay."

"Great!" She takes a deep breath. "Well, that's wonderful. All I want is justice, Harry, you can see that."

He says nothing.

"Come on. I'll give you lunch. There's someone I want you to meet."

FORTY-SIX

FIRST THING, KELLY SITS down with her small team to review progress. She is encouraged. Matthew has been gathering information on Ozdevco and found that Nordlund
Investments has a direct stake in Mansur's company with
Konrad Nordlund sitting on the Ozdevco board. He gives
Kelly a comprehensive company profile. Kelly herself has
re-established contacts from her previous research and put
together a file of some of the rough, possibly illegal, prac-
tices alleged on Mansur's previous developments.

Hannah meanwhile has information on Phoenix Square,
including the draft of publicity material that Ozdevco's letting agents have been preparing for an extensive marketing
campaign in the *Times'* own property section.

On the strength of this Kelly decides on a direct approach. She arranges an interview later in the morning at
Ozdevco's head office. She and Hannah are received at the
Gipps Tower offices by the projects director and the marketing manager, Chad and Dakoda, both young, attractive,
and strikingly fresh, as if they've just stepped out of a shower
gel ad.

"Thank you for seeing us at such short notice."

"Pleasure," Chad beams and leads them to a conference room.

"Malcolm in your property section has been just fantastic," Dakoda enthuses.

They exchange business cards and sit down. Coffees are ordered.

Kelly asks if they could give them an overview of the Phoenix Square project for an article they're planning.

"Fantastic," Dakoda says. Chad launches into a list of statistics: numbers of square metres, floors, apartments, retail units, parking spaces; the volume of concrete measured in Olympic swimming pools. Dakoda backs this up with Powerpoint, bringing up ravishing animations of the new development on a giant screen. Towers glow against a gorgeous sunset; views from the apartments encompass vast urban panoramas.

Kelly is finding their glib, sunny self-confidence very annoying. "It's amazing what computers can do now, isn't it?" she says, sounding more sour than she intended. "And it all seems to have happened so quickly."

"We've been thinking about this project for some time," Chad says. "It's been a personal priority for our MD."

"That's Maram Mansur, isn't it? Would it be possible to meet him?"

"I'm afraid not. He's overseas at the moment, working on some important international projects."

"Maybe we could speak to him by video link?"

The two exchange a look, shake their heads. "Not very easy at present. Let's see how we go."

"Konrad Nordlund is on your board, isn't he? Is he taking a personal interest in the project?"

"I'm sure he is."

"Is he a personal friend of Mr. Mansur?"

A sudden frown. "I really couldn't say. Let's concentrate on Phoenix Square, shall we?"

"Okay. You actually submitted a development application for the project only in August, soon after the problems in Crucifixion Creek came to a head. You seem to have got your approvals remarkably quickly."

"Mm. The development was deemed sufficiently important to be assessed as a State Significant Project, and approved directly by the Minister for Infrastructure and Planning and his department, rather than the local council."

"So there were no objections?"

"Well frankly, just between us, everyone was desperate to see the end of the old Crucifixion Creek. Everyone appreciated that this was a new beginning, a wiping of the slate."

"A wiping of the slate," Kelly repeats. "That's a good title. But you haven't been so lucky on some of Ozdevco's other projects, have you? Some of them have been quite controversial."

"DISE." The projects director grins, his teeth alarmingly white.

"Sorry?"

"Do It Somewhere Else. It's the same everywhere. We all want progress and fantastic new projects, just not near us."

"There were allegations of intimidation and vandalism of neighbouring properties on your Central Coast development. The police were involved, yes?"

"I don't think . . ."

"And on the Gold Coast there were allegations of corrupt payments to the local council."

"I'm not sure where you're going with this. Ozdevco

Properties is a highly respected company with the highest ethical standards. You . . ."

"Mr. Mansur was a close friend of Derryn Oldfield, the former police minister, who committed suicide rather than face trial for his involvement in the Crucifixion Creek crime ring. Now Mr. Mansur's company is redeveloping the site. Is he overseas to avoid being questioned about his role in that scandal?"

Chad and Dakoda stare at Kelly, then at each other. The projects manager leans forward slowly and picks up the business cards. He reads them for a moment, then takes out his phone and begins to tap.

Kelly says, "We just need clarification . . ."

But Chad holds up a hand at her without raising his eyes from the screen. "Kelly Pool," he says, "crime reporter. You've come here on false pretences, haven't you? You'd better leave."

"Look, I don't think you can sweep those past events under the carpet. A few answers . . ."

"I'll call security, shall I?"

"Okay, okay. We're going."

He escorts them to the front door and closes it firmly after them. As they wait at the lift, Kelly turns to Hannah, trying to think of something funny to say. Hannah looks as if she'd rather be somewhere else.

WHEN THEY GET BACK to the office Kelly unpacks her bag at her desk, then goes downstairs to buy a ham roll from the sandwich shop around the corner. When she returns, she sees Catherine Meiklejohn deep in conversation with Hannah.

They turn to look at Kelly, then the editor comes over to her. "My office, Kelly."

"Close the door. I've just been given a grilling by marketing, who wanted to know how come one of my reporters has caused Ozdevco Properties to cancel a major advertising campaign they were planning in the *Times*. Apparently they're going to the *Herald* now. And Malcolm is livid. He's a personal friend of their projects manager, who claims you were offensive, aggressive, and determined to portray his company as a cowboy developer." She pauses. "So what's your story?"

Kelly blusters. She wants to be cool and rational but she can't. "I may have been . . . *robust* in my questions, Catherine, but they were just full of bland *ad-speak* crap, and there's something sick about what's going on at Crucifixion Creek. The speed they're building those towers, like glossy tombstones on the graves of murdered children . . ."

"*What?*"

"There's a conspiracy!" Kelly plunges desperately on. "Ozdevco's CEO is in hiding overseas from the police, and the woman who was in control of those stolen children is being sheltered by the Nordlund family, who are investors in Ozdevco . . ."

"Stop, stop! Did you say Nordlund? Konrad Nordlund?"

"Yes!"

"And . . . what? You're saying he was involved with Crucifixion Creek?"

"Well . . . possibly, yes, very possibly."

"You've got evidence of that?"

"Not explicitly, not yet . . ."

"Do you read the paper? Our paper? The business section?"

"Not really, but . . ."

"Last month Konrad Nordlund bought a thirteen per cent stake in the *Times*. He now sits on our board."

"Oh . . . no, I didn't know that . . . But . . ."

Catherine's face closes down. "You haven't got over what happened to you, have you, Kelly? I shouldn't have let you go and do that interview without finding out what was on your mind."

She sighs, takes a deep breath. "I've told Hannah to prepare a general interest piece on Phoenix Square. She says she's got enough material to do that. It'll go out under both your names. She may do a follow-up spread for the Saturday magazine. I want you to write a letter to the Ozdevco managers you interviewed, unreservedly apologising for any misunderstanding and telling them that you had absolutely no intention of casting doubt on the integrity of their company or its owners. Let me see it before you send it. Then I want you to go on medical leave, and I want you to get help. Our health fund offers psychiatric services. I'll be sending them a report. Do you understand all that, Kelly?"

She feels her face glowing pink, her stomach churning, her throat tight with anger and mortification.

"Yes," she croaks.

FORTY-SEVEN

THE HELICOPTER DROPS THEM on the grass landing strip behind the homestead. Amber leads Harry into the house
through the rear porch, full of boots and wet-weather gear,
pungent with animal smells.

"Bathroom's over there if you want to freshen up,
Harry. I'll be in the kitchen. Beef sandwich okay?"

"Perfect."

The bathroom fittings must be original, from when
Axel Nordlund, the Swedish patriarch, built the place in
1900. Harry notices cracked tiles, damp stains, signs of age
and neglect. It doesn't look as if Konrad Nordlund has spent
any of his millions on the family home.

He finds Amber buttering bread in a kitchen big enough
to cater banquets, with ranks of copper pots hanging from
hooks.

"Want to carve?" She points to a huge joint of beef lying
on the bench. He gets to work with an antique horn-handled
knife when a voice calls, "Hello?" from the hallway.

"In here, Luke," Amber cries, and a good-looking young
man comes in. Harry notices how Amber's face lights up.
"Harry, this is my friend Luke Santini, Harry Belltree."

They shake hands.

"Harry and I have had a really good talk," she says.

"Oh yeah?"

"Harry really understands where we're coming from."

We? Harry thinks. She's trying too hard. He wonders if they've had a disagreement about this. "Where do you fit in, Luke?" he says. Luke's dressed in jeans and T-shirt, ankle boots. His hand is soft in Harry's grip. "You work with the horses?"

Amber says quickly, "Oh no, Luke's a city boy. Melbourne. He comes up here to unwind, don't you?" She slips her hand under his arm. "Where's Dylan?"

"I left him with the others in the stable," Luke says. "He wants to have lunch with them."

"Okay." She sounds reluctant, as if that wasn't what they'd agreed. "Well, we're just making sandwiches. How about a glass of wine?"

Luke nods and goes off while Amber stacks the sandwiches on a plate and leads Harry out to the veranda. They sit on cane chairs at a table with a view of the mountain. Luke appears with a bottle and glasses.

"Luke's heard all about you, Harry," Amber says. "What happened to your parents. Luke works in environmental education. For Sustain, the international foundation? Anyway, he's very concerned about what's happening up here. Aren't you, love?" She's trying to prompt him out of his silence, but he appears to dislike the word.

"Mm," he says after a pause. "Obviously. Anyone would be. You're a police officer?"

"That's right."

Amber cuts in quickly, "Harry's said he'll help us, Luke. We'll help each other."

"Hard to see how." He reaches for a sandwich and takes a bite.

"Well, we've discussed it. Harry can help us prove Konrad's been corrupt in his dealings with the state . . ."

"What, you're an expert in fraud cases, are you, Harry? Finance specialist? Corporate watchdog?" He reaches for the bottle of wine. His accent is hard to place. Almost American; not quite.

"No."

"Homicide, that's your thing, isn't it? Human, not environmental." He thumps the bottle down and makes an exasperated snort. "Think I'll pass on lunch." He gets to his feet and walks away.

"Luke!" Amber jumps to her feet but he doesn't pause.

"I'm sorry." She sinks back into her chair. "He can be a bit intense."

"Doesn't like the fact I'm a cop? I get that a lot."

"Yes, well, don't worry about him. I want to work with you."

"Okay. I can't promise anything, but I'll follow up any information you can give me, and I'll be discreet."

"Thank you."

"How's that staff member of yours doing, who had the accident?"

"Craig? Oh, he's still in hospital, the John Hunter. Karen, his wife, phoned me last night. They'll keep him there for a while, till he's stabilised. He'll lose the sight in one eye, I'm afraid."

"You said they were here the night my parents stayed. Did Karen meet them?"

"I suppose . . . yes, she must have. She cooked a meal for us, and made up the rooms. Yes, I remember your father talking to her. She's a brilliant cook. I didn't realise how much I depended on her until she and Craig left."

"They left you?"

"For a while, to look after Karen's sick mother in Sydney. Why, is it important?"

"Oh, I was just wondering if my father might have said something to her when they were here. Maybe I should talk to her."

"Yes, fine. I'll give you her number."

When they've finished their sandwiches, Amber takes him back out to the waiting helicopter. As it rises up into the air Harry watches Amber's diminishing figure hurrying back to the house.

They pass over the forest and out across the farmlands around Gloucester and Harry turns to the pilot. "How long you been doing this?"

"Got my licence six years ago, been working for Nordlund Pastoral four years."

"What, ferrying Amber around?"

"Yeah, that. Bringing in guests and so on. They have cattle leases out west, and I go out there mustering sometimes. Little R44 chopper. That's real flying." He laughs.

"I can imagine. Amber's good to work for?"

The pilot turns to give Harry a warning look. "She's me boss, mate. Yeah, she's good. Had some tough breaks."

"Oh yeah?"

But he doesn't elaborate.

"Dylan seems like a smart kid."

"Yeah. Great little fella. Wants me to teach him how to fly. Poor kid's got a crook leg, though. Hip dysplasia, due for some more treatment soon. I'll be flying him down to the hospital next week."

"What about his father?"

"Dunno. Some bloke she met in Europe, apparently."

"Not Luke Santini, then?"

"Luke? Not as far as I know. Lotta questions, mate."

"Sorry. It's a great place she has there."

"Yeah. You got a stud or something?"

"Stud?"

"Horses. Thought you might be buying horses. Didn't reckon you as a farmer."

"Oh, no. Just a social trip. I'm new to the area. Amber wanted to give me an overview."

"Right, well, this is the way to do it, sure enough."

When they get to the Newcastle terminal Harry goes back to his car and drives out to the John Hunter hospital. He shows his badge at the information desk and checks their records. Craig Schaefer was admitted at 2:43 p.m. on Sunday the twenty-fourth and underwent an emergency operation that evening. The following morning he discharged himself against the advice of his doctors, and has not been in contact since.

"Monday morning," Harry repeats. "Three days ago."

"That's correct."

FORTY-EIGHT

1:28 A.M. HARRY WAITS in the hire car parked on the street between his hotel and the Throsby Creek bridge. He sees the headlight of a motorbike turn the corner at the far end of the street and come toward him, slowing to a stop outside the hotel. The bike's light and engine go off and the rider crosses the street into the shadows beside his Corolla. Harry waits for several minutes, then he sees the figure return to the bike. It moves out into the street and as it rumbles past Harry ducks down. Checks its numberplate as it continues on over the bridge. He starts the hire car and catches sight of the bike coming off the roundabout up ahead. Follows it onto the Industrial Highway then off, towards the coal facilities on Kooragang. Through the flood-lit landscape of gantries and conveyors, between the dark steel hulls of ships on one side and the darker mountains of coal on the other, and finally to the bike's destination in the car park of NRL. There are a dozen other vehicles there in front of the brightly lit building. Harry parks in the shadows at the perimeter and watches through the chain-link fence as the biker emerges into the light, taking off his helmet, and walks in through the front doors. A black leather jacket, a glimpse of a face, Anglo, dark hair.

Harry turns around; goes back to the pub to check his car. There's no sign of tampering, but what was the guy doing? Harry drives away, out onto the link road to the motorway to Sydney. When he reaches their home in Surry Hills he grabs a few hours' sleep. He rises at dawn, goes out for a long run, showers, has breakfast and checks the number of the bike. Vince Scully. An address in Wallsend, Newcastle.

Harry is packing a few things that Jenny has asked for when the phone rings.

Deb Velasco.

"Harry, you in Sydney?"

"Yes."

"Good. We've been invited to meet with Capp again, you and I, together with his lawyer, Horn. They've come up with a deal."

He's surprised. "They asked for me?"

"They did. You're free, are you?"

He says yes, and they arrange a time to meet at Long Bay.

He phones Jenny and tells her he'll be delayed. She says not to worry, but he hears the disappointment in her voice. Maybe Aunt Meri and her menagerie are getting stale.

THEY'VE OBVIOUSLY BEEN CONFERRING for some time when Harry and Deb arrive. There's a mess of butts in Capp's ashtray and several pages of scribbled notes in front of Nathaniel Horn. Capp seems cheerful, Horn's hooded eyes giving nothing away. They get down to business.

"My client has decided to take advantage of your offer to drop charges in exchange for information," Horn intones.

"That wasn't what we offered," Deb objects, and there is

an opening skirmish, two wrestlers circling at the start of a bout. Harry and Capp sit back and watch, arms folded.

When some kind of preliminary understanding has been reached they move on to specifics. Capp claims to have information about the Ash Island murders. Divulging this will inevitably result in police actions that will place him in jeopardy if he remains in prison. He therefore requires a guarantee that he will be released and all charges against him dropped.

Deb lights a cigarette and explains that it's impossible to give such a guarantee without testing whether the information is correct. In any case Capp can be held in secure confinement in jail for his safety.

Capp rams his cigarette into the ashtray and snarls, "Waste a fuckin' time, Nat. Told ya. Cunt's fuckin' useless. Get someone else—the commissioner."

Horn, in his usual grinding monotone, suggests a break while he confers with his client, during which Inspector Velasco might discuss the offer with her colleagues.

Harry and Deb retire to a vacant interview room, where she phones her contact at the prosecutor's office. He tells her the DPP has pretty much made up its mind to drop the Capp case, so anything she can get will be a bonus.

She rings off, irritated. "What can he tell us, Harry?"

"Well, it won't be the truth, which is that he ordered all three of them to be killed."

"You reckon he did?"

He nods.

"Okay," she sighs. "Let's see what he has to say."

They return. Horn is sipping at a glass of water. "Well?" he says.

"I am authorised to tell you that if Mr. Capp provides us with information that leads to a significant breakthrough in the Ash Island murder investigations, leading to arrests and charges being laid, then Mr. Capp will be released on bail and the charges against him reassessed with a view to having them dropped."

"No, no, no." Horn shakes his head. "That won't do. I can tell you now that my client's information will lead to such a breakthrough and arrests, but he must first have a clear commitment to drop the charges against him—a guarantee, binding, in writing."

They haggle, first about the guarantee, then about the sequence of events. Will Capp be released *before* the police actions or *after*? Will the charges be dropped as soon as the first arrest is made, or after a murder charge is brought?

Deb digs her heels in, but after a while Harry can see that Horn knows he's going to get his way. It's only a matter of time.

Finally an agreement is hammered out, a form of words agreed, and the two police leave the room again for Deb to obtain a written document signed by an officer of the DPP. They return with it, hand it over to Horn, who nods and makes what passes for a smile.

Finally, Capp gets to tell his story.

"Marco Ganis, Tony Gemmell, the Chinaman— Cheung. That's your three bodies."

"That's been in the papers," Deb snaps.

"In that order," Capp insists. "That's the order they were killed and put in the swamp."

That hasn't been released. Deb says nothing.

"And there's a fourth."

"A fourth body? Who?"

"Don't know the name. Just what I've been told, a fourth."

He isn't the greatest storyteller, but he has an attentive

audience. After resigning from the Crows, he says, Tony Gemmell, their former president, went off and did a deal with another, much larger, Sydney gang to run drugs for them up to Newcastle, where he had contacts. The gang agreed to give him a try, and he recruited Marco Ganis to help him.

"What gang?" Deb demands.

"Couldn't tell you, boss," Capp says blandly. "Let's just say they have several Sydney chapters—west, south-west, and south—and in other cities."

At some stage, he goes on, they discovered that Ganis and Gemmell were skimming. They were duly chastised and their bodies dumped up in Newcastle. The gang then dealt directly with their distributors up there and continue to run a flourishing business. The Chinaman was just a dumb punter. He bought drugs from one of the suppliers in Newcastle and paid in US dollar bills which turned out to be phoney, and so he was dealt with.

"It's just a story," Deb says. "Nothing we can use."

"I can give you the address they take the drugs to, the main distributor. There'll be evidence there for sure—names, quantities. They keep records, see. You'll be able to find out from them who did the killing."

Deb grumbles. It's thin. Not a single name.

"You have nothing to lose, Inspector," Horn reminds her. "No arrests, no deal."

They wind it up.

As they get to the door, Horn says, "Sergeant, a word with you please."

Deb looks at Horn, then at Harry, raises an eyebrow and says, "See you outside." She's wearing more make-up than usual, Harry notices. He wonders if she's got a new boy-friend.

When Capp has been taken away, Horn says, "I was astonished to see you at Kramfors Homestead the other day. Ms. Nordlund was extremely upset by your visit. I insist on knowing what you were doing there. What was this *personal* business you spoke of?"

"Amber knew my parents, Mr. Horn. I was interested in her recollections. I'm thinking of writing a biography."

"You?" Horn shakes his head. "Your father had a way with words. I wasn't aware that talent had been passed down to you."

Harry makes to leave and Horn slides in between him and the door.

"I'm warning you, Belltree," he hisses. "Amber Nordlund is a fragile woman with a history of psychological disturbance. On behalf of her family I insist that you leave her alone."

"You're doing a lot of insisting, Mr. Horn. I wonder why." He reaches for the doorhandle and swings the door, pushing Horn aside.

"What was that all about?" Deb is waiting for him in the visitors" foyer.

"I think he wanted to see if we swallowed Capp's crap. I didn't say one way or the other."

"But you think it is crap."

"Yes."

"Well, there's only one way to find out. I'll get on to Newcastle to set things in motion. I take it you want to be there?"

"Yes, yes, of course."

Another call to Jenny; he probably won't make it tonight. He gives her a few more names to follow up, including Scully, the bike rider.

FORTY-NINE

YOU WAS . . . WE BOTH . . . *fuckin scattered, yeah?*
  Too right, bro. Off me head.
  Yeah. We feel remorse though. Right, brother?
  Dead set. Anyway . . . fuckin threatened us, but.
  Shouldn't have killed him, course not. But bashin a dealer's doin society a favour.
  Fat cop said they couldn't even get dental records [laughs].
  Like a smashed pumpkin, bro!
  Lotsa remorse though.
  You reckon they're recordin this?
  Kelly yawns. They were recording this, and now she has to listen to it, along with a full courtroom. They are pleading not guilty.

She has done exactly as Catherine instructed, written notes to the Ozdevco pair so sickeningly apologetic they might have been composed by Dakoda herself, then gone upstairs and grovelled to the marketing director and to Malcolm in property. She looked over Hannah's shoulder as she put together their "joint" piece entitled "Phoenix Square to lead south-west renaissance," which is about as nauseatingly bland as it could be. She even went to the psychiatrist. She talked about the nightmares, the sleeping difficulties and the struggle to come to terms with what happened, but also the feeling that the worst was over and that she could see light at the end of the tunnel.

Then she saw Catherine again and begged to be allowed to work, and Catherine relented and told her to cover this miserable bloody trial. It drags on, and Kelly's mind turns to the Pandanus Trust. Matthew, who is proving very diligent, came up with the name just before Ozdevco was declared a no-go zone. Along with Nordlund Investments, Pandanus Trust is the other major investor in Ozdevco. Together they own sixty per cent of Mansur's company. It is described as a charity investment fund, and registered in Vanuatu. This caught Kelly's attention, for the Pacific archipelago has cropped up before in relation to Crucifixion Creek: Derryn Oldfield was Australian high commissioner out there before becoming a member of the New South Wales upper house; he met up with Alexander Kristich there; the raid on the Crows clubhouse turned up invoices from a Chinese company in Vanuatu; and most recently, Mansur's yacht *Rashida* was sighted in Port Vila.

However, that's as far as Matthew has been able to go. When the judge calls a break for lunch, Kelly looks up the number on her phone of a contact she has in Vanuatu.

Brad, an Australian expat, runs a hamburger joint on Port Vila harbour, and Kelly can hear the sizzle of frying meat in the background, or maybe it's the buzz of flies. After she's explained what she wants he asks her who's paying. She says she is, a private job, and adds hopefully, "Mates' rates?" He laughs and says he'll get back to her.

FIFTY

IT TAKES HIM A while to work out where they're about to go. He didn't get it from the plans and the aerial shot, and it's only when Colquhoun shows them the image of the front of the place that Harry realises Frank Capp has fingered Dee-Dee Perry's Tattoo Studio in Islington. He groans to himself, certain now that they're being sold a pup. But given his current status he keeps quiet. They can find out for themselves.

It's late afternoon when they set off, the unmarked cars and white vans. Dee-Dee will have customers getting a little work done on their way home. Some vehicles peel off to go round to the service road at the rear. Harry is with Ross, the atmosphere still cool. They follow Colquhoun and his Strike Force Colyton in through the front door, and sure enough there are three men in work gear sitting reading magazines while Dee-Dee operates on a fourth. They all look stunned as Colquhoun brandishes the search warrant and announces the raid. The customers are identified, searched, found to be clean, and dismissed, one with a half-formed octopus tentacle crawling up his neck. By now Dee-Dee is protesting loudly.

Harry goes through to the back and lets the other crew

in. The front of the premises is a brick-built single-storey former shop, the rear an attached fibro storeroom lined with racks of shelving. Behind it is a small yard in which Dee-Dee's little Pulsar is parked, embellished with her signature tattoo decal.

They get to work, searching drawers, boxes, shelves. Harry listens to Dee-Dee arguing with Colquhoun. A detective is working his way along one of her shelves, pulling her pretty little pot plants out of their tubs one by one, and Dee-Dee squeals as if he's pulling out her hair.

"It's a common hiding place for drugs," Colquhoun calmly explains.

She yells, "Not in my place it's not," just as the officer tips a flowerpot upside down and three bags of white powder tumble to the floor.

Dee-Dee stares at them, dumbfounded. "That's not right," she splutters. "That's just not right."

"Yes indeed," Colquhoun says gravely. "Do you have a safe, Ms. Perry?"

It's in the corner, hidden behind a batik curtain. She taps in the combination and the door swings open and more plastic bags spill out. Her mouth drops open, but this time no sound emerges.

An officer comes in from the back shed, wanting keys for the car and a steel cabinet. Colquhoun opens Dee-Dee's handbag and hands them over. A few minutes later the officer returns. "Boss!"

Harry follows them through to the shed, where several men are clustered around the cabinet. Inside they've found scales, empty plastic bags, spoons. At the foot of the cabinet is a steel toolbox, which they drag out into the light. Inside, beneath a top tray heavy with tools, is a metal cashbox.

They lift it out and open the lid. Inside is a wad of banknotes, which they remove. Then they become very still.

"Boss?"

"Yes? What've you got?" Colquhoun ambles over, stares down and mutters, "Shit."

Harry moves closer and gets a view of what they've found at the bottom of the box. Four yellowed human fingers.

Colquhoun calls for a crime-scene team and orders everyone out. As they go Harry sees Dee-Dee standing between two policewomen in a corner of her studio. She is looking dazed. Her eyes register Harry and she stares at him as he passes, as if to say, *Did you do this?*

FIFTY-ONE

FOGARTY'S STRIKE FORCE IPSWICH takes over, their room on the third floor of the police station becoming the clearing house for information coming in from the raid.

A mobile phone has been found in Dee-Dee's safe, with the names and phone numbers of several known small-time drug dealers. Teams have been sent out to bring them in.

As the evening wears on, fingerprint evidence filters in: Dee-Dee's prints on the cash box and on a couple of the banknotes inside. They also have fingerprint ID on the four fingers. They belong to Logan McGilvray.

Towards eleven Fogarty calls the team together. An initial interview session with Dee-Dee has yielded nothing, but the physical evidence is overwhelming. Tomorrow a new search of the Ash Island marshes will try to find the body of McGilvray. But in the meantime Fogarty, with Colquhoun nodding by his side, is grimly pleased. He puts everyone in the picture with an outline of Frank Capp's version of events that led up to the raid. "I don't know what Deb Velasco and . . ." reluctantly, ". . . Belltree used to get hold of this information, but it sure paid off." There are murmurs of approval. Deb isn't there, called to a meeting in Sydney this afternoon, and Harry ducks his head in acknowledgement, feeling embarrassed.

They break up for the night. Ross Bramley comes over to Harry, grinning. "Hero of the hour, mate. Even Fogarty loves you. And you owe me a hundred bucks."

"Eh?"

"Sammy Lee! I was right, wasn't I? You got it all arse about face. Sydney was sending drugs to Newcastle, not the other way around." He laughs.

"Dee-Dee's been set up, Ross."

"What! Never give up, do you, Harry? Nobody likes a bad loser."

Harry hands over two fifties and Ross says, "Where're you staying now?"

"Hotel; Marine."

"Decent sort of pub? Come on, I'll buy us a nightcap."

When they get there Harry points up to his window. "That's my room up there." The pub looks busy, music coming out into the street. Harry looks again at his window.

There's a crowd around the bar. Harry says, "I'll have a schooner of New, Ross. I'm just going upstairs to check my room."

"Something wrong?"

"Someone closed the curtains since I left."

"I'll come with you."

They climb the stairs together, along the corridor. When they reach his door they see the splintered frame. Harry pushes the door. It swings open and they step inside.

"Jeez, mate," Ross says after a pause. "Not very neat, are you?"

Every drawer has been pulled out and tipped onto the floor, the mattress is half off the stripped bed, the tray from the fridge is lying in a pool of half-melted ice cubes.

"You've been done over."

"Yeah."

"Scum. I'll call it in."

Harry steps through the mess, trying to see what's missing. The last time he was here was when he left, soon after 1:00 a.m. yesterday, with an overnight bag. He went out to the hire car to follow the bike, then on to Sydney. He didn't leave much behind. A few bits of clothing ready for the laundry, his two history books—there they are on the floor, ripped apart—a bottle of whisky, two-thirds full. That seems to be gone, along with some loose change in the glass ashtray by the phone.

He says to Ross, "Let's go downstairs and talk to the manager."

It takes a few minutes to get his attention through the throng. "Someone's trashed my room," he says.

"What's that?"

They move to the quieter end of the bar. "Within the last two or three hours, I'd say."

"Sheesh. Didn't see anything, mate." He speaks to the two barmaids. They shake their heads.

"Okay. We've called the cops. We'll wait outside for them and take them up. Notice any strangers in here tonight?"

He shrugs. "Sorry, it's been busy."

A patrol car arrives with two uniforms and Harry and Ross take them upstairs. Ross gives them a statement and they say they'll get someone to go over the place for prints. "Might take a while though." Harry tells them to help themselves.

When they leave, Ross says, "Reckon you need something stronger than a beer now, mate."

Harry shakes his head. "Next time, Ross. I'm heading off to see Jenny. Should have been there this morning."

He has a word to the manager about giving the police access and the man says, "I remember a couple of guys here earlier, sitting over there, not drinking much. One guy was short, leather jacket. The other was big, an islander. Never seen them here before."

"Thanks. If you see them again, can you give me a call?"

He gets into the car, feeling weary, checks the time. He calls Jenny and asks if it's too late to come. She says of course not, she'll wait up.

She's standing on the veranda when he pulls to a stop, the dog by her side, and as he mounts the steps he sees that she's wearing only her thin nightie on this warm night. He wraps his arms around her, filled with relief, feeling that this is all he wants, ever.

She whispers, "Harry, Harry," and they make their way inside, still clinging to each other, to her room. He strips off quickly and slides in beside her, wanting her desperately.

FIFTY-TWO

KELLY IS EATING HER muesli when a call comes through from Brad in Port Vila. "You're up bright and early."

"We're an hour ahead of you," he says. "Thought I'd better check before I go any further. It's not easy. Vanuatu has a fairly secretive financial system. It doesn't maintain company-ownership details in official records, and doesn't require that company ownership or accounts be publicly accessible. Same for trusts and private foundations. I did find a couple of local press reports on Pandanus Trust, one of a scholarship scheme for disadvantaged students they were funding, and the other a gift of an MRI unit to the hospital on Espiritu Santo."

"So they're a charity?" Kelly is scribbling notes as he speaks.

"Seems so. Question is, where do I go from here? I could fly up to Santo and see if they can tell me more about the people who gave them the MRI. Maybe there was a ceremony or something. Or I could poke around a bit more down here. I know one or two people in the government offices who might be prepared to leak me something for a few dollars. What do you think?"

It doesn't sound promising. It'll cost Brad $360 to fly up to Espiritu Santo. They talk it over and decide against it. They agree instead on an all-in fee for Brad to "poke around" in Port Vila for a bit longer.

FIFTY-THREE

AT THE SAME TIME Harry wakes in the Yarramalong Valley. He gets out of bed and steps out onto the veranda, straight into the smell of coffee, the thrashing tails of dogs, the embrace of the women. He sinks into a chair, relishing the gleam of dew in the sunlight, the sound of birds in the forest, with a tremendous sense of relief. He thinks how idyllic this is compared to the sordid mess in Newcastle, as a huge duck-egg omelette on toast appears in front of him.

It's only later, as he and Jenny go for a walk up the hill behind the house, that he realises things aren't quite so perfect. She walks much more slowly and cautiously than he's used to, feeling the ground in front of her with her stick. And when he thinks about it he can see why—the way ahead is littered with ruts and protruding rocks, with fallen branches and wire fences. It must be like walking through a minefield, her stick an uncertain guide and the little sonar buzzer in her other hand unable to decipher the hazards. Felecia runs free ahead, picking up trails of rabbits and foxes, and that worries Jenny too. "There are snakes." She's echoing Amber's words on the climb to the sacred cave, but without Amber's confidence. That's what it is, he thinks, she's lost her confidence.

They sit on a fallen log and he says, "Must be difficult for you, out here in the bush."

"Yes," she says, hesitating, and then it all comes out. "It's a nightmare, Harry. I mean, literally—I have nightmares of being lost out here. I can't get my head around it, can't make a mental picture of it all. One wrong step off the known way and I'm hopelessly lost. I'm thinking I might trip and fall down the hillside or step into a rabbit hole and break an ankle. Yesterday I stumbled and put out my hand and grabbed barbed wire."

She shows him the bandage on the palm of her hand.

"Sorry, this must sound so pathetic. I mean, I suppose it's very beautiful out here but I can't see that. I can smell its freshness, but now that just seems like a threat. And . . . it's not just that."

"Go on." He gently rubs her back. "Tell me."

"Everything's just so frustrating. Meri tries so hard—too hard. She's always telling me how amazing I am, doing ordinary things, as if I'm an invalid, and she tries to lead me everywhere. And then I'm humiliated when I can't do simple things, like eat a meal."

He knows what she means. Eating has always been a problem. He's tried it himself, eating dinner blindfold, the chop ending up on the floor, the mash all over his hands and the peas in his lap.

"We went down to Wyong yesterday for lunch. I should have had a hamburger but I felt like fish and chips. It came all built up into a sort of stack, served on a wooden board. It was a disaster. The waitress had to get a broom to sweep it all up. She was so upset."

He chuckles, she smiles, they both laugh.

"I know," Jenny says, "I'm being feeble. What is it you cops say? 'Toughen up, Tiger.' Only I haven't been feeling very tough lately. I miss you, Harry. I don't want us to be apart like this. It's made me realise how much I depend on you. Too much."

"Maybe it won't be for too much longer. There have been some arrests in Newcastle."

"Sammy Lee?"

"No. They don't think he's involved."

"But you do."

"It was just a hunch, nothing more really, a bright idea without any real evidence."

"I did a bit of work on him. He has a Malaysian wife and a little girl, a house in Lambton, nothing fancy, a four-year-old Falcon. His wife has an online account with Western Union. Maybe sending money back to Malaysia?"

"Hmm, well, Ross reckons he's a good bloke and half the station eats there. They reckon Dee-Dee's the villain."

"What, the young tattoo artist?"

He brings her up to date.

"And McGilvray's dead?"

"Looks like it."

"So can't I come back?"

"Not until we know the whole picture, Jen. Sorry."

"Oh . . . I did find out something about Jason Tolliver's background. You remember the big waterfront dispute back in '98? Tolliver was an organiser for the Maritime Union at Port Botany then, bit of a reputation as a militant. He was in the media—I've got pictures of him on the computer you can look at. Come on. I'm getting stiff. Can you see a twisted old red gum next to a gate?"

He stands up and looks about. "Yes, I've got it."

"There's an easier path back down to the road from there."

They set off, Harry half a pace ahead and her hand in

the crook of his arm. She says, "So that's why McGilvray's Facebook entries stopped. Karen and Craig Schaefer's have stopped too, by the way. No word on them?"

"Nothing."

"I found out a bit about Amber's friend Luke Santini. He's spent time in America, relatives in Virginia. Became an environmental activist at college there, a campaign to get universities to disinvest their endowment and pension funds in coalmining companies. Moved to Melbourne two years ago to work with an environmental group called Sustain."

"That fits."

"There's some pictures of him in America. I'll show you when we get back. And you have to remember to admire Meri's alpaca yarn. I spun some of it."

When they reach the cottage Jenny takes him to the corner where her computer sits and talks to it for a while. Looking over her shoulder, Harry sees photographs appear, groups of young people, some with placards and banners. The slogan *Burning Rage* appears on a placard and on a bandana across Luke's forehead. He looks angry, face distorted, fist raised.

They search *Burning Rage*, which turns out to be a protest group suspected of arson attacks on mine owners' property—cars and holiday homes—in the United States.

Jenny shuts down the computer and they try to relax and pretend that this is an innocent holiday. Harry admires Meri's fleece, fixes up a sagging gutter that she couldn't reach, and takes them out for a hamburger.

This evening they sit on the veranda drinking tea. Harry feels time standing still, and simultaneously running through his fingers like sand. When he goes to sleep he dreams of a burning cabin in a lonely forest.

He leaves the next day after lunch, heart heavy. There's a tear in Jenny's eye as he turns away.

On the road back he takes a call from Deb.

"Harry, thought I should tell you. They're releasing Frank Capp tomorrow morning. Charges dropped."

"Great."

"Yeah. We'll be watching him."

When he reaches the Carrington pub the manager offers him a drink.

"Don't suppose they've caught anyone?" Harry says.

"Nah. We've put a new lock on your door and the girls have cleaned the room up, good as new. You'll be fine."

He goes upstairs and looks at the restored room. It's as if nothing happened. There is nothing of him here, not even a toothbrush.

FIFTY-FOUR

Brad.

"What have you got?" Kelly reaches for her pad.

"Had a bit of luck with the National Provident Fund. Anyone who employs Vanuatu citizens has to contribute to the fund for their retirement benefits. I know someone who works there and I got hold of the names of a couple of Pandanus Trust employees with Port Vila addresses. Managed to track one of them down and we had a few beers together yesterday. He was catching a boat back to work on the island the Trust owns, up north near Pentecost, place I'd never heard of called Maturiki Island. He said there's a big villa up there and staff houses."

"That's interesting. Did he say anything about the people who own it?"

"He was vague about that, just said the bosses are Aussies and Chinese. They come and go. Pay's good, often not much to do, other times people arrive and they're busy. Sounds a bit like a resort—foreigners come, they eat and drink and talk, sunbathe on the beach, go out to the reef snorkelling."

"Oh yes?"

"You should see the boat he left on to go to work—a

hundred-and-twenty-foot super yacht. Million bucks for sure."

"Called *Rashida*?"

"Nah, name of *Princess Estelle*, out of Sydney."

After she rings off, Kelly does a search for Maturiki Island. The satellite image shows a small, densely wooded island about twenty kilometres away from the much larger Pentecost Island. There is a white crescent beach on one side facing across a lagoon to an arc of surf marking the reef. It's just possible to make out some rectangular shapes beneath the canopy of trees—pandanus trees, presumably.

Kelly thinks about it. Why would a charitable trust own an island? Or a luxury yacht for that matter?

Before she leaves for court she phones Matthew at the *Times* office and asks him to find out what he can about the *Princess Estelle*.

When she reaches the seventh floor of the Supreme Court building on Queens Square she finds the trial in a state of suspension, the press, jury, and officials waiting for the judge and counsel to emerge from discussion. It's over an hour before they appear and the judge informs them, to Kelly's great relief, that the fiasco is at an end, the accused having finally accepted reality and changed their plea to guilty.

Kelly returns to ground level and steps out onto Phillip Street, looking for a cab. As her eye scans the street she sees a woman on the corner of King Street staring at her. For a moment Kelly is paralysed. She recognises the posture, the face. The woman turns and vanishes into the crowd. Kelly runs across the street, dodging between cars, and stands on the corner where Karen Schaefer stood. There is no sign of her now.

She lets her heart slow down, then catches a cab back

to the *Times*. Everyone is busy, preoccupied, oblivious. She finally pulls herself together and checks through the latest updates. There is a report of arrests in Newcastle and a search for a fourth body on Ash Island. She goes to see Catherine Meiklejohn, explains that she's now free, and asks to go back up there. Catherine agrees.

When she gets back to her desk she finds a note from Matthew. The *Princess Estelle* was built in Italy three years ago for its present owner, Konrad Nordlund. So here is another connection, Mansur—Ozdevco—Pandanus Trust—Nordlund. First there was Karen Schaefer, now this. There's something here, but what exactly? She goes to see Matthew and tells him to keep it to himself.

He says, "Of course. We don't investigate Konrad Nordlund, do we?" He's becoming cynical. "Oh, by the way," he goes on, "and changing the subject completely, I chanced upon this odd little item, deep in our archives."

Chanced upon? Kelly smiles at him. "What is it?" She runs her eye over it quickly, then stops and reads it again, an article dated 20 December 2002, from what was then called the Social Editor's desk. "This didn't actually run, did it?"

He shakes his head. "It was spiked. Who wants to read about that sort of thing at Christmas?"

FIFTY-FIVE

HARRY FINDS THE CORNER of a table to perch on as they begin the morning briefing. Fogarty's mood is mixed. On the one hand, prolonged interviews with Dee-Dee Perry have produced next to nothing. On the other, her premises have continued to provide links to the Ash Island murders. They have confirmation now that a jacket found hanging on a hook in the shed behind the tattoo studio belonged to Marco Ganis, while his fingerprints have been found on some of the banknotes in the cashbox.

Fogarty shuffles through his papers and begins on the new schedule of tasks. A large contingent of uniform officers is being brought in to expand the search area for a fourth body; detectives are to interview all of Dee-Dee's past customers; a further sweep of CCTV cameras in the streets around her studio will try to identify other visitors to her premises, including Cheung Xiuying and any other Chinese.

They're running short of ideas, Harry thinks, dreaming up busy-work to keep everyone active until Logan Mc-Gilvray's body turns up. And then what? Despite all the evidence in the studio, they've found no links to the Sydney motorcycle gang Capp spoke of. Capp, who's walking free now, a big smile on at least half his face, thinking of all those mugs chasing their tails up in Newcastle.

When they break up, Harry gets his job from the case manager and heads off to the seamen's mission to reinterview people and show them the film clips of Cheung at Marketown.

The mission is busy. Father McCallum is conducting a service for a group of Filipino sailors and the volunteer is out with the van. Harry waits in the main hall, watching the activity, listening to the chatter of languages, picturing Cheung selecting that checked shirt from the rack. He's hoping something will strike him.

The volunteer returns. They find a free office with a computer and Harry plugs in the USB. Father McCallum comes in and they watch the figures moving on the screen, the two men clearly anxious to help. But in the end they can offer nothing new. The volunteer has no recollection of Cheung having a phone, and isn't convinced that that's what he was doing with his hand raised to his ear. Harry thanks them and returns to his car.

He checks his messages; there's one from Kelly Pool, and he rings her number. She says she's on her way up to Newcastle and would like to meet. He tells her the car park at Horse Shoe Beach at three.

DOGS ARE RUNNING UP and down the beach, chasing sticks into the little waves. Beyond them four tugs are guiding a bulk carrier into the river mouth. A car drives into the park next to her and Harry gets out, comes to her passenger door. She leans across and opens it for him.

"The size of that thing," she says. The windscreen is filled now by the huge wall of steel sliding past.

"Yeah."

"How are you?"

"Good, yourself?"

He looks tired, a bit haggard, she thinks. Not his usual self. "I've got something for you, an old press report, never published. I don't know if it ever made it to a police report."

"Go on."

"Ten years ago, Christmas, Konrad Nordlund took his niece Amber to dinner at the Bennelong restaurant at the Opera House. Just the two of them. At some point in the evening Amber grabbed a steak knife and tried to bury it in her uncle's heart. There was a fuss, a doctor was called, but not the police. The next day the Nordlunds made a statement. Amber was unwell, diagnosed with affective psychosis, or manic-depressive illness. The family requested privacy, and they got it. The story was never published. If it happened today of course there'd be videos all over the Web, but then it just went quiet. As if it never happened."

"Interesting." He nods.

"You don't sound surprised."

He shrugs.

"They've sent me up here because there's been a report of another body on Ash Island. Can you give me any background on that?"

"We haven't found it yet, but there's been evidence of a fourth victim."

"What kind of evidence?"

"Can't say."

"Who is it?"

"They'll be releasing the name of a missing person later today, name of Logan McGilvray . . ."

She gets him to spell it. "A crook?"

"No record, but a recent charge of assault on his wife."

"Drugs?"

"Possibly. They will also be announcing that drugs were found during a raid on a tattoo parlour in Islington called Dee-Dee's Studio. The owner, Dee-Dee Perry, is currently assisting police with their inquiries."

"Okay, so what's the background?"

He stares out of the window as if weighing up what to say. They watch the last tug go past behind the bulk carrier.

"If you were to do a bit of digging, you might come up with the fact that McGilvray was a regular customer at Dee-Dee's Studio. Coming from Sydney, you might also have noticed that this morning a man called Frank Capp was released without charge from Long Bay after being held for almost two months. He was the sergeant-at-arms of the Crows outlaw motorcycle gang, with whom, coincidentally, two of the Ash Island victims, Marco Ganis and Tony Gemmell, were also associated."

"Wow . . ." Kelly's pen is racing across the notepad. When she looks up, he's staring hard at her. "Detective Inspector Deb Velasco from Sydney Homicide has been involved in this, Kelly, and as you know she doesn't like you. She suspects that I fed you stuff at Crucifixion Creek, so you have to make sure you have solid background on anything you publish that doesn't point to me."

"Of course. I'm good at that. Umm . . ." she flicks back through her notepad. "There was a report a couple of weeks ago in the *Newcastle Herald* . . . yes, the twentieth. An explosion in a house in Carrington. Was that connected with any of this?"

"Forget it."

"Come on, Harry. It was, wasn't it?"

He withdraws again, thinking, and she wonders if he's about to get out of the car and leave, but then he sighs, and says, "There were rumours at the time that the explosion wasn't accidental, and that the occupants of the house were a police officer and his wife, who were lucky to escape unhurt. But there's a blanket suppression order in force, pending further inquiries."

"A police officer? Gee, Harry, that's terrible. Who was it?"

"You can ask, but they won't tell you. Anything else?"

"Yes, there is. I was in the Supreme Court on Queens Square this morning. When I came out I looked across the street and saw Karen Schaefer."

"You're sure?"

"Absolutely. She just stood there for a moment, staring at me, then she turned and was gone. It's not a coincidence, Harry. She must have followed me there. I think she was trying to frighten me, and she bloody well succeeded."

"Tell the cops, Kelly."

"I can't, not after what I did. You see? I'm just like you—I have to find out what's going on myself or I'll never have any peace. I've left home, so has Wendy, because Karen probably knows where I live, and I find different ways to come and go to work and look over my shoulder all the time. But I can't go on living like this."

He nods. "Well, you take care." He turns to open the door-handle and a thought strikes her.

"It wasn't your house, was it Harry? That got blown up?"

He turns back.

"It was, wasn't it? My God, you never said anything . . . Is Jenny all right?"

"We were lucky."

Harry's phone rings. He listens to it for a moment. Says, "I'm on my way," and hangs up. "They've found the fourth body. Give me half an hour before you come out there."

FIFTY-SIX

THE MISSING FINGERS ARE the same, but other things are different with this one. The heavily tattooed body is found half a kilometre away from the other sites. Not buried this time, just dumped in long grass and covered with vegetation.

It's a hot afternoon, humid with the threat of evening rain, and the CSO team labours and sweats. After a while the pathologist, Leon Timson, emerges. He's spattered in mud, face red. Someone gives him a bottle of cold water.

"Hello, Harry. It's McGilvray all right. Possible cause of death a massive blow to the skull."

"Like Gemmell," Harry says.

"Not as extreme as that, but more than enough to kill. Come and take a look."

He follows Timson down a trodden path to the edge of the water where McGilvray's body lies sprawled, face down.

"How long ago did he die?"

"Hard to be sure with all that tattooing, but he seems to have that marbling discolouration of the skin that comes four or five days after death. When was he last seen alive?"

"Our last sighting of him was late night, Saturday before last. Has he been here all that time?"

"Good question. I might be able to tell you when he's

cleaned up and on the table. The material that was laid on top of him doesn't tell us much." He points to a heap of branches and leaves stacked on a tarpaulin. "Old debris. Nothing that's been recently broken from a tree.

"There is one hopeful thing, over here . . ." He leads the way back down the path and points to an area of flattened grass just off the road. "Quite a reasonable tyre print, see? Fortunately there hasn't been any rain since he was dumped." He looks up at the sky. "We'll get a cast done straight away."

As Harry walks away Ross catches up with him. "Press are starting to arrive." He nods over to a huddle of people at the barrier. Harry makes out Kelly talking to another reporter. "Fogarty wants us to attend the PM."

"Fine. We should have cameras up here, on the bridge onto the island and the main tracks."

"You think there's going to be more?"

"Who knows."

They walk together to the cars. "Remember when we arrested McGilvray?" Ross says. " 'Loretta.' Didn't see it ending up like this, mate. What the hell's going on?"

"Well, I don't think they can pin this on Dee-Dee."

LOGAN MCGILVRAY NAKED ON the dissection table is something to behold. Ross's eyes roam all over the tattooed surface and he murmurs, "Jesus, will you look at that—he even had his prick done."

Timson is sticking a syringe into one of McGilvray's eyes. "The amount of sodium in the vitreous humour can indicate time of death," he says, and continues with his detailed inspection of the body, pointing out signs of restraints, probably tape, on the wrists and ankles. "Same as Cheung," he says.

He and his assistant turn the body over onto its front. "Ah yes, lividity." He points to the darker areas over the shoulders and buttocks. "After he died he lay on his back for some time, at least six hours, before he was moved."

He turns to the head, carefully probing the large wound on the rear right side. "At least two blows, probably three, and there's a compression fracture here consistent with the shape of a bottle we found in the water near the body."

They take a break while Timson has X-rays taken of the damage to the skull before he disturbs it further.

FIFTY-SEVEN

WHILE KELLY WAITS AT the barrier on Ash Island for the police to issue a press statement, she chats to the same reporter from the *Newcastle Herald* that she met before. The woman fills her in on the theories that have been circulating around the city about the murders.

"There was a bit of panic when people thought it was a serial killer, then the police put it out unofficially that they think it's gang-related." She mentions the names of the local biker gangs. "I know a few of those blokes. Wouldn't have thought they'd get into anything as heavy as this."

"Gangs from out of town, then?" Kelly suggests.

The woman shrugs.

"There was an explosion recently in a house in Carrington, wasn't there?"

"Yes, that was strange too. The coppers have kept very quiet about that. I went and spoke to one of the firies who attended that night and he said he'd been told not to talk about it. He did hint that it wasn't a gas leak though. Said it was a miracle no one was hurt. I spoke to the neighbours and they said the couple who were living there were out at the time. Nice couple, quiet, they said, but they didn't know anything about them, except that she was blind.

Seeing-eye dog, the works. They haven't been around since, apparently."

Superintendent Gibb comes to the barrier and makes his statement. The latest victim is believed to be a thirty-four-year-old local man by the name of Logan McGilvray, resident of Mayfield. The police are very anxious to trace his movements over the past eight days and are appealing for anyone with information to contact them. The cause of death is unknown at this stage, pending a post-mortem.

KELLY RETURNS TO HER hotel and sets up her laptop, spreads out her notes, and begins to compose her article. Facts to begin with: the bleak setting of Ash Island, the fourth body, a recap on the previous three. Then the more difficult part, describing the links between at least two of the victims and the Sydney Crows biker gang involved in fatal shootings earlier this year, and mentioning the release today of their former vice-president from prison without actually saying that it's connected. No mention of the Nordlund family, or Ozdevco or Crucifixion Creek. And the final line: *If you have information about any of these events, or about the whereabouts of a Crows associate known as Karen Schaefer or Donna Fenning, call Crime Stoppers on 1-800-333-000, or contact our crime desk: KellyPool@times.net.au.*

She rereads it and sends it off, then goes downstairs for dinner.

At midnight she gets confirmation from the editorial office in Sydney that Catherine has passed the article without cuts. It'll be on page five of tomorrow's paper.

FIFTY-EIGHT

HARRY TAKES ANNA DEMOS with him to the house in New Lambton Heights. "I always hate these visits," she says. "There's nothing you can say that sounds right."

"Especially if the deceased was a scumbag. But at least his wife's had a bit of time to get used to the idea of being a widow."

McGilvray's father-in-law answers the door, sombre but brisk, obviously not unduly upset by last night's news. "Come in, come in. My wife is with Olivia now. They didn't get much sleep last night."

"I'm sorry to disturb you again," Harry says.

"Oh, it's all right. I know you have to go through a process. Sooner it's all over the better."

"Is she very upset?" Anna says, in a hushed voice.

"My wife? Good heavens, no. It's a bloody relief, frankly. Olivia was contemplating going back to him. She wanted a baby, but she'd held off because he kept talking about covering the infant with tattoos." He shakes his head. "Sometimes I find it impossible to understand human nature. She's bright, had a decent education, knows the difference between right and wrong. And yet for some unimaginable reason she became infatuated with that thug."

"Obviously we're interested in who might have wanted to kill him," Harry says.

"Apart from me, you mean? Afraid I can't help you."

"You don't know any names of his friends, acquaintances?"

"Sorry, you'll have to ask Olivia. I'll get her for you."

He returns with the two women, both looking pale and exhausted. Everyone sits. Harry introduces Constable Demos and himself again, and Anna begins.

"Olivia, we're so sorry for your loss. And we're sorry to disturb you at such a sad time, but in a murder investigation time is of the essence."

Olivia's face crumples and she looks ready to burst into tears.

Anna hurries on. "We'd just like you to help us by telling us the names of Logan's friends—male friends especially. People he was close to, liked to have a beer with, that kind of thing."

Olivia takes a deep breath and begins a halting list of names. Harry writes them down. A couple were on Dee-Dee's phone, smalltime dealers in pubs and clubs. They've already been interviewed. The others sound innocuous, but they'll all be spoken to.

When she's finished, Harry says, "How about someone called Sammy?"

She ponders. "The only Sammy I know is Sammy Lee. Runs the Chinese restaurant."

He nods. "Someone called Tolliver?"

She shakes her head.

"Jason Tolliver? Doesn't ring a bell?"

"No."

"How about Tyler?"

She frowns, thinking. "I think we did meet someone

229

called Tyler. When was it? . . . It was in a pub, but I can't remember which one."

"Can you describe him?"

"Oh no, no. I can't remember."

"What if I show you a picture." He takes out a copy of a photograph taken from the last NRL company report and offers it to her.

"Oh . . . Yes, that might be him. Yes, I'm sure it is. He was big, friendly, very charming really. Well off. I remember now, Logan told me he had a special car, something fancy, like an Asian girl's name . . ."

"Lotus Elise?" Anna suggests.

"Yes, that's it."

"I've seen it around," Anna says.

"Is it important?" Olivia asks. "I only saw him the once, at that pub."

"No, not important, Olivia, but thanks anyway for your help."

She sighs. "If I hadn't left him, this might never have happened."

"That's nonsense, darling," her mother says sharply. To Harry she says, "Tell her it isn't true, officer."

"Your mother's right," Harry says. "There's nothing you could have done to prevent this."

"Did he suffer?"

"No." Harry sees Anna's eyebrows shoot up. "And I know you've already been asked this, Olivia, but are you quite sure you have no knowledge of Logan's movements over the past week or ten days? Or can think of anyone who might know?"

"No. I've no idea."

They leave. When they get into the car, Anna says, "Who's Tyler?"

"Good question."

When they get back to the station, Harry goes to his computer to write up a report. Halfway through, he spots Ken Fogarty circulating round the room, and when he reaches his desk Harry says, "I went with Anna Demos to interview McGilvray's widow and her parents, boss."

"Anything?"

"One thing. I was asking about his friends, and I showed her this picture, of a local man called Jason Tolliver. She identified him as someone she and McGilvray met in a pub. He isn't on the lists we have. I think he's worth investigating."

"Hang on, you've lost me. Who is he? Do we know him?"

"No, no record. He's the head of security at the NRL coal loader."

"So . . . how did you just happen to have a picture of him in your pocket?"

"You remember the business of Tyler Dayspring and the Dark Riders that McGilvray told me about?"

Fogarty folds his arms, staring at Harry. "How could I forget?"

"Well, boss, in the Marvel Comics story, Tyler Dayspring also uses the name Tolliver. So I looked into that name. There's only one in Newcastle—this bloke, Jason Tolliver."

"Who Mrs. McGilvray thinks she once saw in a pub. That's it?"

"Yes."

Fogarty runs a hand through his thinning grey hair, shakes his head. "You astonish me, Belltree. We're trying to run a rigorous homicide investigation here, and you talk about comic books. Get off your arse and go and do some bloody work."

After he's gone Ross comes over with a copy of the *Times*. "Seen this, Harry?"

Harry reads it, frowns.

"That bit at the end," Ross says. "Who's Karen Schaefer and Donna Fenning?"

When he gets a chance Harry finds a quiet spot and calls Kelly. "Just read your article. What are you playing at? Trying to provoke her?"

"Don't worry, Harry. I know what I'm doing."

"Well, I hope you've got someone down there watching your back, Kelly."

FIFTY-NINE

IT ARRIVES LATE THAT afternoon, an e-mail:

Dear Kelly Pool, I can tell you where to find Karen Schaefer. Best wishes, Insider.

Kelly replies: *Dear Insider, Can we meet? Kelly.*

Nothing happens for two hours. Then, as Kelly is about to leave the building, the reply arrives:

Tomorrow morning 10AM, bench in Riverside Park, Strathfield, opposite Dogwood Avenue. I will need $500. Confirm. Insider.

Kelly confirms that she'll be there and leaves, picking up a hire car on the way to her hotel.

It's another sleepless night, trying to think it through again and again, struggling to fight off the demons of memory and fear.

She sets off early the next morning, stopping on Liverpool Road to pick up a roll and coffee at a café, then continues to Strathfield South, where the parklands along the Cooks River form a boundary with Belfield, and finds Dogwood Avenue. She drives slowly, spotting the empty park bench beneath a dense canopy of mature trees. Beyond, the open field sloping down to the river is empty apart from a jogger in a purple tracksuit and a man walking a dog. She continues around the block, getting her bearings, then returns to the street that borders the park and finds a space from which she has a clear view of the bench, about a hundred metres away. It is 7:23. She lowers herself in her seat and eats her roll, drinks her coffee, and waits.

The sun glistens on tile roofs, a plane out of Mascot draws a white line across the pale blue sky, people come and go from the small villas along the street. A woman pushing a baby stroller, an old man on an electric buggy.

At a quarter to ten Kelly sees the jogger in the purple tracksuit again, at the far end of the street. He is wearing a cap on his head and dark glasses and is walking slowly towards her, glancing into each parked car he passes. Kelly's heart gives a jump.

He stops at a white van and as he circles it Kelly quickly opens her door and runs, crouching, into the drive of the nearest house. She slips in behind a dense privet bush and looks around, praying no one's seen her from the houses.

After a few minutes she catches a glimpse of purple through the hedge, a flash of white trainers. She holds her breath as they stop at her car for a moment, then continue.

She stays where she is, motionless until her aching knees force her to straighten cautiously, just in time to see the jogger returning, glancing this way and that. She ducks down again, her mind filled with the image she has just seen, of a white bandage visible beneath the left lens of the dark glasses.

When he has passed she edges forward and sees that he has crossed to the park side of the street, where he is checking a couple more cars. Then he puts a phone to his ear and moves on towards the bench. Kelly slips back into her car again. Two minutes later a green Barina drives slowly past and stops beside him.

A woman gets out, long blonde hair, dark glasses,

shoulder bag. Karen Schaefer had a brown bob, but the build is the same. She goes over to the bench and sits down, while the jogger gets behind the wheel of the car.

Ten minutes pass, twenty. The woman gets to her feet and begins to pace, peering up and down the street. It's the same posture, Kelly thinks, that same inquisitive forward stoop. The recognition makes her heart pound.

Thirty minutes, forty, then the woman jumps up and strides to the Barina. She says a few words through the window and gets in. Kelly watches the brake lights come on, the car pull out and move away. She starts her car and waits until the other reaches the end of the street and turns out of sight, then she follows.

It's not easy. Even with relatively light traffic it's a series of hair-raising choices between getting too close and losing it. The Barina makes a right at traffic lights up ahead. Kelly follows and is blocked on the intersection by oncoming cars. By the time she makes the turn there's no sign of a green car. She puts her foot down and almost misses the glimpse of green on a side street to her left. She pulls in, waits for traffic to pass and does a U-turn, back to the side street. Again no sign of the green car until she's right on top of it, parked in the narrow driveway of a small bungalow. Kelly continues past and pulls in fifty metres on.

She wonders what to do now. She's toying with her phone when a figure appears at the gate of the bungalow, hauling a garbage bin out onto the nature strip. It's Craig Schaefer, sure enough. Still wearing his dark glasses, but dressed now in jeans and a lightweight jacket. He turns back to the house and a moment later a taxi turns into the street and pulls up outside. Now Craig and Karen, blonde wig abandoned, emerge rolling two large suitcases. The cab driver lifts them into the boot and sets off, past Kelly lying flat across the front seats, and disappears over the crest of the hill.

It's a little easier to follow the white cab with the distinctive sign on its roof as they thread their way through suburban streets south and east, then following signs to the airport. She tails them up the departures ramp of the international terminal and drives past as they get out of the cab. She has to go some way before she finds a parking spot. By the time she gets out the cab is moving off and the Schaefers have disappeared inside the terminal. The concourse is packed. Kelly works her way through the crowd, searching, but finds no sign of them. After ten minutes she gives up and returns to her car.

She goes back to the Strathfield bungalow. The street is quiet, no one around. She parks outside and walks quickly in, past the green Barina, to the small garden at the rear. She looks through the kitchen window and sees clean benchtops, vacant shelves. Through another window she sees a bed neatly made up, bedside tables bare.

Kelly walks back out to her car. Notices the bin standing nearby. She opens the lid and there's a plump black plastic bag inside. She hauls it out, throws it into the back of her car and drives away.

She comes to the car park of a small supermarket and pulls in to check the garbage bag. She's disappointed—no bank statements, e-mails, photographs. Just an empty milk carton, a half-finished tub of butter, a browning banana and a few other perishables. Some of the items are instructive, though. A bottle of barbecue sauce, a jar of peanut butter— things that you wouldn't need to throw out if you were planning to return any time soon. And then, at the bottom of the sticky interior, a business card for Luc's World Travel in Strathfield. The name "Lexie" written on the back.

The shop has the logo of a Greek flag above a window filled with bright posters. Kelly goes in and asks the woman working a computer at a desk if Lexie is around.

"That's me. How can I help?"

Kelly shows her the business card. "Karen told me about you—Karen Schaefer?"

"Mrs. Schaefer, yes, of course." Lexie checks her watch. "She should be at the airport now."

"That's right, I saw them off. It was a bit of a rush. Karen was going to give me the details of where they're staying before they left but we forgot. I wondered if you could help me, you know, a telephone number, e-mail address?"

"Of the Grand? Sure." She taps on her computer and reads off a phone number.

Kelly repeats it as she writes it down. "Six-seven-eight, is that the country code?"

"Of Vanuatu, yes."

"And how long are they there, if I need to reach them?"

"Just the one night. After that, when they meet their friends for the cruise, I've no idea. They arranged that themselves. Have you got Karen's mobile?"

"Um, oh hell, no."

More tapping. "There we go."

"Oh, thank you so much."

"How about an Athens package?"

"Sorry?"

"We've got a great deal on at the moment."

"Oh, I wish. Thanks so much for your help, Lexie."

"No worries."

When she gets back to her car, Kelly murmurs to herself, "The Grand Hotel and Casino, Port Vila." She gets on the phone to Brad.

SIXTY

ON THE PHONE AMBER sounds brisk, businesslike. "Harry, can you come down to Sydney? There's a member of our family you should meet."

"I'm pretty busy at the moment, Amber."

"It's important, Harry. You'll find it worthwhile, I promise."

"Who is it?"

"My uncle."

"Konrad?"

"No, my other uncle, his brother Bernard. There were three brothers—my father Martin, then Bernard, and then Konrad. When I told Bernard about you he said that it was time he met you. I think he can help."

Harry checks his diary. "Okay. Nine o'clock tomorrow. Where?"

"Sydney University. I'll meet you at the Parramatta Road footbridge."

Harry googles Bernard Nordlund. He's a professor of economic history at the University of Sydney; the pictures show a balding and bespectacled man, chubby face, rosy cheeks, at various cultural events in the city, a patron of the Art Gallery of New South Wales and Opera Australia.

AMBER IS STANDING IN the middle of the footbridge, hands on the rail, looking as if she might be about to leap down into the traffic roaring below. Harry sees the breeze catch her hair and press the light fabric of her dress against her body, her fragile sex appeal.

"Hi."

"Hello, Harry." A wide smile. "It's great you could make it." She takes his arm as they walk towards the green lawns of the campus. "Bernard's the exception in the family. He doesn't own any companies, gives his money away to causes that interest him, and devotes himself to his studies. I don't think he even owns a car. He has a lovely art deco flat at Potts Point and spends his holidays poking around in old ruins."

They reach the entrance to the quadrangle and make their way through into the cloisters.

"I always feel intimidated coming here," Amber says. "Because I never made it to university, I suppose. Bernard says I have a natural unspoilt mind, open to the world." A half smile. "Of course he's just trying to be kind."

They reach the dark entrance to a staircase and climb a couple of floors, then along a short corridor lit by a window at the end overlooking a narrow courtyard in which young people are sitting, drinking coffee in the sun. They come to a door labelled PROF. NORDLUND. Amber knocks and opens the door.

A figure seated at a desk in front of the window turns and gets to his feet. He hugs Amber and shakes Harry's hand.

"It's a great pleasure to meet you, Harry. I followed your father's career with great interest," Bernard says, beaming. "I don't think we ever met, but I remember attending his honorary doctorate award ceremony here at the university. His speech was inspiring. And Amber tells me you're a detective."

"Harry's hunting for the Ash Island murderers at Newcastle."

"Ah! Fascinating. I've had occasion to study a few murderers in my time—Mengistu Mariam, Leopold the Second, Mao Zedong. But I find it dispiriting. In real life evil is as depressingly banal as Arendt believed. Have you come down from Newcastle this morning? You must be ready for a coffee. Look at my new machine, Amber. Isn't it smart? You put these little capsules in. My students find it only too agreeable—they won't leave me in peace."

While Amber makes the coffee Harry looks around the cramped room, enclosed by shelves packed tight with books. He notices a small print in one corner of a man in traditional Chinese costume seated on a throne. Amber says, "Bernard is a China specialist."

"Oh yes?" Harry says. "Your brother Konrad must find that useful. I understand he has business interests over there."

"No, no! I'm no use to him at all," Bernard says. "My interests are strictly historical. That venerable gentleman, for instance . . ." But Amber interrupts, bringing over coffee cups.

"Come on, let's sit down. About Konrad, Bernard," she prompts.

"Ah." He gives a regretful frown. "I don't like being disloyal to my family, Harry, but we don't always see eye to eye. They have all been great capitalists—my brothers, our father, his father—the kind of ruthless entrepreneurs upon which our country depends, I suppose, and without which parasites like me would not have the time for idle speculation. But we could never get beyond that question—*why?* Why make great fortunes? What was the point? For them, the purpose was the game itself, the accumulation, the success. My brother Martin, Amber's father, acknowledged that there had to be a social purpose to his gains, and he did a number of useful things, especially in the region around Kramfors. But Konrad has no interest in that. He is a ruthless businessman first and last. In my cups I might call him a predator."

"The judge, Bernard," Amber prompts again. "What you told me."

"Yes, yes. Amber explained about your desire to discover the truth about your parents" deaths and your poor wife's injury, and your consequent interest in their staying at Kramfors that night. I mentioned to her something that struck me at the time, and she felt I should tell you. It's this: about a month before the tragedy happened, I had lunch with Konrad. I was trying—without much success—to persuade him his company should sponsor a symposium I was organising, when his phone rang. He answered it and became visibly agitated. At one point he said something like, 'Well he has to be stopped then.' When he finished I said, 'Bad news?' and he replied angrily, 'That bloody judge . . .' before he pulled himself up and changed the subject. Well, I had no idea what he meant and he wouldn't elaborate. But a month or so later when I heard the news, the words came back to me, and I had a terrible feeling. I couldn't help asking myself, was Danny Belltree *that* judge?"

Harry says, "You believe your brother was responsible for my parents' deaths?"

"Oh . . ." Bernard winces. "No, I couldn't possibly say that. He might not have been referring to your father at all. But clearly someone—perhaps the person Konrad was speaking to—felt that drastic action needed to be taken to prevent *a* judge doing something. Might that have been your father? It's worried me a great deal since then."

"Why would Konrad want them dead?"

"Well, I know Amber has her theories, but I have no idea. I suppose judges must upset a lot of people when they have to make decisions that touch on their lives. And I know only too well what Konrad's like when someone tries to block his plans."

There's something almost gleeful in this, and he reminds Harry of a mischievous schoolboy, standing at the back of the mob, urging the others on to a fight. He wonders why he's doing it.

"YOU DON'T LOOK CONVINCED," Amber says as they walk back across the quad.

Harry shakes his head.

"Okay, let's find a seat and talk."

When they're settled she says, "It's the missing link, isn't it? The proof that Konrad had prior knowledge of your parents' visit to Kramfors."

"It's not proof of anything, Amber. And the thing that worries me most is your attitude."

"My attitude! What the hell do you mean?"

"You obviously hate your uncle. Every time you mention his name you curl your lip. It prejudices everything you say. It's some kind of family quarrel, and it makes it impossible for me to get a balanced picture."

"Some kind of family quarrel!" she explodes. "A balanced picture!"

She pushes her face forward across the table to Harry and says intently, jaw stiff, "On the ninth of August 2002 my father flew his plane back to Kramfors from Sydney and disappeared somewhere in the forest near Cackleberry Mountain."

"Yes, I . . ."

"No, *listen*. For three weeks they sent out search parties, helicopters. People came up with different theories—had he diverted north of the mountain, or south? Had he managed to land safely somewhere miles away from the search zone—maybe he was lying trapped somewhere out of radio contact? Try to imagine it, can you? I was fifteen, my mother had died three years before, and I was hearing all these stories about how my dad was either dead or dying alone, in agony, at the bottom of some hidden gully.

"When they finally abandoned the search, Konrad came to comfort me. He gave me a hug, and he stroked my hair, and then he raped me. It happened a number of times."

She pauses, trembling. Harry says, "Did you—"

"I was in shock. I didn't tell anyone. Then I discovered I was pregnant. I kept it a secret until Christmas, and then they sent me to Switzerland. Two years later I came back with Dylan."

Amber sits back, calm now. "So yes. Ten out of ten for observation. I hate Konrad. I hate everything about him. I know him, and I know that if anyone was capable of the cold-blooded murder of your family it was him."

They're silent. Then Harry says, "I'm sorry. That's a terrible story."

"You must hear terrible stories all the time. The point

is, what are we going to do about it? You know people in the media, don't you? Investigative reporters in newspapers or on TV?"

"Why?"

"I want to go public. I want to get someone to take up the story and tell the world the truth. I can't do it on my own, that would be just another wealthy family breakdown story. But with your parents' murder it becomes something much bigger and more serious."

He shakes his head. "No, Amber. You've given me some circumstantial detail, that's all. Nothing concrete to link Konrad to my parents' deaths. No one will touch it. If we tried to go public now he'd call in a heap of lawyers and smother it."

"But making it public will bring out the evidence, Harry! We can begin with the rape; then what Konrad is doing to the farmers in the Hunter Valley and wants to do to Kramfors; then your father's involvement with the native title owners. A step at a time. It's a great story, Harry! Konrad won't be able to stop it. Everything will come out."

"Everything? Does Dylan know that Konrad is his father?"

"No, but he's got to know sooner or later. He's old enough to understand now."

"You'd use him to get Konrad?"

She flushes. Raises her fists for a second before she collects herself. "I want justice, Harry," she hisses. "I thought that's what you wanted too."

"I want to find the truth, not get tangled up in libel suits."

She stands abruptly, unable to suppress her anger. "Well, good luck with that. I *know* what the truth is, and I'm going to do something about it."

Harry watches her stalk off towards the street, then gets

to his feet and follows. He sees her in the distance, hurrying away. Shrugs and turns and hails a cab to Central Station.

AS THE TRAIN HEADS through the northern suburbs he gets a call from Kelly.

"Harry, I've got a lead on Karen Schaefer."

He takes out his notebook and jots down names as she tells him about the meeting in the park, the Strathfield house, and the flight to Vanuatu.

"They stayed last night at the Grand Hotel on Port Vila harbour. Told the travel agent they were meeting a friend to go on a cruise today. My contact in Port Vila has just told me that they've got onto a yacht that came into the harbour this morning. Its name is the *Princess Estelle*, and it's owned by Konrad Nordlund."

"Is that right?"

"Yes. And I think I know where it's going. Have you heard of a company or charity called Pandanus Trust?"

"No, I don't think so."

"It has a stake in Maram Mansur's company, Ozdevco. I haven't been able to find out who owns Pandanus Trust, because it's registered in Vanuatu, where these things are less transparent. However, my contact in Port Vila tells me that the *Princess Estelle* was used to take a Pandanus Trust employee out to an island they own in north Vanuatu, called Maturiki Island, where the visitors are Australian and Chinese. You got all that?"

"I got it."

"Karen Schaefer, the Nordlunds, Pandanus Trust, Ozdevco, Maram Mansur. All connected."

"Yes, I see."

"I'm telling you all this to keep you in the picture,

Harry. Maybe you would be able to find out more about Pandanus Trust?"

"Yes, I'll try."

"Is there anything you can tell me?"

"There was a major crime review of the Ash Island murders yesterday, but basically we're all just waiting for the results of forensic tests, hoping they'll tell us something this time."

When she hangs up he calls Jenny. She's just been outside helping Meri with the alpacas and she sounds refreshed and breathless. He asks her to see what she can find out about Pandanus Trust and the other names. She's happy to have the job.

Later, he thinks, when he sees Deb Velasco in Newcastle he'll ask her to do a crime-scene sweep of the Strathfield house to establish a definite forensic link to the occupant of eleven Mortimer Street at Crucifixion Creek. It's not that he doesn't believe Kelly. But, like Amber Nordlund, she is way too emotionally involved with what's going on. He stares at his reflection in the carriage window. Who is he to talk?

SIXTY-ONE

AS THE TRAIN APPROACHES Newcastle, Harry decides to pick up his car to take it into work. He gets off at Wickham and walks down to the Throsby Creek bridge and on to his street. In the distance he sees cars and people clustered around the hotel. A tow truck is reversed up to his car and appears to be in the process of hauling it up. He is about to run towards the scene when he notices the uniforms. Up on the first floor someone leans out of his window and calls down to the people below.

Harry stops dead, moves into a doorway and pulls out his phone. He calls Ross's number.

"Ross? Harry. What's up? Cops are all over my pub."

"Harry! Shit, where are you?"

"What's going on?"

A pause. "There's a warrant out for your arrest, mate."

"You're joking. What have I done?"

"They know you murdered McGilvray. The DNA results came back."

"That's bullshit, someone's contaminated the samples."

"Your DNA is all over his throat, his wrists, his ankles."

Ross sounds sad, resigned. "Not only the DNA, Harry. Your prints are on the murder weapon."

"What murder weapon?"

"They found an empty bottle of scotch in the mud near McGilvray's body. Fits the fatal wound in his skull."

"Scotch . . . ? I had a bottle of Scotch in my room. The thieves took it."

"You mention that to the cops? You didn't tell me."

"Ross, I . . ."

"And the tyre print, at the scene, fits your front tyre like a glove. Do yourself a favour, mate. Get a lawyer and hand yourself in. I know a couple of names in Newcastle I'd recommend . . ."

Harry switches his phone off. Up ahead he can see a pair of plain clothes outside the hotel, listening on their phones, looking around, then calling to the uniforms.

He leaves the doorway and turns into a side street, breaking into a run as he hears the sound of an approaching police siren. It rounds the corner up ahead and comes toward him as he ducks behind the broad girth of one of the big palm trees that line the street, grown, so he's been told, from seeds brought back by World War I diggers returned from the Middle East. The patrol car rushes past and he runs on, turns down a side street, then another, heading in the direction of the docks. Once he has to jump into cover in a front garden as another car goes by, more slowly, searching.

The small houses become workshops and warehouses. He turns a corner and hesitates, facing a street in which there's no cover—no parked cars, no front yards, just long stretches of high brick walls on both sides. He starts to run. Halfway down a car appears at the far end. There's a gap in the wall ahead, a narrow access laneway, and he plunges into it. It widens into a yard filled with large steel bins.

Behind him he hears car doors slamming. He lifts the lid of one of the bins, full of jagged metal scrap, slams the lid down again and races to the chain-link fence on the far side of the yard, vaults up onto a bin, jumps and hauls himself over the fence. He drops to the ground and scrambles into the bushes growing up against the fence on this side.

Voices now and the squawk of a radio. The clang of bin lids being opened and shut. Then a voice almost on top of him: ". . . dark jacket and trousers, bare head . . . like he's gone into the rail yards . . . dogs, yeah, get the dogs . . ."

Other voices join in, growing fainter as the searchers go back out to the street.

Sucking in deep breaths, Harry looks out across a wide deserted space crisscrossed by the arcs of rail tracks. Ranks of empty black coal wagons stand over to the right; beyond them the dark steel sheds and towers of the coal loaders. None of these will provide shelter when the dogs arrive. He has to move quickly, but where? Beyond the coal loaders are the Dyke Berths and the river, the rail yards on this side surrounded by high security fences.

The mournful sound of a horn echoes across the yards, the rumble of heavy machinery, and he sees a yellow diesel engine emerge slowly from among the dark buildings. As it crawls out into the yards he sees a second engine behind it, a long trail of coal wagons following. He gets to his feet, watching the long procession make its way across the space, and begins to run towards it, reaching the last wagons as the train picks up speed. Between each pair of wagons there is a steel plate covering the coupling and as the last pair comes past he grabs at a handle and swings himself up onto the plate. He crouches into the concave end of the wagon and hangs on, pressing himself back into the steel as the train passes out through the perimeter fence, then across an even larger rail yard filled with long coal trains and into a tunnel. When they come out he sees houses above the embankments on either side, and streets. Another tunnel, a glimpse of a park, the brick buildings of an institution he doesn't recognise, and then the track swings to the north.

The train slows, the wagons clanging as they shunt into each other, a playing field and oval on the left, then an embankment. The train passes under a bridge and Harry jumps, rolling into the shrubs at the foot of the embankment. He picks himself up and sees station buildings ahead. He brushes coal dust and grass from his clothes and walks onto the end of the station platform. The sign says WARATAH.

He can't place it in his mental map of the city, and when he gets to the ticket office he asks if he can get a train to Sydney from here.

"Sure," the man says. "There's a train in five minutes going into Broadmeadow. Change there for the Sydney train."

He buys a ticket and waits on the platform, eyeing the roads flanking the station until the train arrives.

THREE HOURS LATER HE gets off at Central. He moves into the middle of the crowd, hurrying along the platform, keeping his head down, looking for police in the concourse. Makes for the exit and walks down to a branch of his bank in nearby Elizabeth Street, where he withdraws all of the money in his savings account, almost twenty thousand, then crosses over to Broadway and catches a bus heading west.

He gets off at Petersham, and walks to the little shoe repair shop tucked into a side street near the park. It's five o'clock and the sign on the door says closed, but Harry presses the buzzer and gives his name and Ricsi lets him in.

"You need a laundry, not a shoe repairer," the old man says, brushing dirt from Harry's sleeve. "You in trouble?"

"I need a bit of help, Ricsi. A drivers licence."

"Uh huh. What name?"

"Doesn't matter."

"Shouldn't be a problem. Long as you don't want a passport?"

"No, just the licence. And a set of your bump keys."

Ricsi takes his photograph and tells him to come back in the morning.

"Where would I stay around here?" Harry asks, and Ricsi gives him the name of a "half-decent' pub nearby. Harry thanks him and walks back to Parramatta Road, to a Vinnies op shop he noticed from the bus. There he buys used clothes and shoes and a suitcase and makes his way to the hotel. They have a free room, which they describe as "quiet," upstairs at the back. It is clean, simply furnished. Harry unpacks his new clothes, has a shower, and gets changed.

He calls Jenny on the mobile he uses only for her. It's good to hear her voice, warm, enthusiastic as she tells him about her researches. She has managed to discover a good deal about Pandanus Trust and Maturiki Island, not through the official records that Kelly tried to access, but from a variety of web sources.

"Pandanus Trust has three directors," she tells him, "two Australian and one Chinese. The Chinese one is a businessman by the name of Deng Huojin. He's based in Chongqing and is the chairman and principal shareholder of Chongqing Power and Light. Remember them?"

Harry doesn't.

"It was their ship, the *Jialing*, that the missing seaman Cheung was on."

"Okay."

"I got this from a Chinese Web site—I had to translate it. That was interesting."

"I'll bet." Harry yawns. He feels tired. Wishes he'd bought a bottle from the bar.

"The other two directors are Konrad Nordlund and—wait for it—Warren Dalkeith, former premier of our beautiful state."

"Really?"

"Yes. There's a lovely post from this couple who got into trouble in their yacht in a storm off Vanuatu. They managed to get to Maturiki Island and ended up on the reef. These people came out across the lagoon to rescue them, and they were Konrad's two sons, Ryan and Hayden. The couple had a great time with them on the island while the mechanic there made some scratch repairs so they could sail back to Australia."

It occurs to Harry that he really couldn't care less about Maturiki Island or Konrad Nordlund or Deng whatever-his-name-was. It all seems very remote and irrelevant now. He has other, more pressing things on his plate.

He misses what Jenny says next, and she must realise something's wrong. "Harry? What's happened?"

He tells her. She listens in silence, then finally says, "Well, we're going to have to do something about this. Where do we start?"

SIXTY-TWO

KELLY, IN HER HOTEL room in Newcastle, is itching with frustration. The latest police briefing has added nothing new and there's been no word from Harry. What about the forensic results he was talking about? Has he done anything about Karen Schaefer in Vanuatu? She's tried calling him several times, and each time it's gone to voicemail. She tries again.

As she does so there's a knock on the door. She opens it and finds two large men in suits standing outside. She recognises one of them from the briefings. "Chief Inspector Fogarty?"

"That's right." He shows his ID and identifies the other man as a detective senior constable. "Can we come in?"

"Sure."

She steps back and watches them as they circle the room, sniffing, scanning.

"How can I help you?"

"You know Detective Sergeant Belltree, Ms. Pool?"

"Yes."

"Can you tell us where he is at the moment?"

"Odd question. No, I've no idea. Have you lost him?"

"You've been in regular contact with him recently. Why is that?"

"I wouldn't say regular . . ."

"You've called his number eight times in the past two weeks, plus another three times today. What's the nature of your relationship?"

Kelly flares. "You've been monitoring his calls? My calls? Our *relationship* is strictly professional, and entirely correct. I am a newspaper reporter, sent up here to cover the Ash Island murders, and it was natural I would contact Harry, whom I'd known for some time in Sydney."

"So where do you think he might be now?"

The man's belligerence is extremely irritating, but she senses that his hostility is directed as much at Harry as at her. What's Harry done? Have they found out he helped her to cover up her wounding of Craig Schaefer? But why don't they know where he is?

"I have absolutely no idea. Look, if he's in trouble I'd like to help."

"Do you know his wife?"

"We have met."

"We'd like her contact details."

"No, I don't have those." Why don't they have them? "Is this connected with the explosion in the house in Carrington? I've heard rumours that a police officer and his wife lived there. Has there been an attempt on his life?"

Fogarty shakes his head dismissively, and it dawns on Kelly that they aren't worried about Harry's health.

"He's not *wanted* or anything, is he?" She sees the look that passes across the other officer's face just as they turn to go. That's it, she thinks, they're hunting for him.

At the door, Fogarty turns back and gives her a card. "If

you hear from him, or get any idea at all about where he might be, you must call this number, day or night."

Must I?

She closes the door, feeling very disturbed. What can she do? How can she help him? All she can think of is Amber Nordlund, the unexplained link in all of this.

She stands at the window, watching the two detectives get into a car and drive away, then she grabs her bag and takes the lift down to the basement car park.

AS SHE EMERGES OUT of the forest and into the open fields of Cackleberry Valley, Kelly remembers Harry's comment about Kramfors' isolation and wonders if this is a good idea. She doesn't even know what Amber Nordlund looks like, and has no clear idea of what she's going to say.

She pulls to a halt at the end of the drive and switches off the engine. Ahead of her an elderly woman is ushering a small boy with a limp out of the homestead and into the rear seats of a large black Mercedes sedan. A driver in a dark suit closes their door, lifts a suitcase into the boot and gets behind the wheel.

As the car sweeps away, Kelly sees someone, a man, standing in the shade of the veranda, smoking. She gets out and walks towards him.

"Hello. I'm looking for Amber."

The man comes down the steps to her, eyeing her. In the sunlight she sees that he's in his twenties and darkly good-looking. His gaze is disconcerting.

"Is she around?"

He nods towards the paddock beyond the white-railed fence. "That's her."

Kelly turns and sees a woman with long fair hair, no helmet, trotting on a large horse. The young man calls out to her and waves when she turns.

Amber brings the horse to the fence, slips off the saddle, and climbs neatly over the rail.

"Hello?"

"Hi, sorry to interrupt," Kelly says, aware she's gushing. She tells herself to calm down, be cool. "My name's Kelly, Kelly Pool."

"The *Times* reporter?"

"You've heard of me?"

"We were talking about you the other day, weren't we, Luke? You've been covering the Ash Island murders. What brings you out here for goodness sake?"

"Well . . . the investigation's going fairly slowly at the moment, and I thought I'd do some research while I'm waiting, on the region."

"Oh yes?"

"I know Harry Belltree. I believe he's been here?"

"Ah. Yes, he has. How well do you know him?"

"Pretty well. We've worked together in Sydney before."

"I see. And he told you there was a story up here, at Kramfors?"

Kelly hesitates, not sure how to answer that. Amber looks over at Luke, raises an eyebrow, then says, "I think you'd better come inside."

She leads the way into the house, across the hall, to a door leading into the kitchen, where she goes to a large fridge and brings out a jug of cold water. Pours three glasses. "Take a seat. Harry didn't mention . . ."

"No, he's been hard to get hold of the last day or two. You haven't heard from him today, have you?"

Amber shakes her head. "But we were hoping he

might . . . Anyway, you're interested in the coal industry are you?"

Kelly hides her surprise. "Well, yes."

"Harry told you about my Uncle Konrad's plans for this valley, did he?"

Kelly catches the contempt when Amber mentions the name, and senses something interesting. "Actually I'd really like to hear the whole thing from you."

"Right. Do you want to record me or something?" And she starts to tell the story of the fate of the valley that she told Harry at the eagle cave.

KELLY IS DISAPPOINTED. IT sounds like a family feud over their assets. If there were evidence of Konrad Nordlund acting corruptly to obtain the mineral rights, that would be very interesting, but Amber doesn't seem to have that. As it is, it's a human affairs story. Not one for the crime desk.

Then Amber says, "And that's where Harry's parents came in."

"Yes, he told me they stayed here the night before the crash."

"The night before Konrad had them killed, you mean."

Kelly wonders if she misheard. "I'm sorry?"

And Amber launches into the story. She is speaking faster and faster, leaning forward as if she might grab Kelly and shake the truth into her. Kelly remembers Harry's words: *highly strung*.

"You see? The judge had the power to kill Konrad's plans, or at the very least cost him a great deal more money. Of course he had to die."

"I see, yes. Do you have any proof of that?"

Amber shrugs as if it's a small matter. "There may not

be any after all this time, and even if we eventually found it it would be too late—the land council is about to come to a final decision on Konrad's revised offer. There's only one way forward now, to bring all this out into the open, to publish the truth."

"Amber, no newspaper or publisher is going to accuse Konrad Nordlund of anything without proof. Very solid proof."

"No, no. We begin with the story of the threat to the valley, then the dilemma of the Yoongooar, and then the dramatic coincidence of the death of their chief advisor, Danny Belltree. We don't have to accuse Konrad, it'll be obvious to everyone what happened, and he'll have to deny it, and then people will come forward with what they know. Harry and I discussed all this. It's why you're here, isn't it? I asked him to use his contacts with the press to publicise it, and here you are."

It is a great story, Kelly thinks. Hell, it might even be true. The problem is Amber. Kelly can imagine how Harry must have reacted to this obsessive torrent.

Which is still going. "Actually I believe we will find evidence. I'm a director of Konrad's company and I'm getting access to the archives. There must be something—a secret memo, a comment scribbled on a letter, the record of a phone call—something to point to Konrad's guilt. So what do you say?"

"I think it's a very powerful story, Amber," she begins, conscious of how guarded that sounds.

Luke Santini picks it up too, and gives a contemptuous snort, a shake of his black curls.

Kelly turns to him. "What's your role in this, Luke?"

"I support Amber absolutely. This is not some isolated incident."

Kelly picks up the North American intonation.

"It's happening everywhere, the rape of the planet by increasingly ruthless oligarchs. Murder is nothing to them, they do it every day, directly or indirectly. Whole populations displaced and starved. Humans are just another disposable asset to them."

"Luke has a wider perspective, you see," Amber says. "I tend to get stuck in my own little nightmare, but he reminds me that all over the world people are realising these things have to be stopped. We have to fight them and we have to use whatever weapons we can lay our hands on—the media, the courts, the finance markets. Even direct action."

"This is a lot to take in, Amber," Kelly says. "I'm going to need to think about it."

"Of course. And I have documents here, copies of the offers to the land council and their deliberations, maps, a timetable of events I drew up. I can't let you take them away, but you can stay and study them as long as you like."

"Okay, thanks."

Amber hesitates, then says, "There is one thing . . . In your article in the *Times* the other day you said—well, you didn't actually say, but reading between the lines it seemed as if you were making a connection between the murders on Ash Island and some kind of drug ring."

"Yes, that seems quite possible."

"You mean the biker gang—the Crows you mentioned—bringing drugs up to Newcastle?"

"Or the other way round, bringing drugs into the country up here, in the port. There is one thing that I'd like to ask you about, Amber. Harry mentioned that you had a housekeeper here at the time his parents visited."

"Karen Schaefer, yes. She and her husband have worked here for years. Harry asked me about them too. Why?"

"Were they working here last June?"

"June? No, they had to move down to Sydney for a year to look after Karen's sick mother. She died in July and they came back here, to my relief."

"Karen's maiden name was Suskind, yes?"

"I think so, yes. How on earth do you know that?"

"I happened to meet Karen in Sydney last July when I was doing a story, and I did a bit of research. Her mother, Donna Suskind, died in 2008."

"What? No, that isn't possible. She told me herself . . ."

"In Sydney Karen was living under a different name, Donna Fenning."

"I . . . I don't understand."

"How did you find her in the first place?"

"Um, it was when I came back from Europe. Dylan, my son, was just a baby, and someone suggested I needed help to look after him and run the homestead. We got Karen through an agency. She'd been a nurse, and her husband being an electrician and mechanic was a big plus."

"Who suggested it and helped you find her?"

"I can't remember . . . um, I think maybe . . . yes, I think it was Trixie."

"Trixie?"

"Konrad's mother . . ."

"Shit." Luke is staring at Amber.

Kelly says, "I believe she's been—"

"Working for Konrad?" Amber's voice is faint. "Dear God . . . I trusted her with everything, discussed every-thing . . ."

They are silent, then Kelly says, "Well, she's gone now. Have you heard from her lately?"

"No, nothing."

Luke says, "Amber, we have to talk."

"Yes." She runs her fingers through her hair, shaking her head. "I need to think . . . Kelly, let's set you up in the study. I'll bring you all the documents you might find useful. We can meet again later."

Kelly agrees. She follows Amber into a room lined with glass-fronted bookcases and fitted cupboards, with a cedar table and massive desk, a large antique ceiling fan, a stone fireplace with elaborate cast iron grate.

As Amber brings in armfuls of document boxes and rolled plans and dumps them on the table, Kelly studies the volumes in the bookcases, a set of the 1910 edition of the *Encyclopaedia Britannica*, rows of old Baedeker travel guides, Shakespeare's collected works, volumes on botany and agriculture.

"My great-grandfather, Axel," Amber explains. "A great collector. Look at this . . ."

She opens a series of shallow drawers filled with labelled birds' eggs on beds of cotton wool; pinned insects, spiders, bird skeletons, snake skins; test tubes full of different shades of powdered rock, like chemical samples or drugs.

"What was it about the reference to drugs that disturbed you, Amber? Do you think Konrad could be involved in something like that?"

"Hah," Amber says lightly, "I wouldn't be surprised by anything he might do. I'll leave you to it."

SIXTY-THREE

RICSI HAS THE ORDER ready. He hands over a driver's licence in the name of John Brown, bearing Harry's picture.

"Does he exist?"

"He does, a respectable gentleman currently on a six-month touring holiday in Greece. Here's his last electricity bill, genuine, to back it up, and the phone."

"Thanks, Ricsi."

Harry practises the signature on the licence a few times, then pays. He returns to Parramatta Road, where he catches a bus, getting off at the first car sales yard he comes to. He picks a four-year-old Focus—small, dark blue, anonymous—and beats the salesman down with the offer of cash. He signs forms and drives away, the registered owner. He calls Jenny. She has various bits of information for him that she's found on her computer, but first tells him about the fantasy she's been having.

"You come and live with us here, Harry. We keep ourselves to ourselves, and over time they forget about you and we slip away, overseas, and start again."

"I've thought about that too," he says. "But it's a small community, and we'd soon run out of money."

"Yes . . . yes, I know."

"What have you found?"

"Well, the good news is that the police seem to be keeping you in-house. There's been no announcement that they're looking for you, no publication of your picture."

"Right."

"I have some stuff on Sammy Lee."

He listens, making notes. When she's finished he says, "Hang on, Jen. We'll get this sorted."

"Yes," she says, "I know." But it sounds like a sigh of despair.

He goes to a barber and has his hair shaved off. He buys a new pair of sunglasses, returns to pick up his bag at the hotel and sets off for Newcastle once again.

The Marine is quiet, no one in the bar. He slips in through the side entrance and takes the exit door to the yard immediately on his right. There's a row of bins here and behind them a stack of bricks and tiles, the remnants of recent building work. He pulls back the tiles and feels around in the cavity beneath for the sealed package he buried here. It contains the Taurus pistol he bought previously from Ricsi. He slips it under his jacket, replaces the tiles, and leaves.

SIXTY-FOUR

AMBER'S DOCUMENTS ARE OUT of sequence, incomplete and in some cases incomprehensible, at least to Kelly. After grappling with them for a couple of hours she feels no more confident about Amber's story than before. While she works, the silence in the study is punctuated from time to time by the voices of Amber and Luke. Out on the veranda one moment, crossing the hall another, always sounding at odds with one another.

Finally Kelly stretches, rubs her forehead, feeling a headache coming on. She decides to look for a glass of water and an aspirin. In the hall she hesitates, hearing their voices from the kitchen. Luke, impatient, is saying, "Will you leave it! They have no idea."

"But we have to be sure, Luke! Dear God, I don't want to go to jail. Maybe we should just stop."

Fascinated, Kelly edges closer to the door, but her hip brushes against a small table and it creaks. The voices in the kitchen stop abruptly. She has no choice but to call out. "Hello? Amber?"

After a second, Amber replies, "In here, Kelly," and appears at the kitchen door.

"Right, I thought I heard voices. I just wanted a glass of water."

"Of course." Amber smiles brightly. "Or better still, a glass of wine. What do you say? Luke, will you?"

He nods, looking sulky.

Amber says, "How's it going?"

"A bit slow."

"Well, I'm afraid I can't let you take them away. Why don't you keep going and have dinner with us? Stay here the night?"

"Well, if you're sure it's no trouble?"

They take their glasses outside and sit on the veranda in the evening light. A couple of stable hands drive by, heading back to their homes in Gloucester, and Kelly imagines the sense of isolation that Amber must feel out here, pinned to this lonely property as surely as the specimens in her great-grandfather's cabinets.

She puts in another couple of hours on the documents, then shares a roast beef salad with the others. She has been hoping that they'll let something slip, some clue about why they'd be afraid of going to jail. But she learns nothing at dinner, and nothing afterwards when they sit up drinking, talking about the environmental movement and the campaigns Luke has been involved in. He seems to have had plenty of experience, but won't be drawn on his future plans.

Feeling slightly drunk, Kelly says goodnight and goes upstairs. The bathroom is a short distance away from her room, along a corridor overlooking the hall below, and as she returns from it she hears them arguing again. Amber sounds as if she's insisting on something. "Tonight," Kelly hears her say. "After she's gone to sleep."

Kelly doesn't like the sound of that. She goes back to her room, locks the door, and props herself up on the bed. After a few minutes she turns off the light.

It's hard to stay awake, sitting there in the dark after all that wine, and gradually Kelly nods off. She jerks awake at a sound, unable to identify it at first. Feet crunching on the gravel below her open window. She looks out. There is a full moon, and in its cool white light she sees Amber walking away from the house. She disappears into the shadows. There is the sound of a car starting, the rumble of an engine, and Kelly watches a sports car emerge into the moonlight. Luke runs down the steps and there is a murmured exchange before Amber slides over to the passenger seat and Luke takes the wheel. The car moves forward slowly onto the drive, then its headlights come on and it picks up speed.

Kelly grabs her things and runs down to the hall, out through the front door to her own car and jumps in. The sports car is out of sight but in the distance she can still see the faint glow of the headlights. She puts her foot down. She doesn't switch on her own lights, using the moonlight to steer by, and this isn't too difficult until she reaches the unsealed road through the forest. As she hits it the car jumps and crashes over the first unseen potholes and she has to slam on the brakes. She feels wildly unsteady—the drink, the ruts, the moonlight—driving madly to . . . what?

She takes a deep breath and moves forward more cautiously, focusing intently on the treacherous darkness. From time to time she catches glimpses of yellow light up ahead, glimmering among the trees.

But there's no sign of it when she reaches the main road, and she switches on her headlights and drives as fast as she can into Gloucester. The town is quiet as she speeds

down the main street and out the far end into open coun-
tryside. Far ahead she spots a pair of tail-lights.

Despite her haste the sports car is moving faster than
she is, and eventually she loses sight of it altogether. When
she finally reaches the Pacific Highway she puts her foot
down hard and races towards Newcastle, assuming that
their destination is somewhere there. But she's caught no
sight of them as she crosses the Hexham Bridge, and has to
admit to herself that she's lost them. She stops for a red
light near the turn onto the Ash Island bridge and, as she
sits there drumming her fingers on the wheel, she glances
over at the all-night filling station on the far side of the highway. And there is the distinctive shape of the sports car.
When the lights change she drives on until she finds a lay
by. She pulls over and waits.

SIXTY-FIVE

THE NARROW LANEWAY IS deserted, the moon casting dark shadows over the bins and cartons in the yard behind Sammy's restaurant. There is no van here. Sammy is out, provisioning another Chinese bulk carrier, the *Xingjuan* out of Wenzhou, which docked two hours ago.

Harry pulls on latex gloves and feels for the lock to the back door, tries inserting a couple of Ricsi's bump keys until he finds the right one. He gives the key a tap with the butt of his gun as he turns it, and the lock opens. He pushes the door. Steps inside.

There is a pervasive smell of garlic and ginger. Absolute silence, the diners and staff long gone. In the darkness the alarm panel glows on the corridor wall. Harry enters the numbers Jenny has given him, hacked from the computer of the local back-to-base security company. He uses his phone light to begin a search.

To his left is the kitchen. To the right the cold store, the cool room and then the counter of the grocery section with its shelves of dry goods. He explores, opening cabinets and drawers, searching racks of packets and cans.

He hears the sound of a vehicle entering the yard and tucks himself into the space behind a stack of drums of noodles and rice. The slam of a door, voices, fluorescent lights flickering into life. Sammy appears.

He is followed by a big Pacific Islander carrying a large aluminium box. He is wearing a lightweight jacket, and as he leans forward to put the box on the counter Harry notices the bulge in the small of his back.

Together they bring more boxes in from the van until there are half a dozen stacked on the counter. "You've got the key, George?" Sammy says, and the other man nods and produces a small tool from his pocket. "Let's see what we've got."

The Islander takes the lid off one of the boxes and inserts the tool under the lip of the bottom section. He gives it a twist. Lifts the lining, scattered with cabbage leaves, off the base and sets it aside. Starts to take flattened plastic packets out of the cavity beneath, setting them out on the table.

Sammy places them in turn on a set of scales at the end of the counter, tapping numbers into an adding machine. "Eight forty-six," he says. "Plus the pills. Try the next one."

"Sammy?" A woman's voice calls from the direction of the back door, and both men freeze. The Islander backs away from the counter towards the cool room as Amber hurries in. "Oh, I've caught you. Good. This is from the *Xingjuan*? I've got a bit of a problem, Sammy, I . . ."

She stops and turns towards Harry's hiding place. "Who are you?"

For a moment Harry thinks she's talking to him, but then the Islander moves into view.

Sammy, looking alarmed, says quickly, "This is George Taufa, Amber. He's my driver. It's all right."

"Your driver? What are you talking about?" Her eyes go to the plastic bags on the counter and she says, "What are those?"

"It's just your pills, Amber. Don't worry. I think we should . . ."

"No, the other ones, the white crystals." She picks up one of the packets and examines it. "What is it?"

In front of him Harry sees Taufa's hand move to his back, lift the hem of his jacket, and close around a pistol butt. Harry moves quickly out of his hiding place and grips Taufa's wrist, pressing the muzzle of his own gun to the man's temple.

"Relax," he says, and then, to Sammy, "It's a good question. What are they?"

"Harry!" Amber's cry is panicky. Then she sees the gun in his hand and shuts her mouth.

"Looks like crystal meth, Sammy."

Sammy says nothing, eyes darting around as if for escape.

"No, Harry!" Amber finds her voice. "Nothing like that, just party pills, ecstasy," the words tumble out. "They're not harmful, not really . . . And it's for a good cause . . ." She seems to realise how ridiculous this sounds. "It takes money, Harry. We're up against billion-dollar companies."

Harry slips handcuffs on Taufa's wrists, holsters his own pistol and removes the gun from Taufa's belt, tells him to sit on the floor, then steps over to the counter. He puts Taufa's pistol down and picks up the single bag of small heart-shaped pills. "This, yes. But these?" He shows her.

"I don't know. I've no idea . . . Sammy?"

Sammy's brow is gleaming with sweat. Then he breaks into a sudden frantic smile. "Luke!"

They turn as Luke Santini rushes in. He takes Amber in his arms and looks around in consternation. "You okay? What's going on? Sergeant Belltree?" He releases Amber and comes at Harry, hands held up as if in blessing, then grips his arms, "Hey, this is a surprise."

Harry takes a step back, pulling away, then stops abruptly, feeling something hard jam against his cheekbone and a hand close round his throat. Another hand takes the pistol from his holster and he catches a glimpse of the motorbike rider, Vince Scully, and behind him Jason Tolliver, before the gun is whipped against his forehead and he falls.

VOICES, ALL SHOUTING AT once.

Harry tries to focus. Pain is hammering at the side of his head. One voice emerges close by. Luke Santini.

"No, no, it isn't like that. They're our partners now."

"Since when!" Amber protesting.

Harry misses the next bit as a wave of pain roars through his ears. He tries to move his hands and realises they've been handcuffed behind him.

". . . found out what we were doing. Tell her, Sammy."

"The blokes on the dock security cottoned on to it. I had no choice, Amber. I had to tell them everything. They let us go on with it as long as we brought in stuff for them. Meth, very pure, that's what they wanted. I couldn't tell you because I knew you wouldn't agree."

"Damn right!" Amber yelling, furious. "Well, it ends right now."

The room seems to go very quiet. Then Luke says, "Amber, these guys don't negotiate. Don't you read the papers? The bodies on Ash Island?"

"Shut the fuck up!" It's Tolliver bellowing, his voice booming in the confined space. Harry opens one eye and sees him turn his back on them. He has a phone to his ear.

His head and shoulders duck. "Sure. Yep, absolutely. No worries." He turns back. "Sammy, you and George stay here and clean up."

Harry remains limp as they drag him out by the feet and throw him into the back of the van. Amber and Luke clamber up after him and the doors are slammed shut.

SIXTY-SIX

IT WAS EASIER TRAILING the yellow sports car on its journey into the city. When they reach the west end Kelly watches it turn into a narrow street, a Victorian terrace of boutiques and cafés. She drives past, circling the block and returning to pull into a dark spot at the end of the silent street, killing her lights. Ahead of her she sees the yellow sports car parked outside a Chinese restaurant. Amber jumps out and disappears down a laneway at the side while Luke stays in the driving seat. Then he too gets out, goes over to the dark restaurant window and peers inside, hands cupped around his face. He turns away, paces for a while. Pulls out his phone.

The minutes pass. A couple appear and make their way unsteadily towards Luke, who is now sitting against the bonnet of the car. They stop and say something, and Luke checks his watch. He stands up, lights a cigarette and turns away, and they wander on, whispering and giggling as they pass Kelly's car.

Now another car appears at the far end of the street. Kelly doesn't spot it at first, jet black, just a glitter beneath the street light, a big Mercedes gliding up behind the sports car. Luke snaps to attention, grinding his cigarette beneath his heel. A big man emerges from the driver's side, another man from the passenger door, and they approach Luke, talk together, then all three disappear down the laneway.

Kelly gets out of her car, closing the door quietly, and walks along the shadows against the shopfronts on this side of the street. She has no idea what's going on, but is thinking that she should get the number of the Merc. Maybe it will mean something to Harry, if he'll just answer her bloody calls. It's one of those fancy number-plates, red numbers on black, hard to read. She's forced to cross the street to make it out. She's near the mouth of the alley as she writes the number down, then hesitates, hearing a woman's voice from somewhere down there, a cry. The slam of car doors, an engine grinding into life.

She ducks back into a shop doorway as a white van rumbles out onto the street, followed by a man on foot, the big man from the Mercedes. He stops for a moment on the pavement, looking up and down, then gets behind the wheel of the car and moves off. As soon as it's clear, Kelly runs back to her car, which is facing the wrong way. She does a clumsy three-point turn and tears off after them. Catches sight of them again at the far end of Hunter Street, the white and the black, moving at a steady pace northward, retracing the route of the yellow sports car. Kelly wonders if they are heading out to the Sydney road.

They are on the highway, approaching the McDonald's corner with the filling station where Kelly spotted Amber's car, when she sees the vehicles' indicator lights flashing a right turn and a sudden panic swells inside her. There is only one right turn ahead, onto the Ash Island bridge.

She swerves across lanes. Turns off to the left and pulls in. What should she do? Call the cops? But then she wonders. As far as she knows, Amber and Luke are still back at the restaurant. Perhaps they've finished whatever business they had there and are now driving safely back up to Kramfors. Maybe they bought some dope, or just fancied a late-night Chinese. She tells herself she's spooking herself. It's the thought of Ash Island, dark and empty. What are the people in those two vehicles doing, going over there now in the depths of the night? She really doesn't want to know. But she has to know. There is a story here, a big story, and somehow Ash Island is at the heart of it.

She pulls out her phone and tries Harry's number again. Again it goes to voicemail. "Harry," she says, almost a whisper, "It's Kelly. It's 2:45 a.m. I'm at Ash Island, following a white van and a black Mercedes sedan, registration TOLLIES. I'd feel a lot happier if you could come and join me, mate."

Kelly restarts the car and goes back to the lights. They turn green for her, and, heavy with misgiving, she drives across the bridge over the black river and into the bleak darkness of Ash Island.

SIXTY-SEVEN

"I THINK THEY'VE KILLED him, Luke. Dear God, what have you got us into?"

"It wasn't me, for chrissake. You heard Sammy, they found out themselves, ages ago. Which isn't surprising because you were amateurs, you know? Just not very good at crime."

"This isn't crime, it's justice. Using Konrad's ships to make the money we need to fight what he was doing."

"Oh, come on Amber, that was chickenfeed. You take on big coal, you need big lawyers—big, expensive lawyers, and big media, and big politicians. Get your head out of your arse and be a realist for once. These guys are giving us a good deal, a share of their business in exchange for the use of your route." A pause. "Anyway, he's not dead, he's bleeding."

That's true. The blow to Harry's temple opened a gash which has clogged his left eye with dried blood. He forces himself to move, to try to act. Thinking that he must be getting old. His recovery time seems to be increasing.

"Harry . . ." Amber crouches beside him.

"There's a phone in my right pocket," he says.

She feels. "No. They must have taken it."

She takes his handkerchief instead and presses it gently to his forehead.

He says, "Where are we going?"

"I don't know."

Luke speaks. "To Tolliver's house, to talk things through. And listen, Amber—you too, Harry—these guys are fair, but they're tough. Don't piss them around. We're in the drugs business whether we like it or not. We've just got to focus on what's important."

Amber is silent for a moment; then, "Harry's a policeman, Luke. They know that."

"Right, and Harry has to do the smart thing." He sounds impatient.

"What do you mean?"

"Harry has to do a deal with them, just like we do. He has a value."

"A value?"

"Christ, Amber, wake up!" Angry now. "A friendly cop is a real asset to people like this. That's right, isn't it, Harry? I'm right, aren't I?"

"Yes, you're right," Harry says. "But murder's different. What do you know about the bodies on Ash Island?"

Luke turns away. "Nothing. I'm just guessing it was to do with drugs. Doesn't concern us."

"Don't kid yourself. That is a major investigation, dozens of police working on it. Sooner or later they'll get to you. You got a phone?"

"Yeah." He pats his pocket.

"Call them now. If you don't you'll be an accessory to anything that happens. They'll hunt you down, Luke."

"Nothing's going to happen." The van bumps and sways. Luke grabs the side, mutters, "Don't they seal the roads in fuckin' Merewether?"

They slow and come to a stop.

The back of the van opens. Tolliver is standing there, Vince Scully beside him, swinging a short silver baseball bat in his right hand. The darkness beyond them is intense. No houses, no house lights.

"Nice and easy, folks." Tolliver takes hold of Harry's ankle and drags him out, grabbing his arm in a huge fist and hauling him upright. "Out you come, watch your step."

Amber and Luke follow cautiously, looking around—indistinct dark mounds are visible in the moonlight, the stars bright overhead. "Where the hell are we, Jason? You said we were going to your place?"

"This is more private, mate. My home away from home."

Beyond him Harry sees the dark curved hump silhouette of an odd building he's seen before—one of the old radar huts on Ash Island.

Tolliver flicks on a torch and points the way with the beam across the broken concrete apron. "Come on guys, careful does it."

"No!" Amber says. "I don't like this. I'm not—ah!" She gasps as Tolliver grips the back of her neck with his free hand. Scully has taken hold of Luke's arm and is marching him towards the corrugated steel sheet panel that seals the entrance to the hut. He takes a remote from his pocket and points it at the panel, which clicks and springs open a few inches. He hauls the panel open and they are bundled inside. A smell hits them. Stale gas fumes and musty age and urine.

The door slams shut behind them and Scully gives Luke a shove. He stumbles, falls, and swears. Tolliver pushes Harry to the floor beside him, steps back and points the beam of his torch at Scully bending over a gas camping light. It hisses into life, casting a baleful glow over the vaulted space. Harry guesses it was once a maintenance workshop of some kind. There are black oil stains on the concrete floor, oil drums against the wall. A pulley with chains and a hook is suspended from the ceiling and beyond it in the shadows what looks like a vehicle inspection pit cut into the floor. The only piece of furniture is a single heavy chair. Tolliver gestures to it. "Take a seat, Amber, while we get ourselves organised."

Amber stares at it with distaste that turns to alarm as she makes out the duct tape curling from its arms, the stains on the concrete beneath it.

She backs away, but Scully grabs her and pushes her down onto the chair, then stands over them, a gun in his hand, while Tolliver pulls out his phone and turns away to make a call. Harry hears the odd word, ". . . Boss . . . Sammy . . ." but nothing to say who he's calling. Amber meanwhile is leaning forward in the chair, urging Luke in a low murmur to do something, while he looks pointedly away. Harry notices his hand moving to the pocket where his phone is.

"Okay, folks." Tolliver has finished his call and turns back to them. "We've got a short wait until the big man arrives. He'll get everything sorted. Just relax till then."

Harry moves his hands behind his back, searching the floor with his fingers for anything—a nail, a piece of wire—that might help him spring the handcuffs. He feels something, fragments of something hard and brittle, but he can't make out what it is.

Amber is protesting again, rising from the chair, and Tolliver goes over to her and puts a hand on her shoulder, pressing her back. He leans down to whisper something in her ear. Harry can't hear what it is, but when Tolliver straightens up Amber is rigid, her eyes wide with fright.

SIXTY-EIGHT

THE DARKNESS CLOSES AROUND Kelly's car as if she were a thousand miles from civilisation. The mangroves that the headlights move across are alien, twisted things growing out of black mud. There are no lights on the road ahead, no cars.

A bend in the road. Now for a brief instant she does see a tiny prick of light, way off down a side track. She stops, reverses, and turns down towards it, a glimmer in the darkness. Her headlights pick out a building, a dilapidated house with a single lit window. There is an old truck standing outside, but no white van or black Mercedes. She turns around and heads slowly back to the road. She recognises landmarks now that she's passed on her earlier visits to the crime scenes—a stand of casuarinas, and here on the left some crumbling brick walls and a ruined fence. She glances at them as she passes, and almost misses the glint of white in the moonlight. She pulls in to the side and gets out of the car.

Feeling suddenly exposed, Kelly picks her way carefully along the road back to the ruined compound, wondering if she was mistaken. She moves in across the yard between the collapsed structures, careful where she steps, and then comes to a stop. Yes, there it is, a white van. Standing next to it the slight glimmer of moonlight on the polished black Mercedes. They are parked outside a strange curved-roofed building, like a Nissen hut. She makes her way cautiously towards it, and makes out a faint line of light on its end wall. Closer still, she sees that the light is leaking from the edge of a corrugated steel panel.

She reaches out to it, and at that moment becomes aware of light reflecting off the trees by the road, and then the harsh beam of headlights turning into the compound. She scrambles away from the hut and drops down behind the van as a vehicle drives straight at her and pulls up. Peering through beneath the van, Kelly makes out feet dropping to the ground on both sides of the vehicle. The headlights are switched off and she's blind in the sudden darkness. She holds her breath, staring, listening. Then the crunch of a boot right beside her makes her jump and strong hands grip her arms.

SIXTY-NINE

"AH, HERE HE IS." Tolliver strides over to the door and throws it open. "Boss?"

The muffled sound of male voices from the doorway and then a sudden yell, a female voice that Harry recognises. He watches as Tolliver backs into the hut followed by the islander, George Taufa, dragging Kelly Pool. Tolliver grabs her other arm and together they haul her in and throw her to the floor. She grunts as she hits the concrete, and tries to struggle upright, clutching her shoulder.

And then another figure strides in through the doorway, slamming the door behind him. Frank Capp. As he turns towards them the light catches the shattered left side of his face and Amber gasps. Tolliver whispers in his ear, pointing out the captives, and Capp's eye settles on Harry. He comes across and squats down in front of him, puts out a hand and twists his face around so that he can see the bloodied temple.

"Still on the run, Harry? Well, this is as far as you get." He moves in closer and strokes his own ruined cheek. "By the time I've finished with you, you'll be pulp."

"Sorry, wait . . ." Luke is struggling to his feet. "I don't know who you are."

Capp swings around to stare at him. He goes over, grips his hand and Luke winces. "Name's Capp, mate, Frank Capp. You're a friend of this piece of shit, are you?"

"What?" Luke glances down at Harry and looks quickly away. "No, no, not at all. I'm a friend of Jason . . ." He nods encouragingly at Tolliver, who doesn't respond.

Capp tightens his grip. "Jason doesn't seem to know you, mate."

"We're in business together, Frank! Tell him, Jason."

But still Tolliver says nothing.

"What business would that be, mate?"

"The goods . . . from the ships!"

Capp shakes his head. "Nah. Can't say we've heard of you."

"For chrissake, me and Amber here—we set it up, with Sammy."

"Sammy I know," Capp says. "He works for me. But you and Amber here . . ." He shakes his head. "History, mate."

"No, look, you don't—"

"Sit down and shut up."

"You're not listening—"

Capp lashes out with a savage kick to Luke's knee. He falls to the floor, screaming.

Capp turns his attention to Amber. "You're in the hot seat, love."

She looks at him, eyes wide. "My name is Amber Nordlund. My family—"

"Nor-d-lund." Capp turns it over, slurring it through his uneven mouth. "Yes, I know about Nor-d-lunds."

"Well, you'll know they're not people to annoy."

Capp grins. "From what I hear, darlin, you've annoyed them pretty bad yourself."

Amber opens her mouth, but nothing comes out.

She swallows, then tries again. "Luke and I would be very happy for you to take over the shipping business, Mr. Capp."

He nods. "Good on ya."

"We would like to leave now, and you won't hear from us again."

Capp laughs. Then something catches his attention. Harry follows his gaze to Luke, hunched up on the floor. He has got the phone out of his pocket and is busy trying to tap in a number.

Capp roars and runs to him, stamping on his fingers and crushing the phone beneath his heel. He turns and calls to Taufa, who is holding a roll of tape. Together they bind the writhing figure on the ground, hands, legs, and mouth, then drag him upright and loop his wrists over the hook of the pulley chain. With a rattle and a screech Luke is hauled up, up until he's suspended like an animal carcass, feet dangling.

"Now . . ." Capp starts giving rapid orders. Tolliver takes the gun while Taufa and Scully move among the prisoners, searching them, taking the phone from Kelly's pocket. Then they roll a large steel oil drum into the middle of the space and begin filling it from heavy plastic sacks with some kind of white granular material. It isn't until they open a jerry can and Harry smells the diesel that he realises what they're doing. They're making a bomb, a crude ANFO bomb.

Capp hands Taufa a small black box that he places carefully into the mix. Tolliver seals the drum with a heavy lid.

They step away from the drum, moving more warily now. Capp takes a sheet of paper from his pocket, checks it, then thrusts it at Amber.

"Ms. Nor-d-lund," he says, "read this."

She takes it reluctantly, scans it with a frown, shakes her head.

Capp takes out his phone, presses buttons, then holds it up to her. "Read what the paper says—nice and loud."

"I will not," she says loudly. "This is ridiculous."

Capp gestures and Taufa goes over to the bench and picks up a sledgehammer. Takes it back to Capp, who carries it over to the helpless Luke. He swings it in a great arc and smashes it with a hideous splintering crack into Luke's knees.

Harry realises then what the fragments are that he's holding in his fingers behind his back—pieces of human bone.

Amber is screaming.

Capp strolls back to her and slaps her face hard. She stops.

"Want me to hit him again?" he demands.

She shakes her bowed head.

"Then read the paper."

He holds up his phone again and she begins, in a trembling faint voice. "My name is Amber—"

"No, no. Louder! Start again!"

"My name is Amber Nordlund. I speak on behalf of the environmental group Burning Rage. We have learned that lawful protest against the ravages of the coal industry is useless, and that only direct action will have any effect. Accordingly we announce a program of armed assault against its infrastructure, and call upon all people who care about the future of our planet to support us."

Capp nods, puts the phone to his ear, listens, then nods again. "Good."

He's arranging a suicide, Harry thinks, the accidental

suicide of bomb-making terrorists. But we can't be found trussed up like this—he'll have to kill us first, and free us.

Capp is looking around. He picks up his sledgehammer again and comes towards Harry.

"Where's his phone?"

Tolliver gives it to him.

"What's this? Only one number in memory? Who would that be?" A nasty smile forms on one side of Capp's face. "Jenny, right? Blind Jenny. Shame I won't be able to show her what I'm goin to do to you, mate. But I'll tell her. I'll make sure she gets the picture before I put out her lights."

At his back, Harry feels the sliver of bone finally slip into the narrow gap in the handcuff and depress the ratchet, opening the cuff. He springs at Capp with a roar, swinging punches, clawing for his throat. All around him the room erupts, the others running forward, throwing themselves into the melee, punching, kicking. Blows hammer down on Harry's head and ribs and he is finally dragged onto his back, bleeding and barely conscious. He opens his eyes and sees Capp standing over him, gasping for breath, raising the sledgehammer.

"Boss!" Someone shouts, pointing. "Boss, the woman! She's gone!"

They all turn to where Kelly was lying. She's not there and the door is open.

SEVENTY

SHE FLIES ACROSS THE concrete yard towards the line of bushes, scrambles into them, hits a chain-link fence and stumbles on, faster, faster, comes to a break in the fence and plunges through into the soft earth of a field, trips, falls headlong among cabbages, hauls herself up and races on, heart pounding, lungs bursting. Ahead she sees the glimmer of light, the cottage window. She clambers awkwardly over a steel gate and flops into a yard and runs towards the house and hammers on the back door. A dog inside begins to bark.

Come on, come on! She keeps banging and finally the door swings open—an old man holding a shotgun in her face.

"Please . . . please . . ." She can hardly get the words out. "Must call the police."

A small woman pushes into view. "What is it? What's the matter?"

"My friends, trapped by bikers in the huts over there. Please, must call police."

"You'd better come inside, dear. Close the door, Rick."

"I'll get on the phone," he says.

The woman takes Kelly into a sitting room with ancient

armchairs and threadbare carpet, the dog following, sniffing suspiciously at Kelly's legs. She hears the murmur of the old man's voice from the hall and sinks back into a chair, letting her heart slow down.

It doesn't take long, a bell ringing at the front door, male voices, and then the door opens. The two thugs from the hut walk in with pistols and torches in their hands.

"Thanks, Hilda," one of them says, and takes hold of Kelly's arm and pulls her to her feet.

"You boys would lose yer own noses if they wasn't stuck on," she says. "Is this the only one?"

"Yeah, just her."

In her despair, as they march her out of the front door towards the white van, Kelly sees the headlights of another vehicle approaching down the track.

SEVENTY-ONE

HARRY LIES ON THE hard concrete barely able to move. They've cracked his ribs, he thinks, maybe his legs too. He just wants to lie there, go to sleep, but he forces his eyes open, sees Capp over at the door, peering out into the darkness. Tolliver remains, standing over Harry, a pistol in his fist, gazing at Capp. "Can you see anything, Frank?" he calls.

Harry eases his right arm out from under him, stretches out his hand, makes a lunge for Tolliver's ankle and jerks. The big man jumps, steps quickly back, and his heel skates on a patch of oil. He staggers for a moment, recovering his balance, cursing, and his back foot steps into space, the inspection pit. He gives a cry, dropping the gun as he topples backwards.

Harry begins to crawl towards the gun, expecting Capp to jump on him at any moment. It doesn't happen. His fingers reach the gun, clutch at it and he swivels round, aiming it at the man in the doorway silhouetted against a blaze of light from outside.

"Drop the gun, Harry! Drop the gun!"

It's not Capp's voice.

"Ross? Is that you?" *I'm hallucinating*, he thinks. He lets the gun slide from his hand and lies back with a groan.

"JEEZ, HARRY, WHAT'S HAPPENED to you?"

He opens his eyes. It *is* Ross. Harry mumbles, "Bomb . . . gotta get outta here."

"What? What did you say?"

"There's a bomb . . . in that oil drum. Gotta get everyone out, Ross."

"Okay, okay, sure." Ross shouts something to people coming in through the door, then slides his arm under Harry and tries to lift him. He grunts, swears, then calls for help and Harry stifles a cry as he's lifted up and carried out into the fresh night air. All around him people are shouting, lights blazing, vehicles revving. They make it to the road; red, blue lights flashing; an ambulance. Amber is there, a blanket around her shoulders, looking shaken.

"Harry! You're alive! Where's Luke?"

Ross says, "Who's Luke?"

"Inside," Harry says, "strung up on a hook."

"Jesus . . ." Ross shouts suddenly, "No, stop!"

Harry sees Amber's blanket on the ground, her figure fleeing across the concrete apron as the hut explodes in a dazzling white flash. He blinks, and when he looks again she is gone.

SEVENTY-TWO

HE REFUSES TO LEAVE. The ambulance officers do what they can for him, then drive off with Amber. He feels light-headed, barely taking it in. From the scene of the explosion someone reports a body in the inspection pit. Tolliver. What's left of Luke will be harder to find.

"How did you show up?" he asks.

"We've been tracking Kelly's phone to try to get a lead on you," Ross says. "We intercepted a call asking you to meet her on Ash Island."

"Kelly's okay?"

Ross nods, tells him about rescuing her from Scully and Taufa at the farm. "And we got Sammy Lee too, stuffing bags of speed under his floorboards. I'll have to give you back your hundred bucks."

"And you got Capp."

"Who?"

"Frank Capp."

Ross looks blank. "No. Was he here?"

The fog inside Harry's head clears. "Of course he was here! He was behind all this. You didn't catch him?"

Ross hurries over to a car, gets on the radio. Harry follows, wincing with every step. Ross says, "We found four vehicles—Kelly Pool's car down the road there, and a white van, a black Mercedes and a WRX over there by the hut."

"The WRX must have been his."

"Well it's still there, and the bridge across to the island is blocked, so he must be here somewhere."

Another car draws up, Fogarty gets out and Ross hurries over to him. Harry follows, Fogarty staring at him as he listens to Ross. A helicopter appears overhead, a searchlight beam probing the ground beneath.

As Fogarty turns back to the radio in his car, Harry grabs Ross's elbow. "I need a phone."

SEVENTY-THREE

JENNY IS DEEPLY ASLEEP when the phone sounds, buzzing near her ear. She sits up, groggy, fumbles. "Harry?"

"Is that Jenny?" She doesn't recognise the voice, male, rough, slightly slurred.

She says, "Yes . . ." cautiously. "Who . . . ?"

"Jenny, my name's Detective Inspector Tom Carpenter. I'm a mate of Harry's."

Jenny is wide awake now, sitting up, tense. "What's happened? Where's Harry?"

"Been badly hurt, Jenny. He gave me his phone and told me to call you. You're in danger—great danger. You got someone there can drive?"

"Yes, but . . ."

"How far is it to the nearest main road?"

"The freeway? Fifteen minutes."

"Right. What would your nearest junction be?"

"Look, I don't know who you are. Let me speak to Harry."

"Sorry, Jenny. He's gone in the ambulance. I got to come and take you to him. You gotta leave where you are *right now*—drive to the freeway. I'll meet you there. So what junction is that?"

"Tuggerah."

"Okay, good. Park on the southbound slip road and wait for me there. What's your vehicle?"

"A blue Peugeot."

"Right. I'll be in an unmarked police car. Now this is important, Jenny. They're tracking your phone, so you gotta turn it off and leave it where you are. Understand?"

"Yes. But . . ."

The phone goes dead.

SEVENTY-FOUR

HARRY PACES BACKWARD AND forward beside the circle of cops gathered around the radio. He can move more easily now—can't stop moving. Jenny's phone is switched off, went straight to voice mail. No one is answering Meri's house phone either. A patrol car has been sent, but it's still five minutes away along that valley road.

The helicopter roars past overhead again, heading for the river. Then Ross calls out to Fogarty, "Boss! They've found a boat on the river bank. The far bank."

As Fogarty takes the radio, Harry grabs Ross. "He'll have crossed the highway to the filling station, tried to get a lift there. C'mon, let's get over there. Where's your car?"

"Hang on, mate. There's cops all over the place over there. They'll get him."

But then the report comes in of a triple-0 call from an hysterical motorist out on the freeway who claims to have seen a man being shot.

They replay the call. "Two men standing together, then I saw a flash and one of them dropped to the ground, and the other got into the car as I was going by. I slowed down and he came flying past me and I pulled over, reversed back to take a look. I'm with the bloke now. Dear God, covered in blood . . . a big hole in his face."

"Where is this?" Fogarty says, and they get the answer, twenty minutes away down the highway.

Harry says, "I'm betting he hijacked a car over at the filling station and made the driver take him, then decided to get rid of him. Is there a description of the car?"

There isn't.

Harry says, "Capp's got a phone. I don't know the number, but Tolliver called him."

Fogarty nods, tells a couple of men to go down into the inspection pit to retrieve Tolliver's phone. They find it beneath him, protected from the blast by his body, and call back with the last number it rang. Fogarty passes it on to the telephone intercept room at the Newcastle police station, and they wait.

The answer comes back within a few minutes. Capp's phone has been tracked to a point on the freeway near the Tuggerah interchange.

SEVENTY-FIVE

"ARE YOU QUITE SURE about this, dear?"

Jenny hears the suppressed panic in Meri's voice. They're sitting in the car on the slip road, little traffic at this time of the night except the periodic roar of long-distance trucks down below on the freeway. She imagines Meri staring out into the blackness, wondering how long it will be until dawn breaks. And she isn't sure about this, not at all. There was something about Carpenter's voice, an aggressive edge, that jarred. She feels the baby stir in her belly, and spreads a protective hand across it.

"Lights!" Meri cries suddenly. "Coming up behind us. They're stopping."

Jenny hears the slam of a car door, the crunch of feet.

"Jenny? Jenny Belltree?" The voice from the telephone.

"Yes."

She hears the door at her side click open.

"Out you get. Come with me—not you, lady."

Meri's voice. "I'm coming too. She's not going anywhere without me."

"Just do as you're told."

Jenny hears Meri gasp at the brutal force of the demand. She says, "Where are we going?"

She feels hands release her seatbelt, tighten around her arms and pull her bodily out of the car, swing her upright, then half-march, half-carry her up the slope. Then she's sprawling across a car seat. The car door slams behind her. A foul smell of sour sweat. Meri crying out, beating at the car window, and then a loud bang.

A car door slams, the engine starts and Jenny hauls herself upright, reaching for him. Her fingers wrap around his face, a strange uneven shape, and she claws at him. A harsh shout and then a shattering blow splits her skull.

SEVENTY-SIX

HARRY SITS, TENSE AND impatient beside Ross, driving fast in a column of police cars, lights pulsing. On the radio they listen to the target's progress down the freeway towards Sydney—Somersby, Kariong, Calga. A report comes in of a woman's body found on the Tuggerah slip road, identified as sixty-two-year-old Meredith Spooner, shot through the heart. A dog is sitting by her side. The car nearby is deserted.

Fogarty's plan is to stop Capp before he reaches the Peats Ferry Bridge across the Hawkesbury. The freeway has been closed to north- and south-bound traffic and spikes laid south of the Mount White interchange. As they race on, a pale light begins to transform the hills around them, revealing their forested slopes. In this deceptive half-light they pass through the Tuggerah interchange, scattered now with flashing police lights.

Then a hiatus—the target has left the freeway at Mount White. Spooked by the empty road, maybe; the absence of oncoming traffic. He's moving west along Morgans Road, which winds among the fields of the Mount White enclave within the national park forests. He turns off onto a side track and the signal comes to a halt. They trace the address. It has a history, the scene of a drug raid last year. Its owner is another resident of Long Bay Correctional Facility, still inside.

When the cavalcade arrives they find an improvised command post already set up beside the road out of sight of the house. A surveillance helicopter is in place high overhead, ready to transmit pictures to the gathering team.

Harry and Ross crawl up to the fence line with a view of the place, a small timber cabin with a rusting tin roof, set back against the forest edge at the top of a slope. A Ford Mondeo is parked outside, no sign of life. A sick feeling overwhelms Harry, thinking of Jenny inside that place with Frank Capp. It's all he can do to hold back from jumping over the fence and running up there.

The TOU arrive, snipers sent up into the forest to cover the rear of the property. There are closed louvred blinds in the windows, they report, hard to get a view inside.

Then a hostage-negotiation team. Their leader, a middle-aged man you might take for an old-school librarian, talks to Harry, turning over the possibilities.

"So he doesn't know you're alive, Harry?" He has a warm, steady voice, neutral accent.

"Possibly."

"And what'll he do if he finds out?"

"He'll want me to go up there."

"Hmm. How rational will he be?"

"He won't give himself up. He's killed four people in the past few hours, two of them in cold blood. He knows he's not going to escape."

"He may not know we've been able to track him. Why

would he go to so much trouble to take your wife, if he thought you were dead?"

"Because he's evil."

The negotiator thinks this over. "Best to keep you right out of it, Harry. Your presence can only complicate things."

SEVENTY-SEVEN

FIRST THERE'S THE PAIN, the searing pain inside her head. Jenny wakes slowly, trying to remember, trying to understand. The slightest movement causes excruciating stabs of pain behind her eyes. From habit they open, and she sees a dim light.

Light. For the first time in over three years.

At first she thinks it must be some strange discharge inside her brain. But when she moves her eyes, bars of brighter light jump out of the gloom. It looks just like a louvred window. It is a window.

There is a sound, a door banging shut. She lets her eyelids droop, leaving just enough gap to see the man. He is carrying a bundle of things which he drops with a crash on a table, then picks them up in turn—a hammer, an axe, a large kitchen knife, a long screwdriver—swinging them, feeling their weight. There is a pistol stuck in his belt.

He puts down the tools and turns to her, crouches and slaps her face. She groans and turns away.

"Jenny," he says. "Poor little helpless blind bitch. You don't know me, do yer? Me name's Frank, Frank Capp."

Yes, I do. I know you, she thinks. I've read all about you. She mumbles, "Where's Harry?"

"Lucky bastard, should've died. But reckon he'll be here soon enough. We got some unfinished business."

There is a feverish, excited tone in his voice; he can't keep still. She guesses ice—he's high on ice.

Whatever happens, she thinks, I mustn't let him know I can see.

There is a distant growl of an engine from somewhere outside.

"Here we go," Capp says, "Better get ready."

He goes over to the table and picks up the hammer, and then his mobile buzzes.

SEVENTY-EIGHT

THEY LISTEN TO THE conversation. The negotiator begins.

"Frank? My name is Bruno Severini, I am a police negotiator. I am here to help you. We want to resolve this without any further bloodshed. How are you feeling?"

"Feelin?" A harsh laugh. "Fuckin great man. Fuckin outstanding."

"How is Jenny?"

"Oh, she's lookin good man, real good. Tasty. Maybe not for long though."

"Frank, I want you to sit down and take a deep breath and relax. Okay? Can you do that?"

"Yeah, sure."

"I want you to think hard about what I'm going to tell you, because it's important. Okay?"

Nothing.

"Frank? Are you there? We have plenty of time here to get this sorted. We all just need to be calm."

There's a sudden sound of heavy breathing in the mouthpiece. "Listen, I want that mongrel Belltree up here, alone. Got it?"

"Is that Detective Harry Belltree, Frank?"

"Jesus, how many Belltrees ya got?"

"I'll have to speak to my boss, Frank, but I don't think that will be possible. He was badly hurt in the explosion. But you can come and see him for yourself. Just put down your weapons and walk out through the front door and we'll take you to him."

"Listen arsehole, I want Belltree up here. He can crawl on his fuckin belly for all I care. But if he wants to see his little blind woman again before I cut her fuckin head off he's gotta come up here, alone. Got it?"

In the background, faintly, a shout. "Harry, don't come here!"

The phone goes dead.

Severini tries to ring it again, but it goes straight to voicemail.

Harry takes out his own phone. He brings up Jenny's mobile, and after several rings Capp answers. "Harry."

"Yes, Frank."

"Get yer fuckin arse up here. Alone, no guns, hands in the air."

"Okay."

The others try to stop him, Fogarty with a direct order, but when he starts to walk no one holds him back. It should be a long haul up the dirt road on his aching leg. He hardly feels it. He has no plan and no weapon. Only the knowledge of how Capp will want to kill him.

He reaches the front steps, stomps loudly on them as he gets to the front door, which swings open at his touch. He's in a narrow hallway.

"In here, Harry."

He turns and sees through an open door—Jenny seated on a kitchen chair facing him, Capp standing behind her, a pistol in his left fist, aimed at Harry, the other holding a hammer.

"Come on in, Harry."

Harry steps through the doorway, sees Capp aim the pistol at his stomach.

"On your knees."

Harry kneels.

"Hands flat on the floor in front of you."

Capp comes round to him, swinging the hammer in his free hand. "Waited a long time for this, mate."

Harry thinks, now, I have to do something *now*. But the muzzle of the pistol is steady, less than a metre from him, point-blank range, as Capp raises the hammer high above his head.

Beyond him Harry sees Jenny rise silently from her chair and move to the table, where, as easily as if she could see it, she picks up the axe. She steps quickly up behind Capp and swings the blade down hard upon his head.

His whole body convulses, a leap and a twist. He falls to the floor, writhing, and the gun in his hand goes off. Then abruptly the flailing stops and he lies still.

Harry looks down at Capp's body, the bloody axe lying by its side. He notices a splatter of blood on his own shirt and wonders if he's been shot. No, it's Capp's blood.

Shouts, boots, black figures crashing into the room. He goes to Jenny and wraps his arms around her. "Thank God," he whispers. "Thank God." The smell of her hair, the feel of her against him.

"I thought you were dead," she says. Then, "Harry, I have this pain."

"Where?"

"In my side." She shows him, the left side of her belly, and he sees blood.

"Ambos! Here, quick."

Two paramedics run in and pause to stare at Capp.

"No, over here!"

SEVENTY-NINE

HARRY STARES OUT OF the helicopter window at the long line of traffic on the highway down below. Cars crawling towards the city. He feels utterly detached up here. His mind, it seems, refuses to accept that this is possible. Beside him, holding his hand, Jenny lies on the stretcher, hooked up to a drip and an oxygen mask, monitored by the two paramedics. The bullet lodged inside her is so small, just a twenty-two.

Somewhere over Hornsby her hand goes limp and they begin CPR. When they land at Westmead they rush her away to try to save her and the twenty-two-week baby.

Ross finds him in the waiting room. Puts a hand on his shoulder.

"Strangest thing," Harry whispers. "In the chopper she told me she could see me."

EIGHTY

FOUR DAYS LATER HE opens the door to her hospital room. Jenny's sister Nicole is there by the bedside. The two women clasping hands, heads close together, Nicole talking, Jenny pale, nodding in agreement. He waits by the door as Nicole gets to her feet and comes towards him.

"How is she?"

"The doctor was here a few minutes ago. She'll tell you." The smile Nicole gives him is sad. She grips his arm for a moment, then leaves.

Harry takes her seat, seeing the tears brimming from Jenny's eyes.

"How are you feeling, sweetheart?" He reaches for her hand, but she doesn't respond to his touch.

"And your eyes? They're good? The headache gone?"

She turns her face away with a look of pain, as if her recovered sight is a reproach, or a curse.

"I should never have involved Meri," she whispers. "I can't forgive myself."

He begins to form a reply, but she turns back to stare at him. "How did he know, Harry? How did he call me?"

He swallows, feeling that cold lump in his chest. "He got hold of my phone. The one with your number on it."

She turns away again, withdrawing her hand from his. "I thought, when we went to Newcastle, it was over. I thought, a new start, the baby . . ." The tears spill down her cheeks, her head shaking in despair. "I should have known better."

He tries again to take her hand, but again she pulls away. He says gently, "What did the doctor say?"

She sucks in a deep breath. "They can't remove the bullet without endangering the baby. So I told them they mustn't touch it."

"But . . ." They have been very clear about this—lodged where it is, the bullet can kill Jenny at any time, without warning.

"They have to wait," she says. "A few weeks, a month or two, until the baby's old enough to survive. Then they can operate."

Harry starts to object, but she stops him, voice suddenly hard. "It doesn't matter what you think, Harry." The words are like a slap. "This is my decision, not yours. When they've saved the baby, then they can remove the bullet. After that, they've told me I won't be able to have any more children."

A silence, then he says, "I'll support any decision you make, Jenny. Will they keep you here?"

"Yes. But I don't want you to visit me anymore, Harry."

"What?"

"The baby is the only important thing now. I won't have you put it at risk again."

"But it's over now."

She stares fiercely at him. "For me it is. But for you? Have you found out what you wanted, Harry? Have you got to the bottom of it, what happened on that road three years ago?"

He can't answer and she turns away. "Later, if I go and

stay with my mother, or with Nicole and the girls, will they be in any danger?"

"No, no."

"That's what I'll do then. For a while, anyway. Then I don't know."

"But Jenny, we . . ."

"I want you to go now, Harry. This is too difficult."

NICOLE IS WAITING FOR him outside in the corridor.

"She just needs time, Harry. We'll look after her. I'll get help for her."

Numb, he walks out of the hospital and finds his way to his car. He gets in and sits behind the wheel. Stares through the windscreen, unseeing.

ACKNOWLEDGMENTS

At writers' festivals and workshops I am regularly asked about research: How important is it? How do I do it? Today the Internet makes access to information so much easier than when I first started writing crime fiction that it's tempting to think that research is just about accumulating and selecting facts. But it's more than this; it's also about absorbing atmosphere, learning the informal languages that professionals speak but never write down, and getting a sense of what's going on inside their heads. For this you need to speak to people who are involved in the fields that you are trying to bring to life on the page. In this book I have been immensely fortunate to have been helped by some wonderful people, whom I must acknowledge. Of course they are not responsible for any of the words or actions of Harry Belltree and his friends and enemies.

I would especially like to thank Alex Mitchell, Detective Superintendent Matt Appleton, Detective Superintendent Mick Willing, Detective Chief Inspector Wayne Humphrey, Detective Inspector Chris Olen, Dr. Tim Lyons, Libby Dickeson and members of the Blind Book Club at Vision Australia Hamilton, Rev. Garry Dodd, Graham Clark, Colin O'Donnell, Peter Mathews, Darren Shearer,

John and Kirsten Tranter, my agent Lyn Tranter and my publishers at Text: Michael Heyward, Mandy Brett, Jane Novak, and Stephanie Speight. And most especially my wife, Margaret, for her help in so many ways.